THE LAST SISTER

YOUNG PALMETTO BOOKS

Kim Shealy Jeffcoat, Series Editor

THE LAST SISTER

A NOVEL

Courtney McKinney-Whitaker

The University of South Carolina Press

Published by the University of South Carolina Press
Columbia, South Carolina 29208

www.sc.edu/uscpress

Manufactured in the United States of America

23 22 21 20 19 18 17 16 15 14   10 9 8 7 6 5 4 3 2 1

Library of Congress Cataloging-in-Publication Data

McKinney-Whitaker, Courtney.
The last sister : a novel / Courtney McKinney-Whitaker.
pages cm.—(Young Palmetto books)
ISBN 978-1-61117-429-8 (hardback)—ISBN 978-1-61117-430-4
(paperback)—ISBN 978-1-61117-431-1 (ebook)
1. Cherokee Indians—Wars, 1759–1761—Juvenile fiction. [1. Frontier and pioneer life—
South Carolina—Fiction. 2. Cherokee Indians—Wars, 1759–1761—
Fiction. 3. South Carolina—History—1775–1865—Fiction.] I. Title.
PZ7.M478687Las 2014
[Fic]—dc23   2014011484

In memory of Hildy, who saved my life in the wilderness

Contents

Acknowledgments

I am especially grateful to the novel's first and most dedicated readers: Stephen McKinney-Whitaker, my husband; Melanie Cash McKinney, my mother; and Alexis Presseau Maloof and Michelle Nielsen Ott, my dearest friends and colleagues. Emily Elliff, Jacqueline Muir, and Sue Whitaker also read and encouraged. Special recognition is due to Lina and Twitchit, who were there for every word.

PART I

THE ATTACK

I.

December 21, 1759

Dawn

The winter ground is cold and hard against the length of my body. I lie on my stomach, propped on my elbows. The cold of the fowler's metal lock scissors into my fingers as I pull back the hammer and prepare to fire, and the smooth wooden stock presses into my cheek as I eye the length of the barrel and line up the tip with a flash of movement beyond. There's a rock poking into my hip, but I ignore it and stop my breath, conscious of every movement, of every inch of my body hidden behind the fallen log I've steadied the musket on. I pull hard on the trigger.

A half second later, the flint and the frazzle spark, lighting the powder in the pan and sending fire to light the powder in the barrel. In a flash of flame and smoke, the fowler fires and the butt slams into my shoulder, and I grunt with pain despite the thick cloth pad secured there. I glance down at the open pan to make sure there are no remaining sparks and scramble to my feet, brushing bracken from my clothes. I peer into the densely tangled bare vines and branches of the winter underbrush.

"Did I hit anything?" I ask, turning to Mark.

My elder brother leans against a tree, his dark brown linsey-woolsey leggings and shirt nearly blending into the thick bark. He grins.

"Go see."

"She got something that time, didn't she, Mark?" asks Jaime, my younger brother. "Not everybody has that good an aim with a musket, do they?"

Mark shrugs. "Hitting anything with a fowling musket is half luck, anytime, no matter who's shooting. You'd starve to death if you had to depend on it for food. Go get your rabbit, Catie. It'll make a nice birthday dinner for you."

I make to cuff him on the ear as I hand him the fowler, and he grins, his dark blond hair nearly swishing out of its leather tie as he darts out of reach. He knows we're having pork. That's one good thing about my birthday falling in late December. Plenty of meat remains from the fall hog slaughters and deer hunts, and for seventeen years now, Mother has used my smaller celebration to experiment with her Christmas and New Year dishes. Mark's birthday is in March, so he's gotten rabbit or squirrel more times than I can recall. Maybe seven times, all the years since we moved from New Jersey to the South Carolina backcountry when he was thirteen.

Dead leaves crackle under my feet as I push through the underbrush, looking for evidence of a kill. I spot the blood first and lean to pick up a large rabbit by the scruff of the neck. A splinter of shot caught it in the head at about thirty yards. That's not luck, no matter what Mark says. The blood that spilled from the rabbit's skull has melted the morning frost on the leaves around it, turning them a watery pink. As I lift the creature, its hind end snags. I pull harder, but whatever is holding it pulls back. I crouch and find the rabbit's back feet caught in a knot of vines. Grimacing, I pull my jackknife from my pocket. No matter that Mark would have laughed had I not hit anything. I'm sorry to have killed an animal that was trapped. I snap the vines one by one, nicking my thumb as the last one breaks faster than I anticipate. Wincing, I suck blood from the tiny wound.

I turn to rejoin my brothers, holding the carcass away from my gown and overskirt so the dark blue wool won't stain and Mother won't fuss. She'll have enough of a fit when she finds out Mark took me shooting for my birthday. I can hear her now. *It's time to leave the hunting to the men.* And not even to all the men, but to the farmers and the woodsmen. Not to the men like my father, with his university education. If he hunts at all, he should be riding horseback and chasing foxes with a pack of hounds like the lowland dandies of Charlestown, not lying in the dirt to take down a glorified rodent. No, if anything, the backcountry people Mother has been forced to live among should bring my father the glorified rodents and the venison, and when they can afford it, the chicken and the pork. In fact, they do, but that doesn't go a long way toward endearing them to my mother. To her, it's small recompense for living on the edge of the world.

Still uneasy at the way the rabbit died, I swing the body to Mark so he can stuff it in his game bag, and I catch Jaime biting his lip. I cut my eyes sideways at Mark. He has seen it, too. We've talked about this many times, about how strange it is that Jaime, who at ten does not remember a world before the frontier, should be the one most like our parents, the one least able to bear the sight of blood and pain and death. It should be me, I think, because I'm the girl and thus the one mother has most tried to shield. Or it should be Mark, who can remember not only New Jersey but Edinburgh, too, and the way our father's father pilfered shortbread from his wife's cupboards to hide in his pockets for his grandchildren.

But it's Jaime. Not Mark, who is fast becoming a trapper and a trader to rival any Frenchman. Not me. I so quickly learned that the best way to protect myself in the backcountry was neither to flutter my eyelashes and demur when men spoke to me, nor to keep my elbows and ankles carefully covered, but to learn to handle a gun and an ax.

"So," I say to Mark, crossing my arms and lifting my chin toward the long rifle propped against a tree. "I really think I've gone about as far as the fowler can take me."

"Oh, no," Mark laughs. "It took you three tries to hit anything."

Still trying to take my mind off the pitifully trapped rabbit, I protest. "With a fowler, Mark. With an old, cheap fowler. With your rifle, I would have hit something the first time."

Mark pats the cartridge box at his belt. "I can't let you waste my rifle cartridges. It's stupid to waste good ammunition on rabbits and squirrels, anyway, especially when there's plenty of meat waiting at home. And you know Father agreed to cover for us only as long as we promised not to waste ammunition in target practice. You don't need target practice. After me, you're the best shot in the family."

That isn't saying much, but I smile. He might be weakening. And I need him to weaken, because I need to practice shooting the rifle. However little we like to think of it, the war is drawing nearer, and the more skilled I am on both weapons, the safer I'll feel.

I press my fingers into the pad on my shoulder. Bruises are forming in the tender flesh underneath, but because Jaime is here, I keep the smile. "Please, Mark. I could shoot the rifle, and Jaime could try the fowler. He needs practice, you know he does."

Mark shakes his head. "We've done enough for one day. Besides, we need to be getting back to the house. Someday, Catie, maybe I'll take you deer hunting. You can shoot the rifle then."

There will be no *then,* and we both know it. Not because Mark doesn't want to take me with him, but because there's no telling how far we'd have to track a deer or how long we'd be gone, and an overnight trek through the woods would be harder to hide from Mother than a predawn hunting trip on my birthday.

"At least let me hold it," I say, and Mark sighs because he knows I won't give up until I get what I want.

He retrieves the long rifle from beside the tree. With the butt on the ground, the barrel ends at his shoulder.

"It's as tall as you are," he says. "Here, it's not loaded. Just hold it like you would the fowler."

I take the rifle from Mark and cradle the stock between my shoulder and cheek. I slide my left hand down the barrel, trying to get a feel for the balance, trying to learn. It's a heavy weapon. Too heavy and too long. I hold it steady for only a few seconds before the barrel begins to tremble and Mark snatches the rifle from my hands.

"It's too heavy for me to hold," I admit. "I'd have to prop it on something like I do the fowler."

Mark considers. "You held it long enough to fire. You wouldn't have to prop up either of them if you'd learn to shoot faster. That's your worst habit. You wait too long to fire and lose your nerve and your aim. You're decent enough, but you'd be better if you didn't try so hard. You've got to learn to load and aim and fire in one long flow."

I grin. "So you're saying I can fire the rifle?"

Mark laughs and runs his hands lovingly over the dark wood of the stock. "This rifle cost me three years of deer hides. Maybe you can get your husband to buy you one someday."

He tilts an eyebrow skyward. "Speaking of husbands," he adds, meaning to get a rise out of me. "Will I get to see Owen Ramsay tonight?"

I pull my heavy winter cloak from the branch where it's been hanging since before dawn. The weather isn't yet cold enough for me to need the cloak over my thick layers of clothing, and I like to have my arms free for shooting. I tie the ribbon around my throat, hoping the folds of the cloth and the red shadows cast by the rising sun hide my furious blush. Mother has had her eye on Owen Ramsay for me for at least five years. That I've had my own eye on him far longer is something she doesn't need to know. If she thought my gaze had landed in the same place as hers, she'd begin to doubt her own judgment.

My fingers hover at my throat, finding the short necklace of blue ribbons my parents gave me last night. Mother said she wanted me to have it before my birthday dinner. I slide the ribbons through my fingers, working my way around large knots set about an inch apart. I haven't untied them, but

Mother told me each knot holds a pearl, a treasure she took from her father's house when she ran away to marry my father.

"It wasn't stealing," she told me once. "They were my pearls." I'd wondered if she'd been trying to convince me or herself.

"I suppose all the Ramsays will come." I feign annoyance as I pull Jaime's cloak from another branch. The Ramsays always come to our celebrations, as we go to theirs. They are our nearest neighbors, and one of the few families Mother deems fit to socialize with us. Patrick Ramsay, Owen's father, may struggle to write more than his own name, but he can read and has built one of the finest farms in the settlement. His wife, Owen's stepmother, was educated by a private tutor in Philadelphia before her father lost his fortune and she was forced to seek hers. Between the two of them, they suit Mother as well as anyone in the backcountry could.

"Turn around, Jaime." I throw my younger brother's cloak over his shoulders and do the tie, though he's plenty old enough to do it himself. Mark and I never have gotten out of the habit of protecting Jaime, though. Maybe Jaime is our fault.

Mark straps the rifle across his back, slings the game bag over one shoulder and the powder horn and shot bag under the other arm, and picks up the fowler. I take the basket that holds what remains of the food we brought for an early breakfast. I packed it quickly, in big slabs of bread and cheese and smoked venison, so the basket is still very heavy.

Jaime should carry something, I decide. Mark and I are too quick to take care of everything. We've never given him the slightest responsibility. We've never given him the chance to learn much.

"Would you rather carry the basket or the game bag?" I ask Jaime.

He hesitates for a moment, eyes darting between Mark and me.

"Game bag," he answers at last, determined.

"Mark," I call, signaling. He pulls the strap over his head and holds the game bag out.

"Can I carry the fowler, too?" Jaime asks. A rush of affection comes over me. He is trying so hard to keep up, to be brave, to make us proud. I laugh, pleased, and Jaime starts to speak again, but Mark holds up a hand that stops us both.

"Quiet." There's a strange timbre in Mark's voice, and Jaime and I fall silent. I look up sharply. Silhouetted in the morning light, Mark is perfectly still, listening, alert. My mind flashes to a painting of a spotted hunting hound I saw once on a wall in New Jersey. If Mark had a front paw, it would be raised, pointing.

2.

December 21, 1759

Morning

Mark darts a glance at me. "Did you hear that?"

I nod, listening, barely breathing. Though the sun is beginning to warm the day, I feel colder now than I did before dawn. Then it comes again, the sound I have prayed never to hear, the sound Father once promised I never would have to hear.

Seven years ago, when we fell in with a small band of settlers heading south, Great Britain and the Cherokee nation were allies, two great powers united against great enemies: the French, the Creek, the Catawba. The Cherokee headmen even petitioned the South Carolina Assembly to build forts in Cherokee territory to protect the Cherokee towns while their men were fighting the French up north.

But that was before. I recall my lessons with Father, the old newspapers he collected and made me read, the riders who came to our settlement on occasion, spreading news and gossip.

So often Jaime and I were my father's only pupils, as on this day in late November. I looked at the newspapers spread across the table, their close lines of tiny print precious as one of our few links to the world beyond.

"Catie," said Father. "Explain to me the causes of this war." He crossed his hands behind his back, as though he held the answer there.

"Which one?" I asked. The joke was old, and my father's eyes crinkled a smile.

"The causes of all wars are the same at bottom," I answered. "Money, property, control."

He nodded, pleased, and continued his schoolmaster's pacing. "Go on."

"Great Britain is engaged in three wars of concern to us. One on the European continent, one on the American continent, and one here in the colony of South Carolina. The European war is concerned with attaining colonial properties from several European powers, the American war is concerned with wresting control of the interior of the continent from the French, and the Cherokee war . . ."

I faltered. "We need the Cherokee. We can't beat the French without them."

"Consider the evidence," my father prompted. *"Remember, you may have to search far back to discover the roots of an event."*

I scanned the newspapers before me to find the earliest date. 1755.

"Our Cherokee allies went north to help us fight the French," I said slowly. *"But by the time they got to Pennsylvania their help was no longer needed, so they returned home. That's when the trouble began. Among the Cherokee, each man fights by his own say, but the British army doesn't work like that. In our view, the Cherokee warriors had deserted. In theirs, they had not been paid for their service. The returning warriors raided British settlements in Virginia and North Carolina to take their pay in horses and livestock. The settlers retaliated. Violence between British settlers and the Cherokee has been escalating for several years, spreading south."*

"Accurate, if a bit simplified," said Father. *"Jaime, where do the French come in?"*

"French deserters and spies," Jaime chirped. *"Deserters can take refuge in Cherokee towns, but some of them are spies pretending to be deserters. They're trying to convince the Cherokee to ally with France."*

"Many of the Cherokee now disagree on where they should ally," I interrupted, pride smarting from the word* simplified. *"The French have placed a high bounty on British scalps, even those of civilians. They're trying to scare British subjects off the frontier."*

I looked across the table at my brother. From the shade of his skin, it seemed to be working.

"As you know, neither the British nor the Cherokee government wants this war," Father said. *"For us, it represents not only a distraction from the greater conflict with the French but also the loss of a valuable ally. For the Cherokee, it blocks access to desperately needed trade goods. So why is the colony of South Carolina currently at war with the Cherokee nation?"*

"This is a case in which the actions of individuals change things completely," I said, catching at another chance to please my father. *"The Cherokee government is based in the Overhill Towns, deep in the mountains. South Carolina's government is based in Charlestown, on the coast. If the people, the settlers and the Cherokee who live on the frontier, want a war, all either government can do is try to keep it under control. Last month, a Cherokee peace delegation traveled to Charlestown to treat with Royal Governer Lyttleton. Lyttleton is angling for a promotion, trying to show how strong he is, so he took the peace delegation hostage. He's locked them in Fort Prince George, which is a great insult because that fort was built at the foot of the mountains to protect the Cherokee Lower Towns."*

The memory of that lesson sends cold fear drizzling through my body. The trouble with Father is that he contemplates everything with a kind of intellectual detachment, and it seldom occurs to him that events could intrude upon his measured, orderly study. But one of the things I've learned from the rigorous training he gave me in the Greek and Roman classics is that peace only ever lasts so long, and it doesn't take much to upset it. Now, any hope of peace on the frontier is locked in Fort Prince George with the Cherokee hostages, and Cherokee war cries skirl through my ears, high and sharp, mixed with the sickening crack of splintering wood.

I reach instinctively for Jaime, pulling him close under my arm and moving so both of us are behind Mark. Somehow, with Mark here, I feel safe. I feel he will know what to do. That's why he came home, after all, why he gave up the woodsman's life he loved, his explorations of the far frontier. To protect us. To be with us when Father refused to refugee east with other settlers, declaring he wouldn't leave as long as his pupils and members of his small congregation stayed. Once I thought that brave, but now I see it as stupid and arrogant. I understand why Mark and Father nearly came to blows. Mark lives in the real world. He turns to me, and I recoil from the fear in his hazel eyes. I've never thought my elder brother could be afraid of anything.

Mark hands me the fowler silently. He takes off the powder horn and the small pouch of musket balls and shot for the fowler and hands those to me, too. I loop the powder horn around my shoulder and hold the pouch ready. Mark opens the small box on his belt and pulls out a rifle cartridge.

Blood pounds in my ears. "Do you want me to load?"

Mark shakes his head. "I want you to watch me load the rifle. The loading sequence is basically the same as the fowler's, but I want you to watch, anyway, in case you ever have to use it. Then you're going to take Jaime, and you're going to hide until I come for you."

The hot fear in my belly urges me to dart through the woods now, either toward the cabin to fight or in the other direction to hide, but I know moving too quickly can be as dangerous as standing still. I force myself to watch closely as Mark tears the end of the cartridge paper off with his teeth and spits it out. He pours a small amount of powder from the cartridge paper into the pan, pours the rest down the barrel, and covers the barrel with a square of buckskin from his cartridge box. The long, straight ramrod comes out of its storage place beneath the barrel with a metallic scrape that hurts my teeth. Mark places the ball on the square of buckskin and uses the ramrod to push the cloth and ball down the barrel. The ramrod leaves the barrel with another metallic scrape, and Mark returns it to storage. The whole thing seems to take a long time, but I know only about a minute has passed.

"The rifle takes longer to load than the fowler because the ball and the bore inside the barrel are almost the same size. The musket ball for the fowler is a lot smaller than the bore, so it doesn't take as much force to push it down," Mark whispers. "You have to make every shot count with the rifle, but that's not so hard because the tighter fit makes the rifle more accurate. You can aim at a specific target. With the fowler all you can do is aim in a general direction and hope. A piece like that is half luck, any day."

I draw in my breath. "The rabbit was a lucky shot."

Mark nods. "Yes. That's all it was."

He puts a hand on my shoulder. "Do you remember the cave behind Fish Falls?"

I would never forget it. Fish Falls is a waterfall about the height of a man. Mark and I named it that years ago because we liked to fish near there as children. There's a small cave behind it, carved by water and wind. The cave isn't deep. It won't hide us well. But I nod.

"You take Jaime, and you get there," Mark says. "I'll find out what's happened, and I'll come for you as soon as I can. If I'm not there by dusk, you skirt around by the Ramsays' place and see if everything looks safe. If it looks like they've been raided, keep going. You keep going east until you find a place that looks safe. I'll find you, all right?"

"I'd rather stay with you." I'll have to be scared once I leave Mark's side.

"No," says Mark, in the same sharp tone he used when Jaime asked if he could carry the fowler. "I'll find you."

Mark's hand wraps firmly around the back of my head, and he kisses the top of my forehead, hard.

"God bless you, Catie." He holds out his hand to our little brother. "Jaime. Now go, quick. Remember, it's easier to hide than to find."

Mark waits until he's sure Jaime and I are going to move, and then he turns and heads off in the direction of our family's cabin. I grab my flat straw hat from where it hangs beside Mark's cloak and tie the ribbon under my chin.

"Come on, Jaime." I hand him the basket of food and Mark's cloak. I need both hands for the fowler. I wish I could load it, accurate or not, but I'm afraid to try to move quickly through the undergrowth with it ready to fire. I don't want to trip and blow my own head off.

Mark says it's easier to hide than to find, but clearly he's never tried to track me and Jaime. I know we're leaving all sorts of signs, especially after we turn off the well-traveled path and toward the creek bed. The terrain around the wide creek is steeper and hillier than the relatively flat land of the settlements and farms. Fish Falls is on a high rise, and in places I am bent double from a stitch in my side. I envy Jaime his breeches. Mark says they're a bit fancy for the backcountry, but they still look easier to move in than my layers of heavy skirts. I breathe in deeply when we reach the waterfall and take a moment to bathe my steaming face in the cold water.

"In here." I push Jaime and his burdens ahead of me onto the rocky outcropping behind the falls. "Crawl."

The powder will be useless if it gets wet, so I look for a hiding place. In summer there would be plenty, but winter's bare branches will leave the powder horn open to sight. I think of stashing it behind a tree, but that would hide it from only one side. My eyes light upon a rotting trunk covered with debris. I jab the trunk with the butt of the fowler, hoping to disturb any creatures that are wintering there before I reach down. I nestle the fowler along the side of the trunk and cover it and the powder horn with leaves and branches. I think for a minute before dropping the bag of musket shot down the front of my gown, under my shift. If anyone wants to shoot us, he'll have to bring his own ammunition.

I kneel to crawl behind the waterfall. My cloak protects me from the spray, but it's damp by the time I reach Jaime. The cave is only a few feet high, so we have to sit on cold, damp stone. It's only a few feet deep, so we're constantly sprayed by an icy mist.

Jaime's teeth are chattering, and his lips have gone whitish blue. I feel over Mark's cloak. The outside is damp, but the inside is still dry.

"Come here, Jaime."

I settle against the back of the cave, pull Jaime into the crook of my arm, and spread Mark's cloak over us. I rub my hands up and down Jaime's arms.

"There. You'll warm up in no time."

Jaime manages a thin smile.

"Do you want something to eat?" I ask. "Thank God we didn't eat it all this morning. Of course, I packed enough for two armies. I was in a hurry. I didn't want Mother to catch me." I am chattering, trying not to think.

Jaime shakes his head.

"Are they dead, Catie?" he asks, shooting a swift bolt of nausea through my stomach and up into my throat.

"Who, Jaime?" I swallow my fear, though I know exactly what he is asking.

"Mother and Father. Mark."

I debate with myself in the near darkness. I would like to tell Jaime that everything is fine, that Mark will come for us soon, that this won't be the worst birthday I've ever had. For a second, I almost do. But Mark and I have kept Jaime soft long enough, maybe too long. We should have been teaching him to survive the frontier, the way we learned to do. Mother and Father certainly weren't ever going to.

"I don't know, Jaime," I say at last. "I think those cries were coming from the direction of our cabin. But I really don't know." I pause. "Mark will be all right. He knows how to take care of himself, and he won't be taken off guard. He's just going to see what happened. He'll come for us as soon as he knows something."

I don't add that Mark will have been too late to have stopped a war party from doing exactly what war parties do, or that our parents were old and alone. We never should have left them, even if Father was in on our secret and was keeping watch. What could he have done, really? Mark and I knew better than that. I grip the blue ribbons around my throat and say a silent prayer that Mark was too late. I hope he didn't arrive in the middle and try to play the hero. That would be so like him.

Jaime and I huddle together until the sun is high in the sky and the light turns the waterfall to crystal and sends rainbows dancing over the back of the cave. Mark said to wait until dusk, but I can't keep still any longer. I untangle myself from Jaime and tell him to stay still and quiet and hidden, and then I crawl out of the cave, working muscles that cramp and complain. The spray dampens the outside of my cloak again, and I'm shivering as I retrieve the fowler and powder horn from their hiding place.

I straighten and suck in my breath. The smell of smoke wafts toward me, unmistakable, rising from the clearing where our cabin stands. Or stood, perhaps. My view toward the flat land of the settlement is blocked by tree-covered hills.

I should be cautious. I shouldn't leave Jaime alone. If I go anywhere, I should go to the Ramsays' farm. But all I do is reach up and tighten the padding that protects my shoulder from the fowler's recoil. I haven't even considered taking it off.

3.

December 21, 1759

Afternoon

I can move faster downhill, and soon I reach the creek bottom and turn up the steep hill that leads to more level ground across the water. My feet are beginning to ache in my tight leather shoes, and I envy Mark his soft deer hide moccasins more than ever.

I'm safe, I tell myself. *I'm safe.* Everything I have heard about Cherokee raids tells me the raiders strike fast and withdraw quickly. It's been several hours since we heard the war cries, so surely *I'm safe* now. But I don't know what I will find.

I am trying to be cautious, trying to be quiet and quick, trying to blend into the shadows as I move down the path toward home. But I am not quiet enough, because a strong arm circles my waist and yanks me into the underbrush. I get out one yelp before a tall man spins me around and clamps his hand over my mouth.

"Mark," I gasp. "Oh, Mark, thank God."

"Catie," he says, taking the fowler from me with one hand and pulling me to his chest with the other. I look up, searching the features I know better than my own for some sign, some assurance that everything is all right.

"Catie," he says again, investing my name with more sorrow than I knew it could hold.

People who don't know us often ask if Mark and I are twins, partly because our dark blond hair and hazel eyes match so closely, but mostly because we usually don't have to talk to communicate. My face is pressed against Mark's chest, and I can smell fire smoke on him, mixed with sweat and black powder.

"No," I whisper. "No, no, no." I want to keep Mark from talking. I don't want to hear what he has to tell me. I hear my voice growing louder, and I know I should be quiet, but my mouth moves like something outside of me, out of my control.

"Catie, hush," says Mark. My straw hat has fallen back, carrying the small white cap that covers my coiled braids with it. Mark cradles my head against his chest, stroking my hair. "Listen."

"They're dead." My voice is dull. "Mother and Father are dead, and the cabin is burned. I'm not stupid. I know what happens, and anyway, I saw the smoke."

I feel Mark's chest expand as he takes a deep breath, and I press my face into him, trying to hide my eyes and ears.

"Yes," he says. I hate him a little for saying it, but I also know a sweet lie is useless now. Perhaps even dangerous.

"Was it the Cherokee?" I ask, expecting him to confirm that our parents have died in the nightmare we have dreaded for months.

I feel Mark's chest sink as he breathes out. "That's the thing, Catie," he says. "I don't think it was."

I pull back and look up into Mark's face, for the moment too baffled by his words to respond.

"We should get back to Jaime," I say instead. "We have to tell him."

Mark nods. "We'll stay off the main paths. Best to stay out of sight until we figure out what's going on."

My brother takes my arm as we push through the bare snarls of roots and vines that cover the forest floor. I think of the poor rabbit caught in the tangles and rub my thumb and forefinger together. There's a sore place where I nicked myself freeing the rabbit's body. Mark and I are silent for several minutes, both unable or unwilling to speak.

"Not the Cherokee?" I say at last. "Who else would it be, Mark? The French? I know they've attacked British settlements in the north, but they're hundreds of miles from here, surely."

Mark's fingers tighten around my arm, and he glances sideways at me. "Donald Campbell."

"Donald Campbell," I breathe. "I know he's never liked Father, but Mark, you don't attack and kill people just because you don't like them."

Mark grimaces. "For most people, that's true, but you know how hungry Campbell has always been for more acreage. You know he's never liked how Father speaks against crossing the treaty lines and settling or farming Cherokee land."

"Because it's against the law," I protest. "Father is—was—a law-abiding citizen, and he said pushing for more land would cause trouble between us and the Cherokee. And the war just proves he was right. Maybe if people like Donald Campbell recognized that the laws are there to protect us, we wouldn't be in this mess of a war."

"I don't think Campbell ever saw it that way," Mark counters. "Something happened to him back in Scotland. I don't know what exactly, but it's likely enough he lost something. Property, maybe. In his view, it's just the British authorities trying to keep perfectly good land out of his hands. It has nothing to do with treaties or boundaries."

"He's mad," I say grimly. "If he attacked our family over a disagreement of principle, he's mad."

Mark drops my arm so he can use the fowler to push a low branch out of the way. "His mind is poisoned, I think."

A horrifying thought crosses my mind.

"He couldn't have done it alone."

"He didn't," says Mark. "Catie, just let me tell you everything I know once through, without interrupting, and then we'll try to work it out. It doesn't make sense to me, either."

We have nearly reached the creek bottom, and I grab Mark's wrist.

"Tell me before we get to Jaime," I say. "You and I need to work out how we're going to tell him."

I pull my cap from inside my hat and resettle both on my head. Mark nods and pulls me toward a spot where the trees grow thick around the bank, their roots stretching to reach the water.

Mark swings the rifle off his back, lowers himself onto a sturdy, curling root, and gestures for me to sit beside him.

"It was over by the time I got there," he says, wrapping my hands in his. "Father and Mother were already dead, and the cabin had been fired. I could see all that from the tree line. Their bodies had been dragged outside. It looked for all the world like a Cherokee raid, and it looked like the raiders were gone. I was about to go forward to make sure Mother and Father were truly past help, when I felt a hand on my shoulder."

Mark falls silent, his mouth working, fighting tears.

"Go on," I say gently. "Who was it?"

Mark takes a great gulp of air. "Owen Ramsay."

I draw a breath of surprise. "What was Owen doing there?"

"The raiding party hit the Ramsays, too. Owen managed to escape and came to warn us."

Something bright and happy and warm flows through my mind, through the pain and the chill. Owen came to warn me. He left his own family to warn me. To keep me safe.

"But where is Owen, then?" I ask, uneasy. "Why isn't he with you?" He was alive when Mark saw him. Where is he now?

"Owen is going to meet us at Fish Falls tonight," says Mark. I hear him swallow. "The party attacked the house first. Roger had gone out to the pasture ahead of Owen, so Owen is hoping he escaped, too. He's circling back to see what's left and if there's anything to be done, for Roger or anyone else."

Roger is Owen's younger brother. He is sixteen and very smart. Smart enough to have found a way to escape, I hope.

"All right." I nod, my mind darting ahead, weighing options and considering strategies. "You're sure it was Donald Campbell? If it had been a Cherokee raiding party, it would have been an act of war, but this is different. This is nothing short of murder. We have to report him to the authorities at Ninety Six."

Ninety Six is the nearest seat of British government and the only one so far inside the backcountry, so named because it is ninety-six miles from Keowee, the largest of the Cherokee Lower Towns.

I rush on. "Even walking, we should be able to get there by the day after tomorrow if we move quickly."

Mark slides a hand up to my shoulder to stop me. "Catie, I don't think that's such a good idea. Have you heard a word I said? Owen got a good look at the attackers. They were local men, five or six of them at least, led by Donald Campbell. Campbell's always going on about the influence he has at Ninety Six, and he's a dangerous man. I don't think Ninety Six is an option. I'd rather go in the other direction, to be honest."

Possibilities flicker through my mind. I am thinking too hard, trying to distract myself from the loss of my parents and my home with quick actions and words. I am still trying to wrap my mind around this day. Cherokee attackers I can understand. We are at war. That makes sense. Our neighbors and friends attacking us doesn't.

"Fort Prince George, then?" I ask. "If we can't trust the local authorities, what about the British army? This is wartime, so surely they have some jurisdiction. Anyway, after Ninety Six, Fort Prince George is the nearest place I can think of."

Mark shakes his head. "They've been fighting smallpox off and on at Fort Prince George." His lips tighten. "And Richard Coytmore is the commandant there. I don't want a sister of mine anywhere near the man. He and some of the men of the garrison are suspected of raping Cherokee women in the Lower Towns while the men were fighting the French in the north.

Coytmore's only a lieutenant, and the power of commanding even a small fort has gone to his head."

Mark looks me in the eyes. "Don't you go anywhere near him. Promise me."

I swallow and nod, promising, but the concern in Mark's face tears at my heart. Since I learned Mother and Father are dead, I have been too shocked to cry, too consumed with what to do next. Now sobs are gathering in my throat, threatening to tear through my skin. "Mark," I say. "I need to see it. I won't believe it happened if I don't see it."

Mark puts his arm around me and draws me to his chest again. "No, Catie," he says gently. "I'll see it every day until I die. I don't want you to have to."

A fight rises from my belly and into my throat, scattering the sobs before it. "We have to go back. We have to see if there's anything we can do for them."

Mark takes my face between his hands. "Catie, Catie. I went to the cabin. I saw their bodies. Listen to me. Mother and Father were shot and scalped, and the cabin was burned."

It feels like Mark's hands are squeezing the tears out of my eyes. I gasp for breath.

"Is there anything left?" I think of the neat main room and its high hearth, the dishes and cooking utensils clustered so prettily around it. I think of Father's books and papers covering the table and Mother's herbs hanging from the ceiling. She said it was the one useful thing she learned to do as a child, to dry herbs and cover the smell of life with lavender. I think of my own few books, the pretty stitches of my samplers, my clothes.

Mark sighs. "Not much. The ruin is still too hot to search. We might be able to go back later."

"We have to go back," I insist, like a child begging for something insubstantial. "You say we can't go to the neighbors that are left because they were in on the attack, and we can't go to Ninety Six because they may be in on it, too. Fort Prince George is out because of smallpox. And Coytmore," I add, at Mark's glare. "Where in God's name are we supposed to go, Mark?"

Mark lets go of my face and smoothes back a few strands of damp blond hair that have escaped my braids.

"There's Fort Loudoun," he says. "Owen and I talked about it. We're agreed Fort Loudoun is the safest bet."

My voice has grown high and shaky. "Fort Loudoun is over the mountains." My laughter sounds mad and panicked.

"That's the point," Mark answers. "It's far enough away that whatever local nonsense happened here won't have reached them. It's well away from Campbell's influence. It's garrisoned by an independent company of the British army. There's a provincial militia company there, too, under Captain John Stuart. The commandant reports directly to General Amherst, the commander-in-chief of British forces in America."

I laugh again. "Why on earth would the commander-in-chief care about this?"

"He probably won't care about what happened to us," says Mark. "The war up north is what he's concerned with, the battle for the continent with the French. I doubt South Carolina's war with the Cherokee means much to Amherst, but if it goes on he'll be forced to divert troops he needs elsewhere here. So I'd wager he'd be more than interested in hearing any reports of settlers who seem bent on keeping the Cherokee war going. And faking an attack certainly seems like an act that would be at least partially intended to justify war with the Cherokee."

"The Cherokee are the other problem, Mark, besides the mountains. We'd have to go through Cherokee land to get to Fort Loudoun. It's in the heart of Cherokee territory. We're at war with the Cherokee. They'll see us as hostiles."

Mark grips my hands again, the callused tips of his fingers pressing into my skin.

"The Cherokee Path runs directly between Fort Prince George and Fort Loudoun. We'll follow beside it so we don't lose our way, but we'll stay off the main road to avoid being seen."

The panic in my voice has turned to impatience. "We're at war with them, Mark."

"Who is?" he asks. "It wasn't the Cherokee who attacked us. I'd rather take my chances in Cherokee territory than take them here in Campbell territory. A man who would attack his neighbors can't be trusted for anything."

"What about the weather?" I ask, trying one last time to make a bid for going east. "Can we reach Fort Loudoun before winter really hits?"

Mark shrugs. "For all we know, winter may already be in the mountains. Fort Loudoun is still the safest bet. I know how to build a shelter, in case we get caught in a storm. I've had to do it before."

I nod, exhausted and ready to give up my arguments and let Mark take charge. But I don't get to say more, because Mark presses his hand against my mouth. And then, for the second time today, I hear a sound that terrifies me. Voices, loud, varied, coming from our family's land.

"Catie, take the rifle," says Mark, in that quick, firm tone that's getting so much use today.

"Why?" I ask. He barely lets me touch it.

"Because if you're stuck with one or the other, I'd rather you have the rifle. It's more accurate. I'll take the fowler."

Mark shoves the rifle and cartridge box into my hands and motions for the powder horn and shot bag. Quickly, we trade. I stuff the cartridge box into my deep pocket with my jackknife.

"You get back to Jaime, and you stay hidden, and then as soon as it's quiet, you get on your way to Fort Loudoun. Take the road to Fort Prince George first, and from there take the Cherokee Path. Go as fast and as far as you can as quick as you can. I'll catch up with you. I will. Go now, before they get any closer."

"No, Mark." Sobs threaten to tear my throat open. "No, I won't let you. Let me stay with you, please. Please let me stay with you."

My brother holds my face in his hands, his thumbs pressing into my cheeks as that moment imprints itself on my memory. The gray sky, the bare branches, the cold wind that stings my insides as I gulp for air.

"Take care of Jaime, Catie," he says. "I'll see you soon."

Mark spins me around and gives my shoulder a light slap, like you do to a horse to make it run, and somehow it works, and I am scrambling across the shallow creek and up the other side of the creek bed, stumbling up a hill with the weight of my brother's rifle in my arms and the cartridge box solid against my thigh.

Then I hear the shots, and I turn around.

4.

December 21–22, 1759

Afternoon–Dawn

I lower my body to earth and crawl to a concealed place behind a swell in the ground. I have climbed high and fast, and from my hiding place I see everything clearly. Mark is an excellent shot, but he's armed with an old fowler that is nowhere near as accurate as his rifle. *A piece like that is half luck, any day.*

Lying on my belly in the dirt for the second time today, I bite the paper end off a cartridge and load the rifle carefully, repeating Mark's every instruction under my breath as I do. I have to rise on my knees to ram the ball down the barrel, exposing my body, but I drop quickly back to the ground, out of sight.

Far below me on the path, I see Donald Campbell mounted on a brown mare. Campbell, well into his fifth decade, is nearly an old man, and his heavy frame is no match for Mark's quickness or for a pursuit. That must be why he's riding. His face is red, both with exertion and with streams of vermillion dye like that the Cherokee warriors use to paint their faces when they go to war. He has tried to wash it off, but it has left his face streaked with stripes that look like blood.

I recognize the two men accompanying Campbell on foot by their builds and gestures. They are men of the settlement, at least a decade younger than Campbell. Men I have known since we came here and thought I could trust. But vermillion dye lines the creases in their skin, too.

I know Mark could beat Campbell in a fair fight. I also know this is not a fair fight. Campbell is armed with a rifle much like the one I hold, and I see another on the horse. His men also carry rifles. Hidden in the trees, Mark quickly reloads the fowler and fires, and my heart lifts at a shriek of pain from Campbell. He has dismounted to use his horse as a shield, and he snatches at his bleeding thigh, screaming at his men. He can't be badly hurt, though, because he takes the rifle from the horse. He knows where Mark is. He heard the shot.

Run, Mark, run, I beg silently, and Mark does run, darting among the trees. A lucky musket ball from the fowler downs one of Campbell's men. Hit in the stomach, he falls to his knees, where he wavers unsteadily for several minutes as the fight continues around him.

I know it will take Mark at least a minute to reload, and Campbell's other man is creeping through the trees, using the sound of Mark's second shot to work out my brother's location. I want to yell, I want to scream at Mark that the man is approaching him from behind, but my mouth has gone dry, and I can't get sound through my throat. It's unlikely Mark would hear me, anyway. From up here, my words would be lost on the wind.

I wait, the warning frozen in my throat, but it doesn't matter because Mark is a better woodsman than I, and he knows when he is being hunted.

He spins from his hiding place and plunges his knife into the second man's throat, up to the hilt. He yanks the knife out, dropping the man where he stands, and finishes loading the fowler.

Donald Campbell is still on the path, and his back is to me now. He has tied a cloth around his injured thigh, and he stands steadily. Probably the shot only grazed him. From where I lie I have a clear shot at his back, as long as he stays still. I move my hand to the lock and pull back the hammer. I draw in my breath.

That's your worst habit. You wait too long to fire and lose your nerve and your aim.

My brother dies while I am getting up the nerve to fire. I hear the crack of a rifle, but it isn't mine. Mark has circled through the woods and back to the path. His shot misses, and Campbell catches him full in the chest before he can reload. For a moment, all I can see is the dark stain that spreads over Mark's shirt, and then Donald Campbell flips him onto his stomach, wrenches his head up by his long hair, and takes his scalp. I see the silver flash of the knife that does it, and then the pitiful flap of my brother's skin waving lightly in the breeze.

The world shrinks to a needle's eye. I squeeze my eyes shut, understanding now what Mark meant when he said he would see our parents' bodies until he died. *Please let him not have felt it,* I pray. *Please let him have died instantly. Without pain.*

It takes me a moment to remember I have the rifle, and the rifle is accurate, even if the fowler is not. Campbell is too busy inspecting his injured thigh to consider whether his most recent victim's sister is aiming to kill. I could kill him. I could shoot him right now. For a moment, I line up the tip of the barrel with Donald Campbell's twisted brain. But then I realize the rifle's report will reveal my position. If I miss, he will come after me or find others to send after me. And what will happen to Jaime then?

Forgive me, Mark. But I know what he would have said. He would have told me to go. Dragging the rifle, I crawl away as quietly as I can. I stand when I am sure Campbell won't be able to see me. My whole body feels wobbly, possibly because I haven't eaten more than a few bites today. I push forward, though, thinking of Jaime. I am doing this for Jaime. That's why I didn't fire, why I didn't avenge my brother's death when I had the chance. And because I don't want to be scalped. Oh, dear God, I don't want to be scalped. The image of Mark's bloody hair rises in my mind, and my stomach rolls. I manage to turn to one side to keep from vomiting down the front of my gown, but the world goes black for a few seconds, and I return to consciousness to find myself on my hands and knees. Sharp little sticks and pebbles cut into my palms as my body tries to purge itself of this vile day. My stomach cramps so painfully I have to bite back screams as yellow bile scorches my throat and tongue. When I am able to stand again, I pull myself up and go to find the only other survivor of Donald Campbell's massacre of my family.

When I reach Fish Falls, I dump the powder out of the pan so the rifle won't fire by accident and stow the rifle and cartridges in the same place I hid the fowler a few hours ago. I rinse my mouth with water from the falls, spitting furiously to try to clean myself. I wrap my cloak around my shoulders and crawl into the cave. Jaime is waiting for me, shivering with cold and terror but unhurt. I draw him inside my cloak, as much to calm myself as to warm him. I thank God he can't see my eyes. I want to cry. Every moment I feel I am going to. But I can't. The tears simply won't come. The sobs are squatters in my throat. I try to tell Jaime what has happened, but I can't tell him any more than I can loosen the tears.

"Have you seen Owen Ramsay?" I ask instead. Mark said Owen would come tonight. We have to wait here until he comes, anyway, and after seeing what Donald Campbell did to Mark, I don't want to leave my hiding place.

Jaime shakes his head, wriggling against me. "Catie, you're hurting me," he says. "Let go."

I have been gripping Jaime tight enough to crush the breath out of him, and my muscles protest as I loosen my hold.

"Are you worried about Owen?"

Of course I am.

"A little," I answer. "The Ramsays' place was attacked, too, but Mark saw Owen later." My heart beats over my brittle voice as I wonder if Owen has met Mark's fate. And behind my heart beat the questions: *Why? What was the point of this? Why did Donald Campbell kill my family? Why did he make it look like a Cherokee raid?*

Jaime looks up, his face pale and fearful under his fair hair. "Tell me, Catie," he says. "Just tell me."

I want to cry, but all I can do is laugh bitterly. My words come out in a rush, and I tell Jaime how Mother and Father and Mark are all dead, but telling it does not make it real. It sounds like a sad story I heard years ago and learned by heart. I don't tell Jaime everything, though. I don't tell him about Donald Campbell and the faked Cherokee raid. Perhaps I will tell him later, if it will make him less afraid of passing through Cherokee territory.

"What are we going to do, Catie?"

Jaime is looking to me, as I have always looked to Mark. Mark. I will never be able to look to my elder brother again. All I have left is Mark's plan.

"We're going to Fort Loudoun," I say. "There's an independent company of the British army there, and a provincial militia company, too." I press my lips to the top of Jaime's head. "We'll be safe there. Won't you feel safe with the army?"

I am asking Jaime but talking to myself. I don't know. Armies aren't known for being terribly safe companions for young women on their own. I remember what Mark said about Lieutenant Coytmore and the Fort Prince George garrison.

It is sunset by the time Jaime cries himself to exhaustion, and freezing in the cave. Dark comes early on the longest night of the year. Mother once told me that the day I was born, she lit the lamps at three hours past noon. I pull out the basket of food and thank the person I was this morning for carelessly packing so much. Jaime manages to eat, though the trapped sobs keep me from swallowing, and he falls asleep beside me as soon as it is fully dark. I drift in and out of restless sleep all night, too alert and too afraid to ever sleep deeply. I feel the vibrations of the waterfall and long for my own small bed in the cozy attic of a home that is gone forever.

In the morning, I am stiff and sore from spending the cold night on the damp rock. Jaime moans in his sleep, and I wake him quickly, wishing there were someone to wake me from the terrible dreams I got hints of last night, the terrible dreams I know are coming. A sense of unease for Owen's safety comes over me. He was supposed to join us last night, but he never came.

I crawl out to check on the rifle and cartridges, and I see we can't stay here long. I look down toward the clearing where what's left of our cabin smolders. There's a band of men gathered, one on horseback, three or four on foot, though I can't get a clear count from this distance. Donald Campbell is coming after us, but it looks like he has given up playing Cherokee and is pretending to look for survivors. He is looking for survivors, to make sure we don't survive long. After what I saw him do to Mark, I am sure of that. Well, he can have me, say the sobs in my throat. After I stood by and let him kill Mark, I don't deserve life. But I won't wait around for him to kill Jaime. Jaime he cannot have.

Jaime emerges from behind the waterfall, and I motion to him to stay down.

"Get the food and the cloaks," I tell him quietly. "We'll have to hope to meet up with Owen on the road. We can't afford to wait any longer."

5.

December 22, 1759

Morning

It's easier to hide than to find, I tell myself as I lead Jamie away from our home and away from the rising sun. If I can keep the sun to my back for the next few hours, I'll know we are moving toward the road that leads northwest to Fort Prince George. The main roads are the only way I know to get to Fort Loudoun, and while they may be dangerous, I will be lost entirely if I don't stay near them.

It's easier to hide than to find. Mark first told me that years ago, after I chided him for coming back empty handed from a hunt. The game bag is slung over Jaime's shoulder, the strap crossing his chest, and he holds the awkward basket by its handle. I could carry it more easily, but I am dealing with the long rifle, and Jaime is too short to carry that. I've tried strapping the rifle across my back like I've seen Mark do, but my shoulders are too narrow, and the rifle drags. I hope I will be able to load quickly if I must. I know the loading sequence, but it takes so much more strength to ram the ball to the bottom of the barrel. It takes so much longer than it does with the old fowler.

It's easier to hide than to find. I am breathing fast, from exertion and terror, and the cold winter air is crushing my chest. I don't dare stop while we're still on territory familiar to the searchers. They know every rock and tree as well as I do. I remember Mark's declaration that he would rather take his chances with the Cherokee than with Donald Campbell, and now that I've seen what Campbell did to Mark, I would, too. We have to go a few more miles before we rest. Maybe the searchers won't follow us into Cherokee territory. Maybe they'll be afraid. But I remember how Donald Campbell just killed and scalped at least three of his neighbors, and I don't think he is afraid of anything much.

Jaime keeps pace with me, though his legs are much shorter. I am weighed down by the rifle and slowed by the heavy layers of cloth around my legs, but I remind myself those layers will keep me warm tonight. For the first time, too, I am grateful for the sturdy stays that encase my body from waist to armpits. They are strong where I am weakening, and I know without them my back would be aching. I am grateful that Mother, for all her social graces, understood that clothing of the frontier must be strong and supportive, and she even quietly mocked the Charlestown ladies who laced themselves into clothing so tight they could not breathe.

Jaime pants beside me, his cheeks apple red from the cold.

"When can we stop, Catie?"

"Not yet," I say. "Maybe in a few hours. Maybe at noon. We have to get away from the search party."

"Catie, that doesn't make any sense. If there's a search party coming after us, then someone knows we were attacked. They'll help us."

I consider what I might say. *No, they won't. Donald Campbell turns out to be a madman who wants our whole family and the Ramsays dead for no good reason.* That would terrify Jaime. I need to find a way to tell him slowly, once we are out of danger.

"The frontier isn't safe," I say. "You know how many people are refugee-ing east. We're just going the other way. Fort Loudoun is the safest place for us now. Mark told me to go there, so that's where we're going. Mark would know where we'd be safest."

"Doesn't it take nearly two weeks to get to Fort Loudoun?" asks Jaime. "We can't walk for two weeks straight. We have to stop sometime."

"Not far now," I lie, thinking uneasily of Lieutenant Coytmore and smallpox and hoping we don't run right into a real Cherokee war party. I feel I might be sick again. I have to find a way to get food past the sobs in my throat, or I'll be throwing up that horrid, scorching bile once more.

I hear Mark's voice in my ear, so concerned, so brave. He was so ready to give up his life for me. *It's easier to hide than to find.* And somehow I know it is time to stop.

Part of me feels the search party should have overtaken us long ago, but we had a good head start, I counted fewer than five men, and chances are they assumed we headed east. They don't know we know who they are. They never would have expected us to walk right into Cherokee territory. They can't know our exact direction, and they will have fanned out to cover as much territory as possible. Though it's a lot of territory for only a few men to cover, I feel hunted.

My legs are aching and trembling as we spread Mark's cloak under a rocky outcropping I hope will hide us from searchers. The slab of rock juts out of the earth, forming a small covered space. I sit under the shelter and ease off my tight leather shoes. I turn them over, inspecting the soles. They are thin, not designed for long treks through the wilderness, and though they are holding up for now, I fear they will soon wear through. I fumble in the basket, tear off a chunk of bread, and hand it to Jaime. I tear one for myself and lean back against the earth, chewing. Maybe we should rest here for the afternoon and continue on at night. The rock and earth will shield us from the worst of the elements, and Jaime doesn't look as if he can walk another step. I don't feel I can, though my legs seem to have other ideas, and the muscles tense and throb as if they want to stand me up and walk on their own.

"Can I have more bread?" Jaime asks.

"No." I pull my knees up to my chin and massage my aching feet and calves through my wool stockings. "The food has to last us all the way to Fort Loudoun. You're lucky to get that much."

My words are waspish, I know, but Jaime irks me. I just lost my family, too, but he's the one who got to cry last night, the one who gets to complain now.

And then I hear something that snaps me out of the annoyance of exhaustion and grief. Voices calling for us, calling us by name. The sound echoes through the woods, the tone so kind, so concerned. So deceptive, like the sirens that lured Odysseus's men to their deaths. I want to go to them. I recognize the voices, and I want to go to them and tell them the Cherokee killed my family and beg them to take us home and take care of us. But the Cherokee didn't kill my family. These men did, these men who are looking for us, to finish us off.

We are trapped, trapped like hogs run into a pen. My mind flashes to the rabbit I killed yesterday morning, tangled in vines, unable to move out of my firing line. I wondered why it didn't run. If we try to escape, we will definitely be seen, so I pull Jaime close and draw back as far as I can under the great rock overhang.

"Not a word," I whisper in Jaime's ear. "If you speak, you'll get us both killed, so for God's sake, be quiet."

I close my mouth and motion to Jaime to do the same, so the searchers won't hear our breath. It's hard to breathe evenly when my heart is beating so fast I feel it wants to run up my throat and out of my mouth. I hear the voices, far off, but coming nearer, ever nearer. Maybe we should have run. But maybe the searchers won't see us. As long as they stay on the other side of the overhang, they won't see us. Thank God I haven't heard any dogs.

Above my head I hear the report of a rifle, and I smell black powder on the breeze.

It's easier to hide than to find. I repeat Mark's words over and over in my head, like the answer to a catechism. Perhaps I should be praying, but the words serve me as well as a prayer.

The men are standing on top of the overhang now. I hear their feet scrape across the thin layer of soil that covers the rock. Then I hear the steady sound of a horse at a trot, the vibrations in the ground growing stronger as the horseman draws nearer. The gunshot was a signal. My hand travels to my throat, searching for my mother's pearls. I grip the blue ribbons, twist them in my fingers, will myself to stay hidden.

From above, I hear Donald Campbell's voice, and the sobs that have been stopped in my throat since yesterday awaken. My vision clouds with sudden tears. I fight hard against sound, swallowing sob after sob until my belly fills with them.

"Where are they?" he asks sharply. "I told you not to signal unless you were sure you'd found them. I've a vast deal of territory to cover." He speaks with a highland accent so thick his words are all but lost to my ears, and I strain to understand what he says. Mother always tried to keep us away from the highlander Scots, fearing we would start talking like them.

"Could be a trail," says one voice. It's an older man, one of the first members of the small congregation my father gathered in the backcountry. When he could spare their labor, he sent his sons to the school my father kept at our dining table. His name is Michael Ross, and his hair was gray ten years ago. He's no tracker. They haven't found us yet.

"You think we'll get them?" asks another. "You sure?" I recognize that voice, too. It belongs to Sam Murray, a tentative, twitchy young man I would not have credited with the gumption to murder two families.

Campbell snorts mightily, reminding me of a horse. "It doesn't much matter. If we don't catch them, the Cherokee or the winter will. They don't have a chance of surviving out here on their own. They're fancy folks, soft in the end, for all they've been on the frontier the better part of a decade. And it's just the girl and the little boy." He spits, and I flinch at the sound. "It's not as if their parents could have taught them anything about surviving the mountains. Not a chance in hell."

"You don't think they might have met up with the other one, do you?" Sam asks. "The Ramsay boy who got away, the older one. Any word on him?"

I keep quiet, by some miracle, though a fierce spasm of emotion shakes my frame. They count only one escaped Ramsay, the elder brother. Roger may be dead, then, but Owen is still alive. And he knows we are heading for the safety of Fort Loudoun. He will have to take a similar path. We will find each other.

I hear the frayed patience in Donald Campbell's voice. "We will find him, as we will find the Blair children. If they have gone east, as I suspect they must have, we will certainly find them. And if they have gone west, as I suspect they would fear to do, the Cherokee or the winter will finish them. Either way, no one will question that they either died in the attack or were taken prisoner by the Cherokee."

Sam Murray's voice comes again, high and panicked. "You don't think we have anyone else to worry about, do you? You don't think he would have told anyone but his family and maybe Patrick Ramsay? He wouldn't have written it in a letter, say? Philip Blair was all for rule of law, you know. It would have been hard for him to know what happened to those Cherokee women and not report it."

"Philip Blair was a damned fool, Sam Murray," growls Campbell. "But not as much of a damned fool as you are. He wouldn't have written it in a letter. And you told him under protection of confession. He shouldn't have told anyone. Whether or not he did is another question."

"I think that's Catholics," says Murray doubtfully. "I don't know that Presbyterians follow that rule."

"You shouldn't have said a word to him," says Campbell. "If your conscience hadn't taken to pestering you, we wouldn't be here now."

Murray sounds close to tears. "I didn't know you were going to take it that far. You said we just had to scare them, teach them a little bit of a lesson so they'd want to give up more land, move the legal line west, and then we could settle whatever land we wanted."

My head pressed against the clammy earth, my mind moves rapidly, raking through possibilities of what Sam Murray could be talking about. Then I remember something that happened last summer, something Mother and Father whispered about but tried to keep from me. I remember Mark's warning about Coytmore's attacks on the women of the Cherokee Lower Towns while their men were away fighting the French. One blazing August day, the bodies of four Cherokee women were found near the treaty line that forms the border between British and Cherokee territory. Every time I think about what happened to them, I taste metal in my mouth. The women had been brutalized, raped with knives, their bellies torn open. They had been scalped, too, and left for the wolves. Something similar had happened to another group a few miles south, weeks earlier. The attacks on Cherokee women had become almost routine, but no one talked about it openly. Mother and Father tried to shield me from the knowledge, but Mark told me about it in detail, believing knowledge would be my best protection, in the end, for there had been similarly vicious attacks on white women in the same vicinity. I had assumed those attacks had come from the Cherokee, in retaliation, but now I am beginning to wonder. Donald Campbell is so very terrible.

Murray is right about one thing. If Father had known who the perpetrators were, he would have felt bound by honor and morality to report it. Protecting a parishioner's confidentiality didn't extend to condoning murder. Not for my father, at least. He had his faults, but that wasn't one of them.

"Now, Sam," Campbell continues. "I had no idea you were going to grow a conscience over the savages. These are dangerous times, Murray, and a conscience is an inconvenient thing. How do we know your conscience won't start bothering you again? You might report to the Commons Assembly next, or to the royal governor himself."

Campbell pauses. "And you've wasted my time, calling me here before you've even found the Blair children. They could be miles away by now. Which is why this has to be done."

Sam Murray screams to wake the dead, a piercing ray of sound that rings silver in my ears.

"Hold him," says Campbell.

Murray keeps screaming. I hear his feet scraping over the rock, shuffling on fallen leaves. The sound continues over my head, Sam Murray running in place as Ross holds him for Campbell.

"Oh, take it like a man, won't you?" Campbell's voice. "You know, the Cherokee honor a man who faces his execution bravely. They mock the ones who scream."

Murray shrieks, reminding me horribly of the sound of hogs at the slaughter. I crush Jaime against my chest, blocking one ear with my body, the other with both hands, trying to protect him from this.

The screaming abruptly stops, though I didn't hear the shot that would have killed Murray quickly.

"Leave him," says Campbell.

Ross must have shoved Murray's body over the rock, because it falls heavily from the sky and hits the ground in front of us with a hollow thump. The body rolls heavily onto its back. Murray's eyes are wide and staring, fearful. His scalp is gone, and the skin of his forehead peels forward. I see what cut off his screams so quickly. Campbell cut his throat.

I hold Jaime for a long time, rocking him gently back and forth, waiting until I am sure Campbell and Ross are gone. Jaime is crying, silently, to his credit.

At last I stand. I straighten my stockings, tighten the ribbons at my knees, and slip my feet back into my shoes. As we pass the body, I try to bring myself to say a prayer for Sam Murray's soul, but I can't do it. I never had a quarrel with the man before, but I remember what Donald Campbell said. None of us would be here now if Sam Murray hadn't grown a conscience and brought my father into whatever this is.

We will not stop again until we reach Cherokee territory. I feel a strange kinship with the Cherokee, though I know they might kill me. We are victims of the same madman. Mark was right. We will be safer there. And maybe the Cherokee won't attack a woman and a little boy. Many of them speak English. Maybe I can tell someone what happened even if I don't make it as far as Fort Loudoun. And then I realize to the Cherokee I won't just look like a woman. I'll look like a woman with a gun.

6.

December 24–27, 1759

I push Jaime hard after Sam Murray's death. Trying to put as much distance as possible between us and Donald Campbell, I set a breakneck pace that squeezes every drop of the scant daylight, and often I push us on after dark. On Christmas Eve, we skirt Fort Prince George and meet up with the path that leads to Fort Loudoun. Mindful of my promise to Mark, I keep as far away as possible, but when we reach a rise that overlooks the fort, I can't help but look curiously down at the small structure. A log palisade stitches a diamond in the ground. At each of the diamond's points is a bastion in the shape of an arrowhead, and the space inside is dotted with small buildings. The Cherokee hostages are being held in one of them, the fact of their captivity driving the war on. What would it take to stop it, I wonder? If the hostages were freed, would that help? Could anything stop the war now?

If it weren't for the war, I could pass through the mountains without fear of attack. If it weren't for the war, Donald Campbell would not have found such an easy scapegoat for his crimes in the Cherokee, and he might not have attacked my family. But Campbell wants this war, clearly, if he attacked those women and used a Cherokee disguise to settle a private score. He thrives on violence, but Sam Murray's words tell me the real reason Campbell wants war. He wants to win. He wants an excuse to acquire more land, but he must always appear to be a law-abiding British citizen. No one can know he is fanning the flames of conflict, which is why my family had to die.

I remember I must not linger here, and I shoulder the rifle again and put my hand on Jaime's back to turn him around.

From Fort Prince George, the path passes west through the Cherokee Lower Towns at the base of the mountains. The Cherokee Path will take us past the Middle Towns and on to the Overhill Towns, where Fort Loudoun is located. My goal is to get us to Fort Loudoun without encountering another soul, British or Cherokee. I don't know whom I can trust, so unless I have to, I will trust no one. I didn't think of the Cherokee towns being so close to the path before. I frown. There are other paths, I know, narrower, less traveled ones. We will have to leave the wide Cherokee Path and hope and pray we can manage to stay on course.

That night, poorly sheltered by a few thin pines, I give Jaime an extra bit of bread and cheese in celebration of the holiday. Christmas was always a bit of a contested point in our house. Father didn't entirely approve of it, and Mother, who was reared in the Church of England, wouldn't give it up. Fixing a large, celebratory meal was a small thing, really, but it made her happy. Happy in the way that leads to sadness, for I often saw tears in her eyes at the end of the day.

We spend three days climbing steadily into higher reaches. We are lucky that winter seems to be waiting this year and that the Cherokee seem to have pulled back into their clustered towns for the cold weather. But we are lucky for only a little while, because we are well into the mountains when it starts to snow. Flurries, at first. Frost that melts in the morning sun. A taste of what will come.

Our food is running low, but if we ration it carefully we will have enough for several more days, by which time I hope to have reached Fort Loudoun. According to the traders, it should be a fairly easy journey of about ten days from Fort Prince George. But that was in peacetime, when travelers could take the main road without fear of attack. It will take us longer by the back ways, the little used trails clogged with underbrush. And that was for a strong, healthy, well-supplied man. Not for a woman with a little boy who is beginning to cough. Not for two people who use up all the food in their bellies before they can replace it.

We must reach Fort Loudoun by the new year, I tell myself. January's weather will be much worse than December's, and it is only a few days away.

I am counting the days, trying to keep track of time. Somehow it comforts me to know the day of the week and the date. But the days begin to bleed together. I learned to read by the first chapter of Genesis, but for the first time in my life I feel the rhythm of evening and morning, because it is all I have to guide me.

And there was morning and there was evening. And there was morning and there was evening. Morning. And Evening.

The sixth day.

We camp in a circle of evergreens that blocks the wind. I rest against a thick trunk where two trees have grown together and pull Jaime to me. We are wrapped in our heavy cloaks, and I spread Mark's larger cloak over us. *Oh, Mark,* I think, feeling the sobs sharp in my throat. *I wish you were here. I wish you hadn't played the hero. You could have run with me. Why didn't you run with me?* I know why, of course. If Mark hadn't held Campbell's party off, it's likely they would have found all three of us then. The pain of Mark's absence is like that of an amputated limb, raw, like a piece of my own skin has been ripped away and left my innards unprotected.

I can forget Mark during the day, when I have to think about where I'm going, about avoiding contact with anyone, about keeping Jaime on his feet and moving. But he haunts me at night, with his absence, and I am so sad and so angry all at once. If he were here, I could put some of this burden on him, this burden of bringing Donald Campbell to justice, this burden of keeping Jaime alive. But Mark is not here, so I have to shoulder it all myself, and that makes me hate him only slightly less than I hate Donald Campbell.

The thought of Donald Campbell brings an acid burn into my throat that eats through the sobs. *No crying,* I tell myself. *No crying yet.* It's too dangerous to cry, too draining. I will cry when I am safe, when Jaime is safe, when Donald Campbell has been brought to the gallows and can no longer hurt us. When tears are a luxury I can afford.

Jaime coughs, recalling me to the one member of my family who is still alive.

"Sit up," I say, propping his back with my hands.

"I'm so cold, Catie," he says. "Can't we build a fire?"

"I wish we could, Jaime." My voice is gentler than I feel. I'd like a fire, too. There are all sorts of things I'd like. A hot mug of cider and a warm bed come to mind. My mind starts to wander, and somehow Owen Ramsay slips into that bed with me, his body warm against mine. A memory warms my cheeks, a memory of summer and Owen's lips on mine, hot and sweet.

"We can't build a fire, Jaime," I continue, ripping my thoughts away from things I cannot have. "We're trying to hide, remember? And I know it doesn't seem so, but it's still warm enough without one. We won't freeze to death."

And if we do, I add internally, *freezing to death is peaceful enough, in its way. It's a better death than Mark or Mother and Father had.*

Jaime coughs again, and I am reminded there are plenty of ways the cold can kill us without simply freezing us to death. I wrap my hand around Jaime's forehead. It's like a caress, but I'm searching for a fever. He's still cool. Maybe the cough is only an irritation in his throat. Lord knows my own throat is dry and scratchy enough from the frigid air.

I give Jaime a piece of smoked venison to chew and pull him back to my chest. Maybe I can keep him warm with my own body. I gaze through the higher branches of the evergreens to the cloudy night sky. *Please don't snow,* I beg. *Please.*

"Do you want to hear a story, Jaime?" I ask, and he nods. I have developed a talent for lying, for making up stories to keep Jaime calm and distracted. Dredging up old memories has helped me, too, helped me to avoid the recent past by focusing on things that happened long ago or didn't happen at all.

"What kind of story do you want tonight?"

"New Jersey," he answers. "I like New Jersey stories. Maybe we could go back there, Catie."

"Maybe," I agree. I haven't thought about it. I haven't thought of anything past getting us safely to Fort Loudoun before winter arrives in earnest. I settle against the tree and hug Jaime tighter.

"Tell me how it starts," I prompt.

"Mark was little when you moved there," says Jaime. "And you were just a baby."

"Not even. I was born in New Jersey."

"I want to hear about the bear in the laundry," he says.

I draw a breath. It's an old story, a story that has become funny in the retelling, though out here in the wilderness, I have a hard time finding the humor in it. It must have terrified my mother.

I close my eyes against the dark.

"Mother and Anna had been doing laundry all day," I begin. Anna was the daily woman who came in to help Mother. Mother found help easily in

New Jersey, but there was a shortage of servants in the backcountry. "And they had made a meat pie for dinner."

"Where was Father?" Jaime prods.

"Who knows?" I answer. "At the church, maybe, or out visiting a parishioner. In any case, he wasn't home. Mother had put Mark and Mary in the back garden to play, and she left them for a few minutes. She also left the pie to cool on the back wall. It was a small garden, and it was bricked in, so they should have been safe enough."

Mary was my elder sister, the child between Mark and me. She didn't live long after that, taken in a fever, and somehow in my memory she exists only in this one afternoon, the timeless afternoon when a bear breached the gate of our back garden in pursuit of a meat pie.

"It was your fault," says Jaime. "You were crying, and Mother left them to get you."

"It was my fault," I agree. In family lore, I have taken on the role of the villain.

"In any case, the bear must have wanted the pie, but it managed to get itself tangled in all the linens on the line, and by the time Mother heard Mark yell, it had dressed itself up in bed linens so that it looked like a great lady going to the theater. Anna got the kitchen pans and made such a racket that the bear ran off, taking half our linens with him."

"And so the pie was saved," finishes Jaime.

"And so the children were saved," I correct. "Think what might have happened if a bear had gotten to Mark and Mary."

A shiver runs up my spine. For a moment, while I was telling the story, I forgot Mark and Mary were gone.

"Father thought it was hilarious, of course, when he heard about it. Mother didn't."

Mark told me that, years later, after the story of the bear had been rehashed and Father had had to wipe his eyes from laughing at the notion of a bear dressed in our bed linens. Mark said he could never, before or since, remember Mother sobbing like that. I didn't understand it then, but the past week has given me perspective. Her children had been in danger. Her laundry had been ruined, her fine linen soiled and stolen.

I remember Mother sobbing one other time as though her heart would break. It was when I was nine and Father announced we would be moving to the southern backcountry east of the mountains so he could preach to the Scots and Scots-Irish Presbyterians and teach their unlettered children.

Maybe he couldn't help it. For a decade, he had been preaching to a small congregation midway between New York and Philadelphia and taking on pupils to prepare for Harvard. The church door and the door of our house beside it looked out on the Delaware River, and in autumn the enormous leaves of the hardwood trees turned the color of pumpkins, but I think the peaceful beauty of the Jerseys bored him. He had come to America for adventure, not realizing how ill suited he was for it.

Mother had sobbed and sobbed. I'll never forget her face when she said she thought New Jersey was the frontier. Frontier enough for her, anyway. But not for him. She said he'd get her babies killed.

And look at that, Mother, I think, rubbing slow circles into Jaime's temples to put him to sleep. *He very nearly has.* I think again about my and Mark's protection of Jaime, our coddling of him, and I think I know why we did it. There were four other children between Jaime and me, but we lost them all in one way or another. Jaime was the only one we got to keep.

7.

December 28, 1759

I haven't yet had cause to fire the rifle, and I hope to avoid it. I have a limited number of cartridges, and the report is so loud it would attract attention for several miles around, especially here in the mountains, where sounds echo. I know Mark gave me the rifle in case I needed its accuracy for hunting, but I won't need to hunt until the basket is empty. In any case, I don't dare build a fire to cook meat, so I put the thought out of my mind. We will simply have to reach Fort Loudoun before we run out of food. The attack was a week ago today, and we left the morning after. This is our seventh full day of traveling. Though I know it's a deception, I console myself with the notion that Fort Loudoun can't be far away now.

I practice loading the rifle the morning after I tell Jaime the story of the New Jersey bear, because far away below us on a ridge, moving east, I see a Cherokee war party. I admit to myself the other reason Mark wanted me to have the rifle: in case I must shoot a person. There are only a few men, four or five perhaps, though we are so far away it's hard to get an exact count. Their straight, black hair is pulled back from their faces, which are red with vermillion dye. The war goes on, then, and surely the British garrison at Fort Loudoun will care to hear of Donald Campbell's part in it.

The weather is against us that day. It's the strange combination of snow and ice and rain that is somehow colder than any one of those can be alone, the kind of near-freezing chill that sinks into your skin and drenches your bones. I almost give in and try to start a fire with the flint from the rifle, but I remember the war party and realize everything is too wet for the fire to take, anyway. Instead, Jaime and I find a little shelter under a slab of rock mostly buried inside the mountain. It keeps our heads dry, though we have to stand all night, leaning into the earth. Our shelter blocks the wind and keeps us from getting completely soaked, though our feet and the bottoms of our cloaks are drenched.

Jaime's teeth are chattering, and his skin is so pale under his fair hair that it scares me. I make sure he's wrapped tightly in his cloak and then throw mine and Mark's around both of us.

"In New Jersey, this is nothing," I say, though I know I am lying. These mountains have more to throw at us than New Jersey ever dreamed of. "The Delaware used to freeze over in winter, it was so cold." It did freeze over, with ice only as thick as a pane of window glass.

"Did you skate on it?" Jaime asks. He's wanted to ice skate ever since Mother told him about the year the Thames froze with ice so thick Queen Elizabeth hosted skating parties all winter. That was close to two hundred years ago, but it's all the same to Jaime. In his mind, England is a place and a time rolled into one, and everything that ever happened there is happening all the time. He's the one who listened to Mother's stories about growing up as the youngest daughter of an English baronet, about her life before she met the second son of a second son who was bound for the Church and the New World. It strikes me that perhaps I should have listened more closely, perhaps I should not have been so quick to embrace the backcountry, to let Mother's early life slide into the darkness of myth. But I learned from Mother, all the same. I learned when something is gone, you must let it go, or you'll go mad with grief. I am glad I learned. That's the only way I've survived the last week.

"We skated on the Delaware all the time," I lie, my lips so cold they can barely form the words. "Someday I'll take you there, and you'll skate on it, too."

"You and Owen?" Jamie asks.

My cheeks are too red and pinched with cold already for Jaime to tell I'm blushing, but I'm grateful for the sudden warmth in my face.

"Why me and Owen?"

"Aren't you going to marry him?"

"He hasn't asked me," I answer, casting my eyes skyward for any sign of mercy from the elements. "So I can't say."

"But you've always been going to marry him, haven't you?"

For someone I think of as terribly naïve, Jaime doesn't miss much. I have been planning to marry Owen Ramsay almost since the day I met him, the day our families set out southward together from Philadelphia. Owen Ramsay is bound so closely to my childhood it seems as though he has been part of me for as long as I can remember myself. And I didn't plan to marry him because he was handsome or because he would inherit a decent plot of land or because his family had enough breeding for Mother's taste, though I didn't mind that he was one of the few boys who could both read and write for miles.

I planned to marry Owen Ramsay because we got on so well together, because we never ran out of things to talk about or fell into those uncomfortable silences other people were prone to, and because once when I was eleven he spent an entire afternoon by the creek telling me about the pharaohs of Egypt, the early pharaohs who really had been Egyptian, before the Greeks and Macedonians took over and pretended. The only real Egyptian pharaoh I was familiar with was the one in Exodus, so it was a great pleasure to find out there were more, even if no one knew very much about them because their doings were recorded in one of the lost languages of the past. I knew about Cleopatra from Father's volume of Plutarch, the Roman historian I read in secret since Mother didn't think he had anything appropriate to tell me. I smuggled the book out, and together Owen and I read the story of Cleopatra presenting herself to Caesar in a roll of carpet. Plutarch led us on to other old Romans, who led us to the even more ancient Greeks and to stories that thrilled and terrified.

Not long after, Owen began to ignore me completely, to spend more time with his brothers and mine, to treat me like something he either had outgrown or hadn't quite grown into yet. It was around the time of this strange and silent separation that Mother decided Owen Ramsay would just about do for me, and because I was furious over his sudden desertion, I let her make her plans, but I pointedly ignored Owen Ramsay until about a year ago. That was all right, because I ignored him in a way that ensured he felt it, so when I chose to take notice of him again, he felt he'd been pardoned. By that time, I had added certain other attributes of Owen Ramsay's to my list of reasons to marry him, though the pharaohs remained on that list. The boy who spoke to me of pharaohs was more real than the one who ignored me for four years.

"Yes," I answer Jaime. "Yes, I've always been going to marry Owen, and I suppose if we ever go to New Jersey, he'll come with us."

"I like Owen," mutters Jaime, nearly asleep despite the cold and our uncomfortable position. "I hope he's alive."

My heart freezes as cold as the air at those words, but an old tale cracks free and rises to the surface of my mind, an old Greek story I discovered alone one day when I was thirteen. There were three sisters called the Fates who were quite literally spinsters. The first sister spun the thread of life when a baby was born, the second sister measured the length of the baby's life, and the third sister cut the thread when that life was over. They had long, complicated names that meant something special, but to myself I called them Spin, Measure, and Cut. They terrified me. I took my fear to my father, knowing Mother had no more use for the Greeks than she did for anyone else who wasn't raised on her father's manor. Father never saw my fear. He only became very excited that I was interested in the Fates and showed me a terrible illustration in one of his many terrible books. It was another wheel, one with a king at the top and a man being crushed to death at the bottom, and he said it was a medieval interpretation of a similar idea. I was clumsy at the spinning wheel for weeks, leading Mother to despair of my ever developing the ability to spin flax neatly into thread.

The last sister hasn't gotten to Owen, I tell myself. Cut has been so terribly busy lately. He's alive. He has to be. Maybe he's ahead of us, or maybe he has taken a different route altogether. He is alive. We just haven't met up with him yet.

8.

December 30–31, 1759

By our ninth day on the run, it is Owen who haunts my thoughts and not Mark. I know Mark cannot come for us, but Owen still could. I have lost so much that I can't lose Owen, too. I must believe Owen is alive because I will run completely mad if he isn't.

It's nearly dusk, and I dread the way the cold will intensify when the winter daylight is gone. The emptiness in my belly makes the cold feel even more cruel than it is. There's only a little cheese and smoked venison left, and at last I have agreed to let Jaime go to a small creek and try to catch a fish or two. He showed me where they gather in a shallow pool, and he has at least a chance of catching the small fish with his hands. I'd like to make a net, but I have no cloth to spare. We need all our clothing for protection from the elements, so I don't dare risk it until our food is gone.

I am so hungry and cold I decide to take a chance on a fire tonight. I lean against a tree, so tired and sore with walking all day and sleeping all night on the hard ground. I drift into a pleasant dream about Owen and how he will find us and how I can let him take some of this burden from me, care for Jaime, find the way to Fort Loudoun, make Donald Campbell answer for his crimes. My treasonous mind floats back to reality, and I find myself wondering whether it's better to freeze to death or starve to death. It doesn't even strike me as odd that I don't really care which it is. I am beginning to want this over.

A shriek, high, wild, inhuman, shreds my dreams and stabs through my spine. I have never heard a scream like this, never, not even in Donald Campbell's imitation of a Cherokee war cry. It tears the cold winter twilight apart.

I am scrambling in the basket for the large kitchen knife when I hear the second scream call my name, this one small and human and infinitely less powerful. Jaime. I pick up the rifle and the cartridge box. For a second I hesitate, uncertain if I should load and then go to Jaime or go to Jaime and then load. Fear wins, and I know I must see Jaime first.

When I reach the water's edge, I see Jaime standing on the other side, where the bank is higher. His back is to me, and his arms are up in front of his body. I see the silver flash of his jackknife in the air, and my merciless mind calls up an image of Donald Campbell's blade slicing through my elder brother's flesh. But that image dissolves as I watch a tawny animal three times Jaime's size knock him to the ground. Though I have never seen one, I know what it is. I have heard stories, stories of lambs and children carried off, of dogs disemboweled. A sleek, secretive beast. A cat of the mountain. A catamount.

"Jaime, I'm here!" I yell, hoping the noise will both distract the catamount and let Jaime know I heard him call for me. I rest the butt of the rifle on the ground and pull out a cartridge. The animal lifts its gigantic muzzle from the ground, its mouth sticky with blood I hope is its own and fear is Jaime's. I call to Jaime to stay quiet now I have taken the animal's attention from him. The catamount approaches the bank and begins to pad back and forth, looking for an easy way down the steep slope. It nestles on its haunches for a moment and then pounces, easily clearing the creek. I bite the end off the cartridge, pour most of the powder down the barrel, and wrap the ball in the rest of the paper. I pull out the ramrod. This is the hardest part. I have to use my body to hold the rifle up and use both hands to ram the ball to the bottom of the barrel.

It sticks. I can't get the ball to the bottom. Briefly, I consider shooting the ramrod at the catamount, but then it is almost on me, and I lose my hold on the rifle. All I have left are the kitchen knife and my small jackknife.

The cat is silhouetted against the dying winter sun, a gigantic shadow. I raise the kitchen knife, though to use it I would have to be so close that the beast would have no trouble killing me. Every one of its claws is worth two knives. I think about making a dart to pick up the rifle, and that's when the cat springs. The knife falls from my hand when the cat slings me onto my back, and it pops into my head to be glad I am not holding a loaded rifle, which could have misfired in the fall and hit me or Jaime. The fall to the ground knocks the wind out of me, and the pressure of the cat's paw on my chest makes it hard to get air.

We're tussling on the ground. I'm scrabbling my fingers in the cat's face, going for the eyes. I shove my thumbs into the cat's eyes, hoping that will give me a chance to reach the knife. But when I take my hands away from its face, the cat lets out a shriek of pain and fury, one of those cries that shatters the air, and slashes wildly at my chest. Searing, stinging pain cuts across my body, hot and cold at the same time. I manage to reach the kitchen knife, and just as the cat opens its jaws to go for my throat, I plunge the knife into its side. This throws the cat off, but it doesn't kill it. It gives me a second to roll away, though, enough time to scramble for the rifle. This time the ramrod slides down the barrel easily, the way it always did for Mark. I remove the ramrod and pull out another cartridge. I rip that one open with my teeth and pour a small amount of the powder into the pan, hoping it is enough to make the gun fire but not enough to make it explode in my hands. I pull back the hammer until it locks and swing the weapon up to my shoulder.

You wait too long to fire and lose your nerve and your aim.

The ball lodges in the catamount's hip, nowhere near its brain. The cat is slowing, though, and I don't think it will be able to follow me up the other bank to Jaime.

A few yards downstream, a row of slippery rocks provides a rough bridge. Carrying the rifle in one hand and the cartridge box in the other, I rush to it, knowing I have to run even if the cat chases me, because if I stand still it will kill me. I rush across the mossy rocks and up the tangled roots that form a natural ladder in the bank. I drop to the ground when I reach the top, hoping twilight clouds the cat's vision. I am lucky it isn't fully dark, when the cat's glowing eyes could see me easily. I crawl toward Jaime. *Good boy*, I think. *Stay still.* First, I have to kill the cat. Then I can take care of Jaime.

My hands are steady as I reload the rifle, but again it takes all my strength to force the ramrod to the bottom of the barrel. The cat is slowing, so I find a good place to prop the rifle so I can be sure of my aim. Before I can fire, the cat sits heavily back on its haunches and its front legs slide forward. It shakes its head once. It may be dying now, but I'm not sure, so I aim and fire a ball into its brain.

In a few minutes, I am certain the cat is dead. I loosen my grip on the rifle. My hands were steady while I was shooting, but they are shaking now, and I put down the weapon and grip them together to stop the trembling. I wasn't afraid while I was fighting the catamount. I didn't have time. But now I am shivering all over, and I can't stand. I curl into a tight ball, hugging my knees against my chest, until I have recovered, until I have convinced myself that I am still alive, that the cat didn't kill me. And then I look at Jaime. Between his head and chest is a mass of blood and bone. He is dead. The cat ripped out his throat.

I feel my eyelids press together tightly, and I rest my forehead against my knees. I reach out to Jaime and begin to pat his shoulder. I pat over and over, as if that will bring him back to life. I keep expecting him to sit up, to say something. It's dark when I stand, aimless, detached from my body, and wrestle Jaime's knife out of his clenched hand and find the cartridge box on the ground. I pick up the rifle, marveling at its heavy awkwardness. I try to lift it to my shoulder again and find I can't. I have no idea how I managed to hit the catamount the first time with no support for the rifle but my own arms, which are now aching with exertion.

I half slide down the bank and cross the treacherous rocks, which is so much easier now that I don't care if I slip and drown. I walk over to the cat and look it in the face. If it weren't Jaime's killer, I could be sorry for it. It looks like a large housecat. The tangy scent of blood permeates the air, cutting through the smell of black powder from the rifle, and I realize it's not coming from the cat, who really didn't bleed much. I can smell it so strongly because it's coming from me, from the swipe the cat took across my chest. There's a lot of blood, but I still feel all right, if numb is all right. An insistent instinct warns me away from my kill, away from this horrible place, to avoid the scavengers that will come and could present as much danger as the cat. I can't stay here, not even to be with Jaime. A cool reason saturates my brain. Jaime is dead, and I am still alive. The sooner I get away, the better I'll feel.

I find the kitchen knife on the ground and return to where the cloaks and what remains of our food are piled together. I wrap my own cloak around my shoulders and pick up Jaime's and Mark's cloaks from the ground, and my mind begins to play its merciless tricks. Two hours ago, I told Jaime to take off his cloak so he wouldn't get it wet in the creek. Only an hour ago, Jaime was alive, a burden and a blessing I had to carry, but now he is gone, gone so quickly I cannot wrap my mind around it, cannot yet believe it happened. Ten days ago, Mark was alive. I look at the tiny, perfect stitches around the hem of his cloak, stitches done by my mother's hand. Ten days ago, Mother and Father were alive, too. Ten days ago, on the last day of my childhood, though I didn't know it then, I argued with Mother over mud stains on my cloak. Such a stupid thing. Less than two weeks. Less than two weeks ago, I had a family and a home, and nothing was really my responsibility. Until Donald Campbell took my family and my peace.

In a daze, I pick up the food basket and drop the knives and the cartridge box into it. I wrap my brothers' cloaks around my body, pick up the rifle, and start walking. The steady movement helps burn the nervous energy still pulsing through me, but as I walk my chest begins to hurt badly. I am feeling my way through the woods, and trying to move in the dark is making me dizzy. When I reach a hand tentatively toward my chest, I find the other reason I am disoriented. Blood loss. I add bleeding to death to my list of ways to die.

I put down the heavy rifle and basket, unable to carry them any longer. If other predators find me tonight, they'll be able to finish what the catamount started, because I can't fight them like this. Shooting them will be my only chance. I prop myself against a tree, reload the rifle with great difficulty, and wait through the long night.

In the morning, I feel my chest gingerly. The blood has dried my shift and bodice to the wounds, and I don't want to remove my clothes because I'm afraid of starting the bleeding again. For now, the layers of cloth are serving as a plaster and probably holding my skin together. My stays feel off, in the wrong place, but I can't find the energy to care or to do anything about it. I've managed to sit in a patch of sunlight, and I wrap myself in the cloaks and drift in and out of sleep all day. The stinging doesn't stop, and by evening it has turned to a dull, throbbing pain. My throat is parched, and I wish I could get to water to cool the rising heat I feel in my body, but I can't move.

I lie there, stroking the blue ribbons around my neck and thinking of the three sisters and how busy they have been. In my mind, the blue ribbons become the thread of my own life, and I grip them in my fist, wondering if I can snap them from my throat myself or if the last sister will have to do it for me.

The wild beasts come only in my dreams. I know they are dreams because the beasts don't have their own faces. Their heads have been replaced with the heads of humans, with the faces of my neighbors, of people I thought I could trust. The catamount has Donald Campbell's face, and it stalks me, growing larger as it draws nearer, until finally it towers over me and Campbell's mouth opens to reveal terrible fangs. The fangs are ready to clamp down on my throat when I feel a pull on my legs that snatches me out of the way. But now I am in the grip of another, of something I cannot see, and that is more terrifying than the worst thing Donald Campbell can do to me. My chest screams with pain as I spin through a tunnel of fire.

At last the movement stops, but now I am still and so cold. I don't know if I am awake or dreaming. I am in a nightmare place where I am all alone but tormented by the faces of my family's killers. Warm hands touch my skin, burning away the cold, turning me over. Another face appears above me, but this one I don't recognize. It is hazy, ringed with a dark halo, like someone dragged a painting through water before it was dry. From a long way off, from outside the tunnel of fire, I hear a voice calling to me. And then a great wind rushes at me, forcing me through the tunnel. I feel myself moving quickly, faster than I have ever run. I become the ball in the rifle, rolling down the barrel, ripping through the trees. The wind screeches in my ears as I fly past branches and through a chill and driving rain. Then the movement stops as the world goes black, and I drop into oblivion wondering whose dark heart is my target.

PART 2

THE SHELTER

9.

January 7, 1760

Afternoon

When I wake, I believe for a moment I am back in New Jersey, in the small chamber I shared with Mary and with the tiny twins who lived such a short time. I am very young and have been ill, but now I am awake and hungry for the first time in days. Mother will come soon with warm broth and cool cloths, and I will be safe and well again. I run my hands over the rough bedding, thinking my soft linens can't be here because they were stolen by a bear, and the bear itself rumbles through a momentary dream that ends before I can register it. But I know something is not right. I don't want to wake. I want to stay in my cozy chamber, listening to the breeze off the Delaware. I huddle, curled in this place between sleeping and waking, as my mind sorts through itself, pulling reality apart from dreams. At last I open my eyes, uneasy because I am still not sure what is real and what is not, but I know I should have been awake long ago.

The dream evaporates as my eyes open. I am not in my chamber in New Jersey. I am not a small child anymore, and never again will my mother's cool hands feel my face for a fever. The truth of loss comes rushing back with a force that makes my stomach turn, and I close my eyes against it, willing the world to stop spinning around me.

Try as I may, I can't keep my eyes closed. I am in the strangest enclosure I've ever seen, and given the variety of materials the poorest families of the backcountry use to build their homes, I've seen some rather odd structures posing as houses. On either side, two facing walls of solid stone lean into each other to meet at a point twice the height of a man. I am tucked into a corner by one of the stone walls, so I have to twist my neck to see what's behind me. The back wall is a slope of earth that fills in between the mono-liths, except for a point at the very top where a gap allows smoke from the fire to flow out. The gray light that falls from the opening tells me it's late afternoon.

At the base of the earth wall, midway between me and the facing rock, is a crude hearth made of stones stacked together and anchored with dried mud. A low fire burns, and I note with gratitude that an iron bake kettle crouches on three legs beside it, so there must be something to cook. The fourth wall reminds me of the rough cabins poor families sometimes throw up along the frontier. Notched pine boughs are fitted together, and the gaps are filled with mud and pine needles. I look for a way to come and go and realize there must be a door in the pine wall. A large dark blue blanket covers it, probably to stop the heat from escaping.

I didn't get here on my own. This becomes alarmingly evident as I begin to examine myself as closely as I have been examining my surroundings. I am lying on a thin pallet stuffed with what I take for more pine needles. I reach out a hand to touch the rock wall and pull back in shock at the warmth. Of course. The stone reflects heat into the room. That's why it's so warm, much warmer than the small fire alone could make it.

My cloak is spread over me like a blanket. I'm beginning to feel almost too warm, but when I try to pull the cloak off and sit up, the pain that rico-chets through my entire body reminds me of the catamount, and of Jaime, and of the reason I've lost some time and can't remember how I got here. I lie back and inspect my body as well as I can without rising. Most of my own clothes are nowhere to be seen. My shift, stays, and shoes are certainly gone; I can feel that much without looking. I run one foot over the opposite leg. I still have my wool stockings. I pull myself up to glance over my body. My thick under petticoat remains tied at the waist, but my wool overskirt and gown are gone. I am wearing a man's brown shirt that ties at the neck. It's far too big for me, but the blousy sleeves have been pushed up and secured with strips of cloth above my wrists.

Now that the initial shock of waking in such a strange place is wearing off, I'm acutely conscious of the dull pain emanating from the right side of my chest. I reach my left hand tentatively under the shirt. Cloth folded into a thick pad covers my right shoulder and breast down to the bottom of my ribcage. I pat around and find it is held in place by a band of cloth that wraps across the other side of my chest and all the way around my back. I know better than to remove the bandages, but I can't help it. I need to know how badly injured I am.

By working my fingers underneath, I manage to loosen the band of cloth that holds the pad in place. I carefully lift the pad with my left hand, wincing as the cloth peels away from the wounds. I cast my eyes downward as best I can, but I have to use my fingers to ascertain the damage. Pain billows at the pressure of my touch as I slowly follow each line of torn flesh. The wounds are sticky, though with blood or pus I can't say. The surrounding flesh is warm, but not hot, and I hope this means I've passed through the worst inflammation.

But the cat got in a good swipe; it did more damage than I thought. The uppermost slash starts at my right collarbone, passes between my breasts, and tapers out at the bottom of my ribcage. The two in the middle start under my arm, cross the rise of my breast, and end just under my breastbone. The cut at the bottom is the shortest, and it must also be the shallowest. If it had been deep, it would have eviscerated me easily. It scrapes along the bottom of my ribcage and the top of my abdomen.

I replace the pad and struggle to secure it with the cloth band as my mind rushes through possibilities of where I could be. I've heard stories of people taken captive by the Cherokee, many treated well, as I seem to have been. There are also men who live alone deep in the wilderness, making their livings by hunting and trapping and trading. Mark stayed with them sometimes, and though they are generally trustworthy, they are as wild as the mountains themselves.

I look around for clues. Beside the iron bake kettle are a few more cooking implements: a trencher, a spoon, a pot. On the other side of the hearth is a cane chair with a blanket folded neatly on the seat. It's hard to see more from my limited angle in the dim light. There's nothing distinguishing. These things could belong to anyone, especially in the mountains, where decades of trading have led the Cherokee and the white settlers to own much the same goods. Whoever found me in the wilderness seems to have taken good care of me, providing me with shelter and treating my wounds, but I dare trust no one. After all that's happened to me over the last two weeks, the only person left for me to trust is myself.

I am looking around for the basket that holds the kitchen knife and Jaime's jackknife, for Mark's rifle or for some other weapon, for anything I can use to defend myself from whoever brought me here and will certainly be coming back, when I hear the pine door open on its leather hinges. The pain in my chest screams at me to be still, but my fear overpowers it, and I struggle to a sitting position. I won't face this lying down. I glance at the bake kettle on the hearth, wondering if I can make a dart for it, wondering if

I have the strength to lift it. A man's hand grasps the blanket over the door. It's a young man's hand, and for a moment I feel a wild hope that it is neither a Cherokee nor a mountaineer but Owen, that he has found me and brought me to this shelter and begun to heal me. I want it to be true so badly I say his name aloud.

But the fantasy lasts only a moment, because the man behind the blanket is in such a hurry to seal out the cold wind that follows on his heels that he whirls into the room, a game bag banging heavily against his side. Snow falls from his leather boots and melts when it meets the packed earth of the floor. In one hand, he's gripping Mark's rifle, and in my panic, I stand, forgetting the pain.

He leans the rifle against the opposite rock wall and turns to secure the leather latch before he smoothes the blanket over the door. Then he turns back to me. He smiles, sweeping his gaze over my body. I feel my cheeks redden under the indignity of being examined by a strange man while in my under petticoat and a shirt I've never seen before, but I stand my ground.

"I never thought you'd be standing so soon," he says. "But I'm glad you're awake. Are you in much pain?"

His voice is deep and warm, but his English is accented, and I grope in my mind for the accent on it, for the sounds of people I've known who have spoken other languages first. It's not French. Then I recognize it, and I wish it were French. My fingers fly to my throat, checking for my blue ribbon necklace with the hidden pearls. It's not there, and I realize my head feels unnaturally light, and my hair is brushing the sides of my face. My left hand moves up and around the back of my head, searching.

I look again at the stranger. I mustn't let him know I'm afraid. He's dressed like any woodsman, in high winter boots and dark brown linsey-woolsey leggings and shirt like those Mark would wear. I swallow. The shirt is remarkably similar to the one covering my own body. He's slightly shorter than Mark and broader in the shoulders. His hair is very dark, and I can tell his skin is very pale beneath the windburn on his cheeks. If it weren't for his eyes, his hair and skin would look like they didn't go together, but the deep blue of his eyes makes them match. I cobble this together with his accent. A highlander. That's what he is, though his accent is nowhere near as pronounced as Donald Campbell's or that of other highlanders I've known. Still. A highlander.

I swallow and clear my throat, hoping my voice doesn't tremble when I speak. I have to get back the things he has stolen from me, and then I have to get out of here. I wonder if he has yet discovered the pearls in the choker. I hope he mistook them for decorative knots.

"What have you done to me?" I ask icily. At least I don't sound afraid. "Where are my clothes? Why has my hair been cut short?"

The smile falls from the highlander's face, and he answers with a short laugh. "Are you daft? Did that catamount knock out your brains as well as half your blood? You had a fever, you little idiot, and I cut off your hair to let the heat escape from your brain."

He sets the game bag by the hearth and straightens, crossing his arms. "I can see it didn't work."

I feel heat rising in my face. I see now that he's wearing Mark's cloak, and an explosion of grief and fury rocks my brain. I stand as straight as I can, truly feeling for the first time the protests of the deep wounds.

"I'll thank you to return my brother's cloak," I say. Exhaustion and pain make my breath short, but still I am imperious, trying to intimidate him. My grandfather was a baronet, even if he did disown my mother and all her children long before I was born.

Pity washes over the highlander's scowl, and I see that pity suits him better. "Does your brother have need of it?" he asks softly. I can tell that, impossibly, he knows, and I hate him for the kindness in his voice because I know I can stand anything but kindness. I've built a wall around myself since the morning of my seventeenth birthday, and if I let a crack get in I won't be able to stop the whole thing from crumbling.

I have no breath to respond, but he swings the cloak off and spreads it over the hearth to dry. He makes a little gesture of surrender.

"The cloak was a godsend to me, I'll say that. It would have made the winter that much easier to bear."

I feel the heat flow out of my face and the energy leave my body. Mark was a better person than I, there's no question. He would never have denied a man the use of his cloak. I feel an urgent desire to sit, an overwhelming feeling that I must get back to the bed before I fall, but I can't make my body obey.

"My brother would have wanted you to wear it," I say helplessly.

The highlander says nothing as he chooses a log from a stack beside the opposite wall and lays it on the fire. He pokes at the flames, collapsing the burned out wood into embers, making the fire blaze with the strength of fresh fuel.

"Was it Jaime's?" he asks, talking to the hearth. "Or Mark's?"

"Mark's," I say quietly. My legs collapse like the burned out wood, and though I expect to crash onto the floor, I find myself back on the bed.

"You talk a bit in your sleep," says the highlander. He looks up from tending the fire and rests the iron poker against the hearth. "You'd better lie down. I'm afraid it wouldn't take much to start the bleeding again, and by the time I found you you'd lost so much blood already that I was afraid to try bleeding you to relieve the fever. That's why I cut your hair instead."

The flush rises in my face again. I had suspected it, but I'm furious to find out for certain that this highlander treated my wounds.

He moves toward where I sit unmoving on the bed. "Let me help you," he says. "There's no shame in it—you've been badly hurt. Nearly torn apart by an animal. They're vicious in these hills. Now, if this is Mark's cloak I've been wearing, then the little one must have been Jaime."

I nod. "Did you find him, too?" I ask. "How did you find me?"

The highlander crouches in front of me and takes one of my hands. He's very close, but his image is hazy. "It's best not to shoot unless you have to. I heard the report of your rifle. I found the little one's body first, but there was no weapon on him, so I tracked you. It wasn't difficult. You left quite a trail."

"Jaime," I whisper. "Where is he?"

The highlander lays a hand on my uninjured shoulder, and I'm dimly aware of being lifted and resettled onto the bed. I feel his hands on my calves as he straightens my legs and my petticoat around them.

"I buried him," he says. "Once I was sure I could leave you alone for a bit."

My vision is dark. I want to thank him, but all that comes out is one of the sobs clamoring for space in my throat. "I left him. I didn't mean to ever leave him."

I feel myself being covered up and tucked in, and I remember now that I've been terribly ill, and I must rest. I must wait for Mother to come and make me better.

"Hush," says a voice that is not my mother's. "You're not well yet. Close your eyes and try to sleep."

Try to sleep. Try to sleep. My father's voice, on the nights I couldn't sleep when I was a little girl.

"My father used to say that," I tell the voice.

"You're raving again."

"I hate my father."

A rumble of low, sad laughter.

"Don't we all?" asks the voice. "Don't we all?"

IO.

January 7, 1760

Evening

I wake to a heavy weight on the mattress. I startle, my hands groping for something I can use to defend myself. The room is darker now that the sun has gone down, the only light the flickering fire, and it takes me a moment to remember where I am. A log pops apart, loud in the silence, like the crack of a rifle, and a small shriek escapes me. Fire reminds me of the sound of rifles, then. It seems unfair.

"Hush," says the highlander, laying a hand on my uninjured shoulder to keep me from rising.

"The fire," I gasp. I woke with Donald Campbell in my mind. "The smoke. Someone will see. Someone could come." I am afraid to tell the highlander about Campbell. I'm sure he doesn't know about Donald Campbell and doesn't know who I am, because if he did I'd be dead already. But they are both highlanders, after all, and who knows the strength of the loyalty between them?

The highlander glances up, understanding. "Oh, the smoke is all right. I make sure to get wood that won't smoke much, and the hole only lets out a bit at a time. In any case, we're deep in the wilderness, far from any trail. You're safe here." He stares at me curiously, as if he's wondering what I'm doing out here, so far from both British and Cherokee civilization. For a moment it looks as if he plans to ask, but he changes his mind.

"As safe as you'd be anywhere in the middle of a war," he amends. "Do you think you'd be able to keep a bit of food down?"

I think I can keep more than a bit down. After ten days in the wilderness on rationed food and who knows how long unconscious and ill, I'm ravenous, and it's making me tetchy. I raise my head, missing the comfortable weight of my hair.

"Stop treating me like a child," I snap. "You can't be much older than I am."

The highlander raises an eyebrow. "I'll have you know I'm five and twenty. What are you? Twelve?"

"Liar," I grimace. "You're barely twenty, if that. And I know when I'm being baited. You can't possibly think I'm twelve."

He laughs. "You have a good eye on you. I turn twenty this month."

I give a small smile of triumph, pleased with myself for catching him, but he turns serious again.

"I'm going to have to move you so you can eat," he says. "Is that all right?"

I nod, and he retrieves a blanket from the hearth, folds it over several times, and slips it under my head so my body slopes upward from the waist. The movement sets off sudden, protesting stabs of pain from the wounds in my chest, even though his hands beneath my back are surprisingly gentle. The warmth of the blanket is comforting, and when the highlander moves away toward the fire and the food, I call to him. I don't know what makes me do it, what makes me wish to mask cruelty under a gesture of goodwill.

"I'm seventeen years old," I say. "My name is Catie Blair. My full name is Catriona. My father named me that, after his grandmother, and my mother didn't like it. She let people assume my name was Catherine. Catriona is so very Scottish, you see."

I expect that to make him angry. Indeed, I said it to anger him, to stop him from being kind to me. I want to be angry with someone, and if it isn't him it will have to be myself. But I think I see the corner of his mouth turn up. He spoons liquid from a small iron saucepan into a shallow wooden trencher and returns with a mixture that both smells heavenly and makes my stomach turn. He lowers himself gently down, careful not to let the broth slop out or to jolt the bedding and hurt me. I've always been given to understand that highlanders are savages at bottom, no matter how civilized the presence of my parents might turn them, but this one is impeccably considerate.

"Catriona is a lovely name," he says. "You shouldn't shorten it." He looks away from me, into the darkness that drapes the other side of the room. "May I call you Catriona?" The vulnerability in his eyes is unexpected, as is the sadness. "I'm a very long way from home, and it would make me feel closer."

I know what my mother would say. This is moving very fast. If he calls me anything at all, which he probably shouldn't, he should call me Miss Blair. But Mother was hanging on to a world she had already lost. I look around the room, taking in the combination of natural and constructed shelter, the stack of logs, the cooking utensils. My brother's rifle is stacked beside a fine-looking musket. At best, the highlander is a thief. It's possible he's something much worse, for surely no one would live alone like this in the mountains unless he had to. I look again into his blue eyes. They are proud and wounded, like he is daring me to laugh at him and will strike a hard blow if I do.

So I'm not going to laugh at this strange, lost highlander. Now that I have something to bargain with, I'm going to bargain with him.

"If you wish to call me by my first name, you'll have to answer some questions for me first."

He laughs softly and stirs the contents of the trencher's shallow bowl. "You're terribly demanding for a person in your position."

I pull myself as straight as I can before my torn flesh protests. "I am trying to determine what that position is."

The highlander nods slowly, as if this is to be expected. "Well, here's what I know. You've been nearly killed by a catamount, it sounds like you've lost at least part of your family, you're an Englishwoman in the middle of Cherokee territory in the middle of a war between the Cherokee and the British, and you are in the care of a criminal."

I look up sharply at his last words, and I feel the fear in my eyes. The highlander straightens, looking vaguely contrite.

"I didn't mean to scare you, Catriona. It seems I've been a criminal most of my life. I forget how it shocks other people. I'm not going to rape or kill you, if that's what's worrying you." His face flushes with sudden anger. "I've seen enough of that for a lifetime."

I breathe slowly out, appreciative that he doesn't skirt the point, doesn't act as if his words should shock me, or as if I don't understand their meaning.

"Why?" I ask tentatively, not entirely sure I want to hear his answer. "Why are you a criminal?"

"I'd like you to try to get something down," he says. "Will you eat if I answer that?"

I nod, and he lifts the spoon to my lips and nudges them gently apart. Strange how much I have forgotten in my brief time in the wilderness. It feels odd to eat from a spoon. I have grown so used to having only a knife and my own fingers. I swallow real, hot food for the first time in weeks and feel it flow down into my stomach, warming me from the inside.

"You can have a very little meat," says the highlander. "Not much. I don't want you to be sick. If you keep this down, tomorrow you can have some cornmeal cooked in water."

He feeds me a few tiny slivers of rabbit meat cooked almost to mush, slowly, lowering the spoon between bites.

"The first time I was a criminal," he begins.

I interrupt. "You've been a criminal more than once?" My eyes run over his body, looking for markers: a brand, a disfiguration, a missing minor piece that might give me some clue as to his crime. But no. Eyes, ears, lips, nose, and fingers are all intact and unmarred.

He smiles. "If you're a very young child the first time, they don't always count it against you. I don't know if there were ever any charges brought against me. I wasn't punished, not directly, anyway, so maybe this is the first time I've been a criminal. But I felt like one before, when the British army was hunting us down. We were always moving and hiding, trying not to get caught. In the end, they ran us to earth the way hounds run down hares."

"You were in the Forty-Five?" I ask.

In 1745, I was two years old and my parents had lived in New Jersey for nearly three years, so my understanding of the most recent highland rebellion is sketchy at best. All I can remember is how, in 1745, a group of highlander Scots called the Jacobites moved against Britain with the twin goals of setting the man they called Bonnie Prince Charlie on the Scottish throne and preventing the union of Scotland and England. Though they enjoyed no small success at first, even capturing the lowland city of Edinburgh where Father was born, the Jacobites were crushed at last on a moor called Culloden, and Britain's wrath was terrible.

I look closely at the highlander before me. "But, no, you couldn't have been. You're too young. You would have been just a child."

The highlander stares down into the trencher, slowly stirring the remaining liquid.

"My father was in the Forty-Five. And as he was a man of some land and worth, the Crown pursued him after the defeat at Culloden. Suffice it to say there's little enough I don't know about hiding from the British army in the mountains."

"And why are you a criminal now?" I ask, my throat tight. "Did you kill someone?"

The grimace forces his face up. "No. Not directly, anyway. It's nothing that concerns you, nothing you need to be concerned about. You're in no danger from me. That's all you need to know."

He sounds so pained I decide to leave him alone, for now. "I'm still very hungry," I say. "Please, can I have something else to eat?"

I know I am being incredibly rude. I've probably eaten most of his food already. But I am so very hungry.

The highlander considers. "I'd gladly give you more, Catriona, but I've treated the wounded before. We need to go slowly. In the morning, you can eat again, if that much stays on your stomach through the night. Better you rest now. You need to sleep in order to heal, and if you're asleep, you won't feel hunger."

"I seem to have been asleep for a long time," I say. "If it's all one to you, I'd rather not sleep now." I don't have the energy to fight with him, but I have no intention of going back to sleep.

The highlander stands and returns the trencher and spoon to the hearth.

"You haven't been in a real sleep. Not a sleep that would have brought you any rest. You've been raving mad with fever for a week. I had to tie you down to clean and dress your wounds, to force water down your throat. Thank God you were too far gone to feel the pain."

"You tied me up?" I ask, tensing again.

"I released you as soon as you stopped flailing and I was sure you weren't going to do yourself a harm."

I bolt up, and he darts toward me.

"You mustn't move like that," he says. "You could start the bleeding again, and then you might be past help."

"I didn't ask for your help," I say, struggling to stand, to show him I'm not helpless. I avoided Donald Campbell. I got Jaime and myself as far as the Cherokee Path in safety, and if it hadn't been for that catamount, I would have gotten us all the way to Fort Loudoun by now.

"I helped you because you needed help, not because you asked for it." The highlander's eyes flash. I have angered him at last. "You weren't capable of asking for it."

Fury floods my face, and the highlander sighs and drops his hands by his sides. He moves nearer, in the cautious way people have around wounded animals. He reaches out and runs a hand down my left arm, trying to take my hand and lead me back to the bed.

"Sleep, Catriona," he says. "You need rest."

He gives me a tentative smile, and the firelight reveals lavender shadows under his eyes. I'm not the one who needs rest. He looks like he hasn't slept in days, yet he has the nerve to order me to bed.

I raise my fingers to my chest, checking for fresh blood, and the pressure makes me wince. I feel my knees bend, and I manage to sit on the edge of the bed. It appears no matter what my mind wants, my body is going to take over.

"At least lie down," says the highlander. "That will give your wounds the best chance of healing."

The flush in my face is from pain now, not anger. I have to lie down because I can't bear the tugging pain of sitting up anymore. The tension eases as I lie back and pull my cloak up with my left hand. I stare down at my cloak. There's a fraying stitch around the neckline that needs to be mended. For a moment I think of taking it to Mother, and then I remember I can't. I wonder how long this will go on. How many more times will I think of the dead as though they are alive? How many more times must the memory come rushing back?

"You know my name," I say, looking up, my voice low. "I don't know yours." But as I look down at my body again, my voice rises. "And I don't remember getting myself out of my own clothes and into this shirt, and there's obviously no one else around, so you must have changed my clothes yourself, which is just . . . just . . . " I trail off, sputtering because I am again so furious and because I don't know what I mean to say.

But the highlander laughs at that, a real, deep laugh unlike any of the snarky barks he's given me before.

"Good God, Catriona, is that why you're so angry with me? Would it help to know it was either that or let you die, or that you were so filthy when I found you that at first I wasn't sure if you were an Englishwoman or a Cherokee? Or that you were covered in blood?"

I open my mouth to respond, but then I close it abruptly. That's the other thing that felt different when I woke, besides the pain. I've had a full bath every week of my life, except in the dead of winter when the danger of cold was judged greater than the danger of filth. Every day, I've scrubbed my face, my hands, and my neck. Mother was determined her children would not be mistaken for grubby backcountry brats.

But now I feel clean, the kind of clean you get from soap and water, for the first time since the day Donald Campbell destroyed my life. The high-lander hasn't only changed my clothes, he's also bathed me all over, which means he spent a great deal of time with my naked body while I was uncon-scious. All the clothes I'm wearing seem very clean, too, both my under petticoat and the man's shirt.

The highlander is smiling, clearly amused, and I wish he would stop.

"You were in grave danger, Catriona," he says. "If I had left you in those filthy clothes, you would have died. You have to keep a sick person clean, everyone knows that, or the fever will certainly take them. I couldn't clean the wounds without removing your clothes."

I say nothing, so he continues.

"I wagered your desire to live would be greater than your modesty, but clearly I was wrong. If it's any comfort, I didn't enjoy it. I had to work very fast, and unconscious, half-starved, mortally wounded women are not a special interest of mine."

His smile melts into a grin, and I'm unsettled by how quickly he moves between kindness and amusement.

"Malcolm."

I give him a questioning look.

"My name. It's Malcolm Craig. And if you'd like to see me naked, to make us even, I'd be happy to oblige you in that, too."

My look of horror makes him laugh again.

"All right. I'll spare you. If you'll try to sleep."

Despite my earlier protests, I'm feeling desperately weak and tired. The physical effort of standing and the mental strain of my verbal sparring with Malcolm Craig have exhausted me. I lie flat and feel the highlander around me, pulling the blanket from under my head and lowering me gently down, tucking the blanket around my body instead. Then the room swings around me, and the world goes dark again.

II.

January 7–8, 1760

Night

The darkness doesn't last. I soon sink into dreams of vermillion-painted Cherokee warriors and kilted highland rebels, of fierce catamounts and bloodied, dead brothers. My family's cabin is an inferno, and I am trapped inside. A low voice calls, a whisper through the flames, seeking me, but not set on rescue. I know I can't let the body that belongs to the voice find me. Desperate, I stumble through the house, which seems to be growing larger instead of smaller with the flames, as though the fire is building, not destroying. The rooms go endlessly on, and I wonder if I have somehow crossed through time and space into the mansion of my grandfather, the baronet. The beams crack and crash and toss up sparks until I am surrounded by fire, and there is no escape. Down a long, narrow tunnel, a wooden door splinters under repeated hatchet strokes, and at last the demon hunting me through this hell crashes through. It's Donald Campbell, no longer a man but a man-shaped form of flesh and fire. He fixes on me with coal black eyes set in a face made of flames. My feet stumble toward him against my will, and when I am close enough to touch, he grabs my arm and pulls me in, smothering me against his blazing chest. I scream and scream, but no one can hear because my screams are consumed by the flames, becoming part of them, strengthening them.

And then the heat rushes away, and I am suddenly so cold. I'm biting down hard, grinding my teeth against the blanket. That's what's smothering my screams, why they are coming out as whimpers. I slowly calm myself. I tell myself again and again it was just a dream, it wasn't real, no matter what it feels like. And I realize I thought I was on fire because my chest is burning, in a way, with pain.

A weight on the bed startles me so that I try to sit up, my mind full of the demon of my dream.

"Hush, sweet," says the highlander, his tone gentle now, soothing in the way one shushes a child or a frightened animal. "You're safe now. It's only me. What's the matter?"

"It hurts," I moan. "It hurts so much." Too much and too badly for me to care what my mother would say about the impropriety of my familiarity with a highlander or for me to care that he's treating me like a child again. Just for a moment, it would be nice to be treated like a child.

"What hurts, Catriona?"

"Everything. My whole body. It all hurts." A dry sob rattles through my chest, jarring the torn flesh.

The highlander falls silent for a moment, his silhouette a dark pool in the shadows cast by the fire. "Is it the wounds from the catamount? Or is something else wrong?"

Another sob shudders through me, and I start to cough, which pains me terribly. "I told you, it's everything."

The highlander's voice remains low and calm, but there's a firmness in it now. "Catriona, I need you to tell me what's wrong. I know you lost your brothers. Are you only upset about that right now, or are you in pain?"

I squeeze the word through clenched teeth. "Pain."

"All right. Listen to me, Catriona. Thrashing about will only make it worse. You have to be still for me to help you."

I nod and squeeze my eyes shut. Tears leak from their corners and run down the sides of my face, wetting my neck. But I make myself still.

"Is the pain worse than it was this afternoon?" the highlander asks.

"The worst it's been."

"I can't tell anything without examining the wound. Do I have your permission to see if anything can be done?" He sounds so oddly formal, so different from the picture of highlanders I've always had in my head, that I would laugh if I had breath. And if I didn't know how badly laughing would hurt.

"You didn't ask before."

"You couldn't answer me before," he replies.

I have little choice at the moment but to trust him, this highlander who is, by his own admission, a criminal, and I nod, breathless with pain. "Please."

I feel the back of the highlander's hand press gently against my injuries. "The dressing would have to be changed soon, anyway," he says. He swears softly under his breath. "Damn. There's heat in it again. I thought we were through that."

The highlander moves away, and I watch the shadows lurch as he lights a pine bough and sets it between two rocks on the hearth. I breathe deeply, trying to focus on the sharp scent of the burning resin rather than on the pain.

"I have to take your arm out of your sleeve," he says. I nod, though I know the movement will hurt.

"Don't scream," he adds. "You can't. The sound could carry for miles. Do you need to bite down on something?"

I shake my head. I can keep quiet, if it is the only thing of any use I can do.

He folds the blanket down at my waist, untucks the shirt from my under petticoat and puts his hands on either side of my waist. He slowly pushes the shirt up until it's bunched below my breasts, and then he grasps my right arm and works it slowly out of the sleeve. I do cry out once, and he shushes me hastily.

"I'm sorry, sweet," he says. "Try to lie quiet."

He lays my bare arm on the bed, bunching the fabric around my neck. The cold I feel on my arm and my exposed side contrasts sharply with the raging heat emanating from my chest.

"Catriona," he says, his voice less gentle, more matter of fact. "Did you unwrap this dressing?"

I know it's useless to lie, and the highlander sighs heavily. "Did you pull it off the wounds? Did you touch them?"

"I needed to know how bad it was."

The highlander pulls down the band of cloth binding the pad to the wounds. The tips of his fingers feel cold against my skin.

"This will hurt," he warns. He pulls the pad off, slowly, because it sticks to the blood the whole way. "You've passed through the stages of inflammation and digestion already, and thank God you were gone from the world. There was a lot of pus." He smiles. "It was disgusting."

I know he is trying to bait me, to get my mind off whatever it is he has to do. I think of my mother and what she would say to any strange man, much less a highlander, undressing me, whatever the reason. The looseness of backcountry morals notwithstanding, she was very strong on the idea that the only man who would ever need to undress me would be my husband. I cast my eyes down my front. In all her warnings about men, in all her fears for me, she never once imagined it would be like this, I'm sure. I thought the highlander was taunting me when he spoke of mortally wounded women, but the jagged tears in my flaming flesh have rendered my breast unrecognizable. It would repulse any man. Mother has nothing to worry about.

The highlander lights a candle from the pine torch and sets it in a pewter holder. He is quick to hide it, but I catch the dismay that floods his face as he examines the wounds.

"It's bad, isn't it?" I ask. "Don't try to lie to me."

"You've reverted to the stage of inflammation." He runs a hand over his dark curls. "I wish you hadn't bothered with the dressing. That probably set the inflammation off again."

I turn my face away from the candle's light. "Is it streaking?" Redness streaking away from a wound tends to betoken death.

"Not yet. It's only hot and swelling. Thank God there's fresh snow on the ground. It'll be even colder than the spring water." He squeezes my clenched fist. "I'll be right back."

The highlander returns with an icy rag. He spreads it over my injuries and presses down, forcing the cold to do battle with the heat. My body sucks the cold away so quickly, and he goes outside to soak the rag with snow again. He does this so many times I lose count, and the thundering silence becomes unbearable in the face of death.

My mind feels strangely cool and empty, detached from my flaming body, like part of me is trying to leave. I close my eyes.

"I've always expected to die," I tell the highlander. "All my life, I've expected to die."

"Well, that's no great boast of your intelligence," he answers. "Everyone dies. Don't talk until you can talk sense."

"My mother was carrying me when my family sailed for Philadelphia," I say. "Do you know how many women miscarry on sea voyages? And then I had all those illnesses children get. But I didn't die. Mary died. The twins died. But I didn't."

"I'd wager you never stopped talking long enough to die."

"Every autumn fever season," I go on, ignoring him. "But I never died. And when the war started and Father wouldn't leave the settlement and go east, I figured I'd die in the war, because there seemed to be no other way." I laugh lightly. "But I'm not dead. My whole family is dead, and I'm still alive. I should be the one dead. I was never a good daughter. It's my fault we left my parents alone. Mark didn't think it was a good idea, but I prodded him, and he always did anything I wanted, in the end. I thought I was a good sister, but I wasn't. I let him kill my brother, Malcolm. I could have shot him, but I didn't. I told myself it was because of Jaime, but it wasn't. It was because I was afraid. I was so scared of him, and I didn't want him to find me. And then Jaime was such a burden, and all I wanted to do was put it down, and then he died. I never thought of animals. I was afraid of the Cherokee and the winter, but I never thought an animal would get us. The bears are in New Jersey, after all. I'm the one who should be dead. I deserve to die."

The highlander lays his hand against my cheek, brushing back the strands of hair stuck there by my tears and fever flush. There's a faraway look in his eyes, like he's talking to something beyond me. Or maybe I am the one who is far away. "No one deserves to die, sweet. You can't blame yourself for living."

My hand waves over my throat. "I had ribbons," I insist. "Blue ribbons. Did you cut them?"

"I took them off you so you wouldn't choke yourself."

"It's my ribbon—my thread—that should be cut. The last sister—she cut all the others, but she didn't cut mine. She cut them into my skin. That's how it must be. Four cuts. Not five. Owen must still be alive."

"You're delirious."

"I want to die," I insist. "I shouldn't be alive."

"That's the fever talking, not you," the highlander says fiercely. "You have to fight it, Catriona. If you want to die, it will take you."

I blink rapidly, feeling my mind return to my body. I look up at the highlander, watching his face glow and darken with the flicker of the flames.

"Malcolm?" I venture. "Why are you a criminal? You never told me."

"Because I'm not a damned fool," he answers. I have to smile a little at that, despite the pain and the heat in my brain.

"Why?" I ask again. "I'm dying. You can tell me."

"You're not dying, sweet," says Malcolm. The cold presses firmly down on my chest again. "Don't talk like that."

"You can't keep me alive," I insist. "Not if I deserve to die. Not if she cuts my thread."

"You don't deserve to die, Catriona. No more than anyone else. If anyone here deserves to die, it's me, and I'm still alive, so you're not going anywhere."

"Are you under a death sentence?"

"Most likely. That's the only sentence I've ever seen for desertion. The lucky ones get the firing squad. The others get the whip."

I hadn't realized how anxious I felt about Malcolm's criminal past until he told me he was a deserter. I feel tension release, even through the throbbing pain. I laugh and hear the ring of madness. Only a deserter. So many people desert. Most likely that means he's less dangerous, not more. His eyes flicker up to my face, shy and vulnerable. Then he looks away and clears his throat. He peels the cold rag away from my chest and goes outside to soak it again.

The laugh released some of the heat in my brain. I feel it ebb away as my mind resettles itself along more familiar lines. When I speak, I sound like myself.

"You don't deserve to die. Not more than I do, anyway, not for desertion."

His face clouds. "Do you think you're the only one who has lost people dear to you? At least it couldn't have been your fault, not directly."

I start to protest, but he interrupts. "Oh, be quiet for a moment, won't you? I'll tell you the story. It will be good to tell someone. You rest yourself. You need to put all your energy into fighting that fever."

He sits by my head and wipes my face with a cool cloth that draws out some of the heat.

"I lost my father and mother both soon after the defeat at Culloden. We were driven back into the mountains, into hiding, but the British army kept coming. The regulars who found my father hanged him there and then as a traitor to the Crown. It broke my mother's heart and her health."

"I'm so sorry," I whisper.

"Don't be," he says harshly. "Hanging is quick enough. In a way, it's lucky the regulars took justice into their own hands. If he had gone to trial he might have been drawn and quartered, and a skilled executioner can make a man live without his insides for hours before he's torn into four parts."

"That couldn't have been your fault," I insist.

The shadow deepens on Malcolm's face as he moves closer, and I feel him lift my left hand. He holds it in both of his, running his fingers over mine as though he is counting, ticking off time. The time that is gone, the time that remains. Measuring, like the second sister.

"My father's younger brother took charge of me and sent me away to school in England. He thought it would be useful if I learned English ways and learned to speak English well. The English, I think, also thought it would be useful."

The highlander pauses, and his hands convulse around mine.

"After the Forty-Five, the English outlawed the wearing of the plaid tartan and the carrying of weapons, even the playing of the bagpipes, except on one condition. If you'd join the British army and fight for the Empire, you could serve in a highland regiment and wear the tartan and carry your weapons and hear the pipes again."

"So you joined one of these highland regiments?" I ask. I consider this. It seems an exquisitely brilliant form of cruelty, forcing a vanquished enemy to fight your battles in exchange for letting them keep the customs that matter to them.

Malcolm laughs bitterly. "I did. Not entirely by choice. When the highland regiments were raised to fight the French in America, the army realized communication would be a problem. Most of the men knew no language beyond Erse, the tongue of the highlands, so the army needed officers who could speak both English and Erse. My uncle thought it would be a fine opportunity for a young man like myself."

"But it wasn't?"

"It was more of a fine opportunity for him. The Forty-Five was nearly a generation ago, and it all came to nothing. He was ready to be British. He wanted a way to prove our family's loyalty, and what better way than to offer me, his nephew and the son of a Jacobite rebel, to serve as an officer in the British army?"

"Maybe he thought it would be good for you. Many men do make good careers out of the army."

Malcolm laughs, but not kindly. "He wanted me gone. He has children of his own, and I was just a means of making their futures a bit brighter by putting my family back in Britain's good graces. He's got the best of it all now, because I can never return. I suppose I've been reported missing, presumed dead. It's likely enough to be the truth."

"But won't your family want to know what happened to you?" I think of my mother and the long silence across the sea. I don't even know my grandparents' names.

He shrugs. "I don't have much family left, but I imagine it would be so much the better for them if I'm dead in the King's service."

He brushes a hand across his face and rubs his eyes with weariness. "I like to think my uncle didn't know what it would be like here, that he thought it would be like sending me to the Continent. From what I've heard, warfare in Europe must be easy. Here it is all wilderness, and you have to build a road before you can even get to a battlefield. That's what we did all through Pennsylvania. Hacked a road out of the wilderness. And the weather here. It's not like Europe. It's so hot, or else so cold. And there are the bugs that suck your body dry, and the brambles that scratch out what blood you have left, and the Indians, who fight brilliantly. I think the English had a plan to get rid of their two problems, the highlanders in Scotland and the native people here. I think they imagined in sending one to fight the other, they might get us to wipe each other out."

"Is that why you deserted?" I ask.

"No," says Malcolm, rising to check the fire. "That came later."

12.

January 8, 1760

Morning

The cold wakes me in the morning, and bright winter daylight reflects off the snow and trickles through the smoke hole. Malcolm must have extinguished the pine torch sometime in the night, but the fire still burns low on the hearth. I look down at my chest, which is covered by the checkered cloth of one of the cold rags Malcolm kept switching out during the night. The rag has dried stiff on top of my wounds, and the exposed flesh that still has feeling is burning with cold.

I glance nervously around for Malcolm before I realize my hand is resting on his dark curls. He is slumped by the bed, asleep. For a few minutes, I leave my hand still. I know he has barely slept since he found me near death in the wilderness, and I feel a pang of affection for the care he has shown me, and a pang of regret that I could not have accepted it with greater grace. Besides, I want to study him, as I haven't really been able to do yet. His long hair has come mostly undone from its leather tie, and the shorter pieces in front curl around the sides of his face. Except for the light shadow of beard, he looks younger in sleep, more like the child he must have been when he lost his parents. I think of Jaime. Malcolm would have been younger than Jaime, only six or seven, left alone to navigate a world of adults. I think of Malcolm's father and wonder if he would have said it was worth it, the uprising that left his son bereft of all he had known. I think of my own father and wonder if he would have brought my family to the backcountry if he had known what would happen to us.

My gaze passes down Malcolm's body to his belt, where he has stuck a long dagger that reaches almost to his knee. It looks cut down from a sword, and the hilt is shining metal molded with intricate knot work. I'd have to hold it to be sure, but it looks like silver. I recognize the weapon from my father's stories of the savage highlanders. This is a highland dirk, crafted for nothing but killing. When a highland warrior engaged the enemy, my father said, he would draw his backsword with his right hand and his dirk with his left. A memory flashes across my mind of the front room in the house on the Delaware. When Father came home, he would draw his pen and riding crop and call that the highlanders had come for Catie. I would shriek and giggle and run. Mother hated that game, and now I understand why. *The highlanders have come for Catie,* I think. *Oh, how the highlanders have come.*

The dirk is not the only weapon Malcolm has prepared. I see no sword, but close by are both Mark's rifle and a Brown Bess musket like soldiers carry. It's quite fine, far nicer than the old fowling piece I learned to shoot on.

At last I know I have to wake Malcolm because I'm shivering with the cold sweat of the broken fever. I don't want to startle him, though, not when he's so well armed. I am suddenly conscious of the slipperiness of his hair between my fingers, so I whisper his name and press my fingers into his scalp, the one part of his body I can reach.

He starts awake, springing to his feet. He spins to face me, as if he has forgotten my presence. When he realizes I am conscious, he unhooks the dirk and kneels beside me.

"Oh, Catriona," he says, grabbing my left hand. "Oh, sweet, you survived the night."

I smile and nod, allowing his relief to spread through me since I cannot yet be pleased on my own account. Though I must say I'm confused that he feels so strongly about the survival of a near stranger.

In the first rush of relief, Malcolm presses my fingers to his lips, but I stop him. "How do the wounds look?" I ask, gesturing with my chin, to remind him I am not out of danger yet.

He pulls the dried cloth off my chest, managing to hide the grimace that crosses his face almost fast enough. "Much better than last night. There's still a little inflammation, but it's receding. You've passed through the worst of it."

He looks uncomfortable for a moment, but then he looks me in the eye. "You know what comes next, don't you?"

Baffled, I shake my head, and Malcolm sighs.

"I couldn't stitch you up before because a curved wound, like one from an animal attack, can abscess if you close it before it's discharged its fluids. I think we can get by without stitching the one on the very bottom, but the others need to be closed or they'll heal badly."

I close my eyes. "I don't think it's ever going to be a pretty sight. It's not in a place anyone will see it much, which is something. At least it wasn't my face."

"Still," says Malcolm. "I'd feel better about your chances if you'd let me stitch it."

I don't open my eyes. "Why does it matter to you? You don't know me. You have no reason to care for me."

I feel Malcolm's weight leave the bed. "I thought once, seeing as I'd lost the future I should have had, that I might like to make my living as a surgeon. I befriended the surgeon who attended the students at school, and he taught me some things. I spent most of my off-duty hours with our regimental surgeon, as well, so I've learned quite a bit."

That makes a bit more sense, then. Keeping me alive is a matter of semiprofessional pride.

I hear sounds from the other side of the room, as though Malcolm is rattling through a bag. I keep my eyes closed, hoping if I don't open them I can forget that he's insisting on tying my skin back together. When I peek, I see him holding a needle as long as my finger to the fire. I watch as he dips the needle into a bowl and it comes up shining with animal fat. All I can think is how the heat and oil are supposed to let the needle pass more easily through my flesh.

Malcolm kneels beside me. "I've been stitched before, Catriona." He pushes his sleeve up. A bumpy white scar runs from elbow to shoulder. "French bayonet. The anticipation of the pain is worse than the pain itself. It'll be over soon, I promise."

He holds up a strap of braided leather that belies his words. "You can't scream. I don't know who's near us, or how far the sound would carry, and a scream could get us both killed. If you need to scream, you bite, all right? Bite hard."

He lays the needle on a fresh rag and crosses behind my head. He fits the strap to my mouth like a horse's bit and ties it under what remains of my hair.

He threads the needle and leans over me, smoothing my hair from my forehead. "Bite, love. Don't scream. Bite."

The first pierce of the needle sets off explosions behind my eyes, and my brain feels like it's trying to burst through my skull. A moan escapes around the leather strap, and it's all I can do to lie flat. I'm surprised Malcolm can keep going with the way my shoulders are heaving, but he is quick and merciless, and I hate him for it. I remind myself he was a soldier and has probably seen wounds much worse than mine. I can't slow the pace of my breath or the twitching of my shoulders, but I imagine being scalped, which helps me keep my moans low.

"One's done," says Malcolm, and I grunt an acknowledgment. He pauses, dipping the needle in oil again and rethreading it. "You're all right. You're going to be all right."

I grip the fabric by my sides, blanket or cloak or my own petticoat, I can't tell. I know only that I'm holding on for dear life, trying to squeeze the pain away.

"One more. It's almost over. Hush, love, you're doing fine. I've seen strong men cry more than you."

If I can't scream, I want to talk, but I can't do that, either. I grind my teeth against the bit, surprised they aren't cracking from the pressure. Leather flakes and catches in the back of my throat, along with the moans and sobs. Just when I think I'm going to gag, Malcolm unties the strap and pulls it from my mouth.

My head falls back with exhaustion. Malcolm looks vaguely green. A squeamish surgeon. Just my luck. "You look terrible," I croak. My throat is dry, and a new kind of pain is heavy on my chest.

Malcolm smiles and goes to the door. He drags in a bucket of snowmelt and soaks the rag again.

"We'll keep a cold poultice on it for a few days, to keep it clean and to keep the fever from coming back. It won't be comfortable, but I don't think we can afford comfort." He smiles apologetically. "Bread and milk would make a better poultice than cold water, but we don't have either just now."

As he presses the rag to my wounds, I manage to grab his hand.

"Thank you," I say. "For taking care of me and for burying Jaime. You didn't have to do either. Whatever else you've done, you're a good person in that."

Malcolm doesn't reply until he has built up the fire so that it warms the small room to comfort and heated broth for my breakfast. He slips a heated blanket under my head and covers me with Mark's cloak.

"That means more to me than you know, Catriona. I hope you'll never have cause to doubt it. Here. The meat from those rabbits has been simmering in water all night. It isn't beef tea, but it's hearty enough. It should help you get your strength back."

I feel sorry, mostly because he sounds so sad. But as he helps me eat, I realize it's not his sorrow that concerns me. It's my own. For this morning, when I woke, I was so relieved to be alive. After weeks of wishing I had died with Mark, or frozen to death in the mountains, part of me was happy I survived the fever. It seems wrong. Malcolm is the first person I have known, and this shelter is the first place I have inhabited, since I lost my family. My life has changed, has moved on, and I want to stop time before it drags me further away from my family. And from Owen. I'm not sure how long the girl Owen Ramsay loved can hang on out here. Catie Blair was clean and cherished, perhaps even vaguely spoiled, for the backcountry. She had beautiful dark blond hair that fell to her waist.

And crashing over these concerns is the marvel that in a single night and morning of fighting my death, Malcolm and I could have transformed ourselves into an entity, into people who refer to ourselves as *we*. We are companions now, sharing the same fate for a time, and I shiver as I realize Malcolm has yet to tell me what he has done to be more deserving of death than I.

13.

January 1760

Weeks pass, the time marked by my painfully slow recovery. I spend the first several days in bed, except for the few times a day I must get up to use the latrine Malcolm dug thirty yards downwind from the shelter. The weather is cold but gentle, and the deep snow begins to melt, leaving a damp chill behind. Malcolm lets me lean on him to walk, but he refuses to carry me, insisting movement will give me back my strength.

I hadn't realized how weak I had become. The days in the wilderness before Jaime was killed, the constant exertion on rationed food, the blood loss and the cycles of fever after the catamount attack, the fortnight under Malcolm's care when I took little but water and strong broth. I never have put on flesh easily, and now I am uncomfortably thin. When I put my hand to my face, I feel the sharpness of my jaw and cheekbones. At night, I trace my fingers along my ribs when I can't sleep. The stitches come out a week after they went in, leaving behind tender flesh that is still not entirely healed. The first time Malcolm lets me try cornmeal cooked in water, I throw it up.

When I can sit up and hold a needle and thread, Malcolm brings my damaged clothing to me so I can begin to repair it. The cloth that was stiff with dirt is now pliable under my hands because Malcolm scrubbed it in a cold mountain stream, insisting dirt would bring the fever back. I start with my shift, which soaked up most of the blood. Because it is made of white linen, the bloodstains will always show. Though I try to ignore the fact that a strange man has laundered my underthings and is watching me repair them, Malcolm seems to have no such scruples. When I finish the shift and move on to my stays, he merely comments, "Those probably saved your life. I'd wager the cat pushed them down, but they broke the force of the blow." When I try them on, I have to pull the laces tighter than ever to get them to stay up.

My neckerchief is ruined by bloodstains, so I set to making myself a new one from fabric borrowed from my shift and under petticoat. The pocket that ties around my waist is undamaged, as is the under petticoat I've been wearing. Of the outer layer of my clothing, the overskirt of dark blue wool is all right, but the bodice of the matching gown is badly damaged, and I break one of the sewing needles from Malcolm's kit on the thick fabric. I wish I were a better seamstress, not only for the look of my clothing but also because of how economical I must be with the thread. It seems to snap twice for every line of stitches I complete. My mother would have done better. I am grateful for the dark fabric because the bloodstains show only as a darkness on the cloth. The stain could be anything.

Together, Malcolm and I decide I won't dress fully until the bandages no longer need regular changing, so when I am able to spend whole days out of bed, I wrap myself in my cloak and spend my days tending the fire and attempting to read Malcolm's Bible, which is frustratingly the only book available and also written in a language I don't understand. I keep the rifle or the Brown Bess near, ready to load quickly at the slightest suggestion of danger. Malcolm spends most of every day outside, attempting to add to our meager store of cornmeal and dried root vegetables by setting snares for the small animals that are still out despite the cold and collecting other edibles like pine nuts. He doses both of us with a tea made from pine needles every other day. To prevent scurvy, he says.

One day I risk mixing cornmeal with water in the bake kettle to form a thick paste. I nestle the bake kettle beside the fire in the morning and cover it with hot ash. I am preoccupied with trying to translate the first chapter of Genesis from memory, stumbling over the unfamiliar words, so I don't acknowledge Malcolm when he returns at dusk.

"Most people don't curse like sailors when they read the Bible, Catriona," he says, setting the rifle against one wall and removing his cloak.

I close the book, resting it on my lap. "Most people don't read the Bible in a foreign tongue that doesn't make sense."

Malcolm smiles, amused. "Erse would make sense if you knew it. I can teach you, if you like."

Boredom makes my answer easy. "I'd like that. It will give me something to do. I've had nothing to do since I made the bread this morning." I hear my voice become nervous. I know I've risked food. "It should be nearly baked now, and even if it's terrible, it's only cornmeal and water, so it should be edible."

Malcolm and I taste the bread, and though it is bland, it is also hot and solid. After we eat, he sits beside me on the wide hearth and we bend over my lesson together, me trying not to think of what my parents would have to say about my learning to speak highlander.

Every night, Malcolm gives me another lesson, and I spend the next day practicing. It keeps me from running mad.

By the end of January, the skin seals around my wounds, though they are still angry pink lashes across my chest and the skin is puckered and twisted like rope. I struggle to raise my right arm, so with my direction, Malcolm helps me dress. I feel much more like myself once I am back in my clothes, but every time I reach under my cap and feel the hair that curls around my ears, I am reminded that I am not, that I cannot be the person I was the last time I dressed in these clothes on the morning of my seventeenth birthday. That life is gone, but as long as Donald Campbell goes unpunished, I cannot see my way clear to a new one.

14.

February 10, 1760

Morning

By the time the ice storms of February hit, my wounds have healed and my body has strengthened enough to allow me to live as normal a life as possible in a shelter made of the mountains themselves, with a stranger who has come to know me in more intimate ways than anyone else in my life. A highlander whose appearance and accent, however mitigated they have been by years in England and service in the British army, would have horrified my parents if they had known he would be the one to care for my broken body after their deaths.

"I'll check the snares first thing today," Malcolm says, one freezing morning when I can see my breath. He rises from his blanket by the opposite rock wall and adds a log to the fire, building it to warm the room. He shakes out his blanket and brushes off the clothes he slept in. "We have no fresh meat, and it feels like there's a strong storm coming. We don't want to be iced in for days without food."

I reach for my cloak, wrap it around my body, and wriggle from beneath the blanket. I pull off my cap and brush my fingers through my short hair, hoping, as I always do, that it has grown longer in the night.

"There's a ten-pound bag of cornmeal left," I say. Not enough to see us through the rest of the winter on its own, but enough to keep us from starving should we be iced in. I speak absently, avoiding the thought the weather has brought to my mind. The worst part of winter comes just before spring. I cannot deny that my body has mostly healed, and after the bad weather is gone, I will have no excuse to stay here, trespassing on Malcolm's hospitality and delaying my family's claim to justice and my own need to see Donald Campbell hang, to feel safe again. Malcolm has asked me so little about myself. He knows my family is dead, but I think he assumes they died in a Cherokee raid, as Campbell wishes everyone to. I can't tell if Malcolm doesn't question me because he doesn't want to irritate my less visible wounds or if he's simply waiting for winter to end so I will leave him in peace and stop eating so much of his food.

When Malcolm leaves, doubly wrapped in Mark's and Jaime's cloaks against the cold, I add another log to the fire. I think about stepping to the door to ask Malcolm to gather more wood for drying, in case we need it during the storm, but I don't. I will gather wood myself later. I don't want him to think me useless.

The fire is high and bright, but a chill takes me, and I press my body against one of the warm stone walls for a moment. I pat down my bed and spread the blanket over it, reaching to smooth the wrinkles. I sweep the dirt floor with a long branch that ends in dried leaves. I wipe down our shared trencher and spoon. I slip my feet into the remains of my thin leather shoes, pick up the blanket Malcolm wraps in to sleep, carry it outside, and shake it clean as best I can. I fold it neatly and put it on the far edge of the hearth to warm. I go outside and gather fallen boughs I judge will burn well and bring them inside to dry. I am trying to live normally in a place that isn't remotely normal. Perhaps I am more like my mother than I thought. I thread the blue ribbons around my throat through my fingers, counting the hidden pearls.

The ice starts to patter down around midmorning, starting a little pang of anxiety for Malcolm's safety. I know he has to set ten times as many snares, at least, as we need filled. It's never certain any of them will catch anything. Animals get at them, and other people, sometimes. And this is winter, so there are fewer animals about to trap in the first place, only the ones that must venture out in search of food. *It's easier to hide than to find.* Mark's voice inside my brain startles me. I wonder if this will happen my whole life, if I will go about my days and come upon my brother without warning, and grieve again for what was lost.

My morning housekeeping finished, I pick up Malcolm's Bible and try to review the lesson he gave me last night, but I can't focus, and the letters swim before my eyes worse than usual. I put down the Bible and try to keep my hands busy checking for necessary repairs to the blankets and to my clothes. As I repair the seam along the inside of my blanket, I find myself thinking of a sampler I stitched when I was little. It had my name and age, surrounded by the alphabet. *Catherine Blair, Five Years, 1748.* It hung on the wall of the front room of our house on the Delaware. Mother traced it out for me and told me to stitch *Catherine* instead of *Catriona.* A little wave of anger crashes in my stomach, and I feel guilty for being angry at the dead for something that happened so long ago. My brothers' neat names gave Mother no such trouble, though she always did prefer the more formal *James* to *Jaime.*

It doesn't matter anymore. The sampler is gone now, I suppose, lost in the wreck Donald Campbell made of my home. I begin to play a game to distract myself from my worry for Malcolm and my guilty anger. I name all the things I can remember from our cabin. I work my way around the common room and kitchen first, then back to my parents' bedchamber and up the ladder to the loft divided by a thin wall. One side for me, one for my brothers, though when Mark was gone, Jaime often crawled into bed with me in the middle of the night. He never liked to sleep alone. I smile at the memory, recalling the odd ends of stories I used to tell him in the dark.

The game does its job of distracting me from my fear for Malcolm so well that I start when he appears around the blanket, stamping and shaking ice from his hair.

"Is it very bad?" I ask. I can hear that the ice has turned needle thin and sharp. It makes little sounds on the rock like pins hitting the floor.

Malcolm lifts his game bag, which I can tell is mostly empty. "I'm sorry, Catriona," he says. "I judged it better to turn back than to try to beat the storm. You won't mind if food's a bit scarce for a few days?"

Food is always scarce. I put down my work and go to him. "Mind?" I say. "I don't think I've much right to mind. I'm trespassing on your charity, as I'm well aware."

His face is red and raw from the wind, and his clothes are spotted where ice has melted into the cloth. I grip his arm and feel how damp it is.

"Malcolm, you're soaked through," I say, anxiety rising again. So often an illness begins in a soaking, and I don't have much practice treating the sick. "You must get warm this instant. Here, let me build up the fire."

"Don't," says Malcolm. "Not until we must. The wood may have to last us several days. I've passed a winter in these mountains. The ice storms can be vicious."

"I'd rather you didn't catch cold," I say, helping him out of the layered cloaks. "I don't need a sick man on my hands in addition to an ice storm."

I spread the wet cloaks beside the fire and move him nearer to it. In the clearer light, I can see he's shivering.

"You're going to have to take off the rest of your clothes, too," I insist, so urgently that I don't hear my words properly until after they've passed my lips.

Malcolm flashes a grin through chattering teeth. "Are you calling in debts?"

I flush and cover it with a laugh. "You must be feverish already if you think that. You can wrap in your blanket while your clothes dry. I kept it on the hearth in case, so it's warm. We've just got to get your clothes dry so you can put them back on."

"You're not a bit of fun, are you?" Malcolm laughs.

"Not a bit," I answer. "Not when there's an ice storm breaking over our heads."

"Well, hide your eyes, then," he says.

I am glad enough to turn away from him. I press my fingers to my face. Cold as it is, my cheeks are burning. I don't know where that exchange came from. Malcolm is kind and generous, that much is clear from the way he has treated me, but never before has either of us indicated there could be anything more to our relationship than survival and courtesy. I can't help but think of Owen, and I can't help comparing the two of them. Owen never teased me like that. Our relationship was always a solemn business, even when we were children. For the first time, I'm forced to wonder which I prefer.

Facing the rock wall, I try to distract myself from the knowledge that I will shortly be sharing a room with a naked man by broaching the subject of Fort Loudoun. *It doesn't matter,* I tell the silent voice of judgment in my head. *It can't matter, not out here. My reputation would be long gone in Charlestown, but this isn't Charlestown. I don't know what this place is.*

"Malcolm." My voice wavers, and I try to catch and smooth it. "You know I can't stay here forever, and I'm sure you don't wish me to."

I hear him moving behind me, peeling off wet clothing and draping it on the hearth. The fire crackles and spits, and the earthy smell of wet wool fills the room.

"I hope you know you're welcome to stay as long as you like, Catriona. I'm glad enough of the company. It's a lonely life out here."

"How?" I ask, faltering, twisting my hands together. "How did you get here? I know you deserted, but that's no reason to live out here alone. Mark told me many deserters live among the Cherokee. What about Chota, the Cherokee city of refuge? Couldn't you live there?"

"I've been there," he answers. "Last year, before the Cherokee war started. Most of the deserters who live in the Cherokee towns are French, you know. That's part of what started the Cherokee war with South Carolina, the English thinking the Cherokee were going to go over to the French."

"The French give a bounty for English scalps," I whisper, studying the patterns in the rock. "Soldiers and civilians, men and women, adults and children. They don't care who."

I sense that Malcolm has stopped moving.

"I didn't want to stay in Chota," he continues. "I didn't mind it, but I wanted to be alone. The Cherokee headmen know I'm here. I have, or had, permission to live in their territory. If they thought it was odd that I chose to be alone, they didn't say anything. But I don't expect every Cherokee warrior I encounter to know I have permission to be here or to care if they do know. Many of them think the headmen are too tolerant of foreign soldiers on their land."

"Do you plan to stay here forever?" I ask, reaching out to feel the rough surface of the rock. "How will you survive?"

"The same way I always have. As well as I can. The goods and food I've been able to collect came from trading I did with the Cherokee and from some destroyed farms I raided on my way south."

I've been wondering how he stocked his shelter against the winter, but it never seemed like the right time to ask.

"You stole from the dead?"

"Better the dead than the living. The dead have no need of their goods. I'll stay here until the British army sails for home, anyway, or until I'm starved out, or killed. I don't have many other options."

I draw a deep breath and speak before I can stop myself, pressing my palms against the rock. "Malcolm, I have to go to Fort Loudoun," I say in a rush. "In the spring, as soon as it's warm enough to travel. My wounds have almost healed, and my strength is coming back."

The only sound I hear is the crackle of the fire. I can tell Malcolm is standing perfectly still.

"Why do you have to go to Fort Loudoun?" he asks, his voice taut and strained, cautious.

"Because Cherokee raiders didn't kill my family," I say. "A man named Donald Campbell did. A terrible, terrible man. He faked a raid on our home, killed my parents, killed Mark. He chased me and Jaime into Cherokee territory, and he only turned back because he figured the winter or the Cherokee would kill us. I suppose he didn't bet on a catamount."

"How will going to Fort Loudoun help?" Malcolm asks.

I squeeze my eyes closed, focusing on the colors that spill into the dark behind my eyelids. "There's an independent company of the British army there. They report directly to General Amherst, the commander-in-chief. I'm going to report Donald Campbell to the British authorities at Fort Loudoun. I couldn't go to the civilian government because Mark was afraid they might be on Campbell's side, in on his plot. Campbell has done terrible things, Malcolm. I have to make someone listen to me. I have to get justice for my family."

Malcolm laughs at that, a bitter bark. "You'll not get it from the British army."

I almost whirl on him before I remember not to.

"That is the only place I can begin to get it," I insist. "I don't expect you to understand. I don't expect you to come with me. But I will go. I'll leave as soon as I'm sure it's warm enough, in another month or so."

My voice has the hard edge that tells Malcolm, as it told my parents and brothers before him, that it will be useless to argue. My mind is made up. So of course he tries to change the subject.

"You can turn around now."

When I do, I give an exasperated sigh. "You're incorrigible."

Malcolm is naked from the waist up, but he has wrapped Jaime's cloak around his hips like an apron. He's terribly thin, I tell myself. Possibly even scrawny. Skin and bone. You get that way when you've spent most of your life hiding from or marching in the British army. But I can't deny that his shoulders are still broad and straight or that I can see every single muscle in his torso and arms, defined by privation and exertion as if they were sculpted that way. The long scar on his upper arm shines white in the firelight. I flutter my eyelids down for a second, demurring in a way I have never before found necessary. I force my gaze back up, making it clear I am appraising him. He'll not get the better of me through shock.

"Wrap up in your blanket before you catch cold," I laugh. "That's the last thing on earth that's going to stop me from going to Fort Loudoun."

15.

February 10, 1760

Night

Malcolm's prediction about the severity of the storm holds true. By evening the heavens are pelting down solid sheets of ice, and though Malcolm and I huddle close to the fire, it can't do much to warm us in the damp cold. We cook the skinny squirrel Malcolm brought back in a kettle of water to make a broth and do our best to warm ourselves with that. When Malcolm tries to give me my daily language lesson, we have to talk over the whistling of the wind and the smashing of ice against the rocks.

"What should we do?" I ask, after a particularly loud burst of wind whips away the blanket covering the door. "Do you think it's safe to stay here? Will the shelter hold?"

"It's as safe as anywhere else," Malcolm answers, peering up at the smoke hole, which allows occasional shards of ice to shoot down and melt in the fire or smash on the hearth. "Here at least we're sheltered and can keep a fire going. The rocks will stand, and if the pine wall breaks, it will just topple down on itself. The cold is the real danger."

As I pick up the blanket and secure it over the door once more, I think of the warmth of my small bed against the rock and of how Malcolm gave it up to sleep on the cold floor with only a blanket. I return to where Malcolm sits on the hearth to keep from having to shout.

"Sleep with me tonight," I say. "We'll keep warmer that way."

He gives me a look of mocked shock. "Miss Blair, I don't know what to say. I thought you respected my virtue."

I cross my arms over my chest, feeling a little tug from the scars that makes my face look cross in a way I don't intend. "I don't respect your honor enough to allow either of us to freeze to death over it. You know I mean sleep and nothing else."

Malcolm laughs and returns to making me identify short Erse words, but we soon warm the cloaks and blankets on the hearth and abandon the lesson for the bed. It's become too loud to hear each other and too cold to concentrate.

Despite the raging storm outside, by the time I'm bundled in bed with Malcolm, I'm warm enough. I tell myself it's really just like bundling, the courting practice where a girl's parents sew a boy up in a blanket and the two spend the night in bed together. Sewing the boy to immobility inside the blanket is supposed to keep the couple apart, but I know in practice those stitches never last long. I know only from hearsay, of course, not from my own experience. Mother thought bundling a vulgar practice. I think of Owen with a strange mix of grief and guilt. Mother's position aside, I always imagined he would be the first boy I bundled with.

We are both wearing as many layers as we can manage, anyway, Malcolm's clothing having dried hours ago. I'm wearing Jaime's cloak and Malcolm is wearing mine. Mark's cloak is spread over us, along with two blankets, all we have except the one covering the door. Stones heated by the fire and wrapped in rags are at our feet, and it's all I can do not to keep my feet on them. I don't think they would burn me through the layers of rags and my wool stockings, but I tell myself it's not worth the risk.

I find it awkward at first, trying to get comfortable in a very narrow space with a man I have shared my life with for weeks. I tell myself firmly that we are simply sharing the bed for warmth, so there is nothing to be uncomfortable about. And I slip my hand between the bed and the rock, where I have concealed my kitchen knife, just in case there is. At last I settle on my back with my left shoulder pressed against the stone wall. I watch the flicker of the fire play over the rock, recalling one of my father's favorite stories, a story about people who lived in a cave and saw only shadows, so they never caught the true shape of anything.

"How is your chest, Catriona?" Malcolm asks, his voice echoing strangely off the wall.

"I told you it's nearly healed. I should be able to stop wearing the bandages altogether soon."

I feel Malcolm shift in the dark and turn my head to look at him. The fire is behind him, so his face is in shadow.

"I was just wondering if you're pressed all the way against the wall because the wounds pain you," he says. "I don't want to hurt you, and if I am, I can get up. I need to make sure the fire doesn't go out, anyway. It'll be near impossible to get it started again in the cold and damp."

"No, stay," I say quickly. "I don't want you to freeze. It's not fair of me to keep you from your bed on a night like this."

I lay a hand gently, curiously on my torn breast, though there's no feeling anything through my clothes. "I will have to be careful of the wounds for some time yet, I think. I can't explain, I know they shouldn't, but—the scars hurt."

"It's the living flesh around them, not the scars themselves," says Malcolm. And then, suddenly and inexplicably, Malcolm has propped himself on his elbow and slipped his forearm under my head. The front of his body presses along the side of mine, and all the layers of cloth between us can't keep me from feeling the searing heat of it. I feel a flush rise in my cheeks. There's nothing improper in this, I tell myself. Keeping warm is the point. It's not his arm under my head or the pressure of his leg against mine that makes me think there could be more to this than practicality. It's the way he took my hand, covered it in his, and tucked them both in the hollow of my stomach. There's something knowing and intimate about that gesture that makes my breath catch.

I lie still, trying to breathe evenly, hoping Malcolm can't feel the change, the sudden increase, of my heartbeat. We've gotten along well enough as cordial strangers for a month. Nothing has to change.

"Malcolm?" I venture, thankful my voice remains steady. "You never have told me why you deserted. Will you tell me now? We're not going to sleep with all this wind, and it will be a good distraction from the storm."

And from other things. I press harder.

"You said you deserved death more than I did, but you never told me why. What did you do?"

If I must be cruel, I must be cruel.

Malcolm is silent for a few moments, as frozen as the world outside, but at last I hear him sigh heavily, and his hand clenches around mine. "All right," he says. "But I must tell you in my own way, so hold your questions."

The tremor in his voice is anger, not passion. I have made a wise choice, if perhaps an unfair one.

"Officers' commissions in the highland regiments were hard to get," he begins. "There were a lot of families like mine who needed to a way to prove their loyalty to the Crown, but my uncle worked hard. He must have written a hundred letters, paid a thousand bribes. I entered the army as a lieutenant when I was seventeen."

He laughs bitterly. "I don't know how much he paid for the army to take me halfway across the world. I didn't know anything about war, and neither did most of the men. They were farmers, cattle and sheep herders mostly, not professional soldiers. If it hadn't been for the sergeants, we would have been completely lost."

Malcolm's thumb has found its way inside my hand and is tracing agitated circles over my palm. The nail has begun to scrape my skin, and I want to take my hand away, but I don't move because I can tell he doesn't realize what he's doing, and I did start him down this path. The least I can do is stay on it with him now.

"I told you we had to build a road to get to our battles. We were set to building one through the wilderness of western Pennsylvania. Our major, James Grant—he's a likeable enough man, but ambitious as the devil himself. One of those who thinks it's better to reign in hell than to serve in heaven, which is the only explanation for anyone who wants to fight in America rather than in Europe."

"Milton," I say, smiling, trying to pull him out of the dark place I can see I'm losing him to. *"Paradise Lost."*

"Grant thought to make a name for himself by taking Fort Duquesne from the French. He did make a name for himself, but not in the way he wished."

Malcolm disentangles his hand from mine and rolls onto his back.

"It was September of 1758," he says. "About a year and a half ago. Grant let his ambition get in the way of his judgment. It was the first independent command he'd ever held. Over eight hundred men. There were Shawnee allied to the French surrounding the fort. We were supposed to wipe out their encampments. Instead, it went the other way. They surprised and surrounded us. Nearly half of us were killed or wounded. Grant and some others were taken prisoner."

"Were you afraid?" I ask. "Is that why you deserted?"

"I wouldn't be ashamed if I had been afraid," Malcolm replies, his voice measured in the darkness. "I would have had good reason to be. I don't know how to explain it. It's like I didn't have time to be afraid. But no, I wouldn't have deserted just for that. I told you I knew nothing of warfare. I was there mostly to be a translator, and God help me, Catriona, I failed at that."

He jerks upright, resting his head on his hands, his hands on his knees. The blankets pulled away from me, I sit up, too.

I put my hand on his back and begin to trace my fingers in slow circles, the way I used to comfort Jaime after a nightmare. "Hush," I say. "That's enough. I'm sorry I asked you. I had no right to."

He shakes his head. "No, it does me good to tell you. They cut us to pieces. And I," he draws a shuddering breath. "I couldn't translate the orders. I don't know why. In battle, some men lose their stomachs, some their bowels. I lost my language. I've spoken both English and Erse most of my life, and I couldn't remember either one of them. Most of my men were killed." He lifts his head from his knees and looks at me. "It was my fault."

I rest the flat of my hand between his shoulder blades. His muscles are tight under my palm.

"I've never been in battle," I say. "The closest I've come to it was the day I failed to kill Donald Campbell. I was so afraid, Malcolm. I would imagine it was kill or be killed, and your orders wouldn't have made a lot of difference, anyway."

"They fired from the trees," he says, ignoring me. "We had no chance. They were too well protected and camouflaged by the forest. We were wearing white shirts over our uniforms. White shirts, Catriona. God help us, it was supposed to keep us from killing each other. All it did was make us easy to pick off."

Malcolm's hands go to his head, and he grips his dark curls desperately, loosening the strip of leather that holds his hair so that it falls among the blankets and is lost.

"My uncle. He managed to secure my commission by raising men from my family's lands. Most of them didn't enlist willingly—they were forced. He threatened to harm their families or burn their cottages. This wasn't their war, it wasn't *my* war, but I led them to their deaths."

Sweat beads on Malcolm's temples, and I pull his hands from his head and take them in mine. "It sounds like this was all Major Grant's fault, not yours. I remember when that happened. It was in the papers. The blame was clearly assigned to Major Grant." I free one hand and brush his hair from his face. "There wasn't a word about a Lieutenant Craig."

"Still," he says, gripping my hands again, so tightly that my joints grate against each other. "I couldn't get anyone else killed. I decided to hide myself in the mountains, to keep my men safe from me. That's why it mattered so much to me if you lived or died, why I tried so hard to keep you alive. I'd hidden from the British in the mountains before. I figured I could do it again."

"But you can never go back," I say, filled with sadness for what he has lost. "You can never go back to Scotland. Or anywhere someone might recognize you and turn you in. You'll never have a normal life."

"There's nothing left for me in Scotland," Malcolm answers. "And when you grow up on the run from the British, you don't really expect a normal life. What's normal, anyway? I'm alive, and that's something. It's more than those poor devils at Fort Duquesne have."

His tone changes abruptly, and I can tell the conversation is at an end. "I'd better go check the fire."

The cold that envelopes me when Malcolm leaves the bed is a shock, and I am so relieved for his warmth to return that I nestle quite unselfconsciously against him. His arms wrap around me, and he kisses the top of my forehead, just at the hairline.

"I'm glad you know," he says. "Go to sleep, sweet. I'll keep the fire up."

I sleep warmly that night, and many nights after, because though the ice storm wears itself out in a couple of days, Malcolm keeps sleeping in my bed. During the day I tell myself there's no sense in his sleeping on the floor when there's a perfectly good bed available. At night I accept that we would have become lovers long ago, except that neither of us can bear to have anything else to lose.

16.

March 5, 1760

Morning

By the beginning of March, it's impossible to imagine there ever was an ice storm. The birds begin their calling before dawn and continue all day. The first flowers are pushing up out of the earth, the green buds emerging from tree branches. Malcolm's snares are beginning to catch more meat as the small animals venture into the sunlight.

"It's a false spring," says Malcolm flatly, when I tell him I think it must soon be time for me to move on to Fort Loudoun. "It won't be safe until April, as far as the weather goes, and when the weather really warms, armies will start to move. It won't be safe to travel in these mountains for a long time, if ever."

I pull myself out of bed and wrap my cloak tightly over my shift against the chill of early morning.

"My life has never been safe, Malcolm. I told you. I should have died when Campbell killed my family in the first place. I certainly should have died when the catamount attacked me. The stays didn't save my life—you did. If I've been spared, it's only so I can bring Donald Campbell to justice."

I open the pine door, eager to soak as much warmth from the sun as I can after the cold winter. I know it's a false spring. But the longer I stay here with Malcolm, the less certain I am I will ever leave. And I have to leave. I feel in my bones that this is a nowhere place, a place to rest and heal that is not real. If I walked away, I would not be surprised to return and find that all of it—the winter, the shelter, and Malcolm himself—had been a fevered dream. I have to leave here, or I will never find a way to move on.

"I have to go," I say quietly. "As long as Campbell is in the world, I have to go."

I hear Malcolm cross the room to stand behind me. He rests his hands on my shoulders. "Wait for true spring, at least. April. Give yourself time to put on more weight and get your strength back before you try to conquer the mountains."

I know he is trying to stall me. By April he will have thought of another argument to try to keep me here.

"Is it justice you're really interested in, Catriona?" Malcolm asks. "Or is it vengeance?"

I stare above my head to the meeting of the stone monoliths so I won't have to look at him. Our time together is limited now, and I have no stomach for an argument.

"It's a mercy these rocks were here," I say instead. "It was clever of you to build around them. Where do you think they came from?"

I feel the movement of Malcolm's head as he glances up. "A rockslide," he says. "Long ago. You can tell by how deeply they're buried that they broke off the mountain centuries ago and fell."

"It's odd the way they lean into each other," I say. "Unusual."

I hear Malcolm swallow behind my ear. "They had to," he says. "If they hadn't fallen into each other they both would have plunged to the bottom of some gorge and shattered to bits."

I fall silent. I'm suddenly not sure we're still talking about the stones.

17.

March 6, 1760

Evening

The next evening I am dozing by the wide hearth because it was indeed a false spring, and a cold rain is drizzling now. I know it will freeze in the night, blighting the flowers that tasted their brief days of blooming and driving many small animals back into shelter, away from Malcolm's snares. After the scarcity of food during the winter, I am still getting used to not being hungry, and I don't want the unfamiliar sense of being well fed to end.

"Catriona?" Malcolm speaks carefully, like he's treading near a snake he doesn't want to disturb. I look up and see he has risen from the chair where he was cleaning Mark's rifle and stands with his arms crossed, gripping his elbows in his hands.

"Catriona, I want you to reconsider going to Fort Loudoun."

I start fully awake and straighten, wincing at the tug the scars give my skin. "Malcolm, we've talked about this. More than once. You won't change my mind, and I wish you wouldn't try. We have nothing further to discuss."

Malcolm drops his arms by his sides and paces the floor by the pine wall. "You're safe here, Catriona. As safe as you can be, anyway. The best thing you can do is to stay here until the war is over."

He lifts his arms, indicating the shelter. "It's nothing fine, I'll grant you that, but it's warm enough, and it will keep you alive. If you leave, who knows what will happen to you? You wondered before how I got all the supplies in here, the sacks of cornmeal, the needles and thread. The Cherokee Path was a busy road, busy with soldiers and traders, Cherokees and settlers. I managed to trade for things I needed out of my army kit, and yes, out of things I stole."

He pushes his hands through his curls. The tie falls to the floor, and his hair swings free around his face. His voice drops.

"But there haven't been any traders here in a long time. That's why the cornmeal is running so low. The only thing that could keep the traders from coming is something they fear more than they love money. They know how dangerous it is. Strong men, seasoned traders, are afraid to wander out here now. But you think you can defy the violence of three nations because you lost your family. You can't, Catriona."

I stand, facing him, straightening the many layers of my skirts, trying to look as formidable, as self-possessed, as I can.

"Mark told me to go to Fort Loudoun," I say. "It was practically the last thing he said to me."

"Your brother thought Fort Loudoun was your best chance of survival. He thought he'd be with you. He didn't think you would try to go alone. Staying with me is your best chance now. He'd tell you to stay."

"How do you know what Mark would tell me to do?" I demand. "You didn't know him."

"I know he loved you. I know he wouldn't want you to risk your life on the slight chance you might be able to get Donald Campbell hanged."

I shake my head. "I have to do this. Someone has to know what happened to my family." I pause, my hand to my mouth. "I can't just let what happened to them happen without even trying to make it right."

Malcolm's voice is low and fierce. "Can you ever make it right, Catriona? Is that even possible? I once thought I could make things right somehow, but I couldn't. There's no way to right a wrong like that."

"I can," I insist. "I can bring Donald Campbell to justice for murdering my family. That would go a long way."

"Would it?" asks Malcolm. "Would your grief be any less? Would it bring your family back, your parents and your brothers?"

I take a halting step toward Malcolm. "It would keep Donald Campbell from ever doing to anyone else what he did to my family. It would expose him to everyone for the monster he is. I saw him scalp my brother, Malcolm. I saw my other brother torn to pieces by an animal. My parents are dead, and I nearly died, and it's all because of him. I hate him, and I will see him dead or die trying, and that's all there is to it." I think of Owen and my family in a single breath, and any hope that Owen is alive evaporates. Campbell took everyone else from me. My hands scrabble at the scars, my fingernails catching on the new seams that hold the front of my gown together.

Across the room, Malcolm stretches a hand toward me. "Catriona. Is it worth giving up your own life? I'm sure no one in your family would want that."

My vision is clouded by rage and tears, but at last I manage to choke out, "What does it matter if I die? There's nothing left, nowhere for me to go. There's no one left to love me now."

A sound escapes my mouth, a low cry that echoes in my mind like the faraway moan of a wounded animal. And then Malcolm crosses the room, faster than I knew anyone could move, and his arms are around me, supporting me before I can sink to the ground, sliding from my waist up my back and around my shoulders, until he is gripping the back of my head. For a bewildered moment I don't know if he intends to kiss me or snap my neck himself to keep me from a worse death, and I'm still confused when his lips touch mine. For all the weeks we've been together, for all Malcolm's intimate medical knowledge of my body, for all the nights I've drawn warmth from his arms, this is the first time we've kissed. I feel Malcolm's hands slip down to stroke my neck, and I wonder where my own hands are. I find my palms pressed against his chest in a gesture that might have been intended to warn him off, but quickly becomes a way to draw him closer as I gather his shirt in my fists.

Malcolm pulls away from me, and his eyes flicker over my face, searching for something, though whether it's permission or condemnation would be hard to say. His hands skim down my body to my waist. He's about to speak when my hands slide to his back and pull him closer, so instead of speaking he kisses me again, and I pull him backward toward the bed, knowing I'm flirting with danger but unwilling to give up everything these kisses are saying to me.

Because in them I can taste everything that has happened to me since the morning of Donald Campbell's massacre. All the grief and fear and pain. And I can taste, too, all the things Malcolm is running from, his lost childhood and lost comrades. And I feel somehow the heat of passion might heal the hidden wounds, or at least make them easier to bear, the way the heat of a fever sometimes burns away an illness. But I remember, too, in some cool place at the back of my mind, that sometimes a fever also kills, and that's why, as I pull Malcolm down onto the bed, I tell myself this is quite lovely, but it can't go beyond kissing. I reach down to check for the kitchen knife hidden in the crevice between the bed and the stone wall. Because, while I've come to trust Malcolm, I trust the knife more, and I can't let him distract me from bringing my family's killer to the gallows.

I don't need the knife, though, because Malcolm's kisses slowly become softer, until he ends with three short kisses on my mouth and finally stops kissing me altogether. I suddenly feel the pressure lying on my side puts on my new scars, and I roll onto my back. Malcolm lies on his side, facing me, one hand crossing my body and resting on my hip, suggesting things I would very much like to know more about. I feel a trickle of guilt when I think of Owen, but Owen is gone, from me if not from the world. I doubt my own life will last much longer, and someone has to heal the wretched loneliness that is tearing me apart.

"I love you, Catriona," says Malcolm. "It would be the crisis of my life if anything happened to you."

I can't help but smile at that. "It would have considerable competition. But you don't love me, Malcolm. You're lonely, and I'm here. That's why you think you love me. Or maybe because you like kissing me. My mother always told me men would say anything to get up my skirts."

Malcolm grins. "That is true. Which is why I'm not going to try to get up your skirts. If I did, you'd think that was why I said I loved you, which isn't fair to me and my entirely honorable intentions. Now, if you wanted me up your skirts, that would be a completely different matter."

I laugh lightly, and I realize it's the lightest sound that has come out of my mouth since the day I lost my family. I take Malcolm's hand from my hip and twine my fingers through his. The action pulls him toward me, and he leans down and kisses my forehead. The kiss is quick, the punctuation on the end of a joke, but it turns into something more serious, more intentional, on the way to my eyelids, and by the time Malcolm's lips reach my neck, his hand is back on my hip, and mine are lost in his hair. He strokes from my hip up the curve of my waist, and his thumb brushes the underside of my breast. His hand moves back to my hip and down the outside of my thigh as his mouth explores my collarbone.

It's not as if this is the first time I've been kissed. I've kissed Owen, of course, and there was a quiet, stolen sweetness to those kisses that I thought was passion. Until tonight. The thick layers of my clothing are useless under Malcolm's hands. I close my eyes and imagine threads of flame lighting everywhere his fingers touch, crisscrossing my body and delving inside it, like fire touched to lines of powder. I am barely moving, but I feel flushed, and though I can see my breath, I can't catch it. I don't want Malcolm to stop touching me, but I know I have to make him because what was half-jesting a few minutes ago is very real now. Those threads of flame are scorching my skin, and I want them everywhere. But I can't have them, not right now, no matter how distracting they are.

I wrench my hand away from Malcolm's head and somehow find the fingers that are trailing those flaming threads. I take his hand and press his palm still against my hip.

"Malcolm," I whisper.

I hear the warm laughter in his voice from very close because his lips are just under my ear. "Catriona," he says. He presses his mouth into my neck. "Sweet." He is not making this easy.

"You could come with me," I say. My words are unsteady. "To Fort Loudoun."

I know what I'm asking. I know it could be dangerous for him. But he can't stay hidden in this shelter forever, especially not alone. It takes a moment for what I've said to register, but when it does, he pulls his head away, though the length of his body remains pressed against mine.

"Oh, Catriona," he sighs. He props himself up on one arm and passes the other over his eyes.

Something breaks inside me, both at the desolation in his voice and at the loss of his closeness. Disappointment falls in pieces into my stomach. I want to be here. I want to be with him. I want to stay. But I press on.

"Fort Loudoun is garrisoned by an independent company. No one there would have any idea who you are. We can make up a history for you."

I don't like the wheedling tone in my voice, but this is all I can think of. I don't want to leave Malcolm. I don't want to leave him, but I have to. I have to go to Fort Loudoun because it is my only chance of ever finding any peace. If I don't go, I'll never get justice for my family. I'll never know if Owen Ramsay is alive or dead.

I don't want to think about Owen. I want whatever I interrupted to go on. I want Malcolm back, so I reach up and tangle my fingers in his hair. I pull his face down to mine and kiss him again. I kiss him gently, calmly, deeply, learning his mouth, until I have forgotten, for the moment at least, all the things I want to forget, and then I nestle close, ready to be warm and comforted and sleeping. I feel him move away from me to tend the fire, and then he climbs back into bed, pulls the blankets up around us, and curves his body around mine. All I want in this moment is to be surrounded by him and to know both of us are safe for now.

I am nearly asleep when I feel Malcolm's lips brush the spot under my ear where my jaw meets my neck.

"I'll go with you," he whispers. "If I can't convince you to stay with me, I'll go with you. I'll stay with you."

I feel my lips curve into a sleepy smile, but cold fear stalks me through my dreams.

18.

March 1760

After that first intense night, Malcolm and I shy away from each other. He spends long hours outdoors, and I take a greater interest in the Bible than I ever have before. Our sleeping arrangements are cautious; though we pretend nothing has changed between us, I can feel that Malcolm's muscles are as tight as mine, and his heartbeat under my ear is as fast. Though I barely sleep for several nights, when Malcolm attempts a return at sleeping across the room, making some excuse, I stretch my hand toward him, and he slips under the blanket beside me. I am prepared for another night of strained politeness, but not for the trembling that grips his whole body.

"Is there something wrong?" I ask, lifting my head from his chest. Maybe I shouldn't have encouraged him to come back to my bed. Maybe he regrets what happened between us. Maybe this is pure stupidity masquerading as romance; my knife aside, I have no doubt he could overpower me if he wanted to. Maybe he's getting sick.

Sighing, he raises himself on one elbow and looks down at me.

"No," he answers. "No, sweet. It's just that I—I don't deserve this, I don't deserve you, not even for a little while. I don't deserve to have you."

A strange, unfamiliar smile plays about his lips, but I recognize that tone from the night he told me about Fort Duquesne. This is all part of his self-inflicted penance for something that wasn't his fault. I see that I must pursue the light of the smile rather than the dark of the tone.

"Well," I say. "To be clear, I'm not going to let you *have* me. Not anytime soon, anyway." I sit up and kiss him between the eyes. "I warn you, I'm well armed."

The smile wins. "I meant have you *in my life*. Here, with me. What are you thinking of?"

The heat in my face tells me I am not used to this yet, but I smile back. "I'm serious. Do you understand me?"

"I would never do anything you didn't want." His smile transforms itself into a grin. "Just let me know what you do want, all right?"

I laugh and pull him down among the blankets with me and lay my head in the crook of his arm.

"I want this, for now," I answer. "I want you here, with me. It's enough."

My Erse lessons end there. Malcolm and I spend the next month learning the details of each others' bodies, the intricacies of clothing. I never knew my clothes could be so interesting, or removed in so many ways. Sometimes I go to the trouble of putting my clothes back on so Malcolm can take them off me again. Everything is so slow, so very detailed. On a warming evening, Malcolm devotes at least an hour to kissing my wrists and fingers, while he tells me about the countryside where he grew up.

Though I know Malcolm has seen the worst of my body already, I am still shy and embarrassed by the scars that cover the right side of my chest. I keep my shift on all the time, anyway, because without it I would be completely naked, and I don't feel prepared for that. One night near the end of March, I end up lying on the bed in only my shift and stockings. My stays are crumpled among the blankets, the rest of my clothes piled over the cane chair.

Malcolm's hand slides up my stomach, hesitating at the bottom of my ribcage.

"Does it still hurt?" he asks.

I nod, nervous. "Sometimes. Not right now." Tears prick the back of my eyes.

"Are you sure?"

"It's just—it's just that it's so ugly," I say. "You know it is. I'm so sorry."

He pulls away from me and smiles. "You're sorry you survived a catamount?"

I trace my fingers along the unmarred skin of his chest, over the muscle, leaving red lines in the wake of my nails, ghosts of my own wounds. I shake my head. "You don't understand."

But I think he is trying. He follows the lines of my scars with two gentle fingers, over my shift.

"I'm sorry you were hurt. But you should never be ashamed of these. They brought you to me, and I can't help but love them for that."

He leans down and presses his lips to the cloth above my scars, kissing the length of each of them. There is no feeling in the dead flesh, only a deep gratitude for Malcolm that lodges like grief among the sobs in my throat. I understand at last what has made him so good. Adversity and pain make some people cruel and some angry and some bitter. And a precious few it makes very, very kind.

But I never let Malcolm's kindnesses toward my scarred body go as far as I want them to. Lying with men tends to lead, sooner or later, to motherhood. There are means of preventing it, but I am not well versed enough in them to trust myself, and as much as I want Malcolm, I know a baby is the last thing I am prepared to deal with now. Deep in my belly is the grim understanding that once I have a child, my obligation will be to the future, and I have not yet discharged my duty to the past.

19.

March 30–April 7, 1760

I agree to wait until the end of March to start our journey to Fort Loudoun, well aware that winter is simply another obstacle to face. And wanting to prolong our time in the relative safety of the mountain shelter as long as possible, because what waits for us outside is unknown and likely enough to be terrible.

We are prepared for a lengthy journey to Fort Loudoun because we must try to pass unnoticed through Cherokee territory. The fastest route would be to travel north from Malcolm's shelter and follow the great river west all the way to the fort, but we can't do that because the river would lead us directly through the Cherokee Overhill towns. The Overhills, the westernmost of the three large clusters of Cherokee towns, are rumored to be the most hostile to Britain. They were the ones who asked the South Carolina Assembly to build Fort Loudoun for the protection of their people while their warriors were fighting the French in the north, but that was nearly five years ago, before the war exploded across the backcountry, and now we will have to go far out of our way to avoid the Overhills.

On the day before our departure, we pack what is necessary in my woven basket and Malcolm's cloth game bag. Malcolm cleans the guns, Mark's rifle and his own musket and pistol, which I pause to admire, turning the metal piece in my hands, noting the engravings that show it is of military issue.

"Is it not dangerous for you to keep your weapons?" I ask. "Won't they mark you as a deserter?"

Malcolm shakes his head as he wipes a cloth over the barrel of the Brown Bess and rests the musket against the wall. "You don't trade away a good weapon if you can help it, though I did lose my backsword. The musket and the dirk are my personal property, anyway. The army issues cheap weapons. Anyone who can afford it brings his own." He shrugs. "I suppose I have my uncle to thank for them."

I bake the little remaining cornmeal into dry bread to carry with us and do my best to salt some thin strips of meat. We carry the blankets rolled on our backs. We cannot move quickly this way, but supplies are more important than speed, and we cannot move quickly, in any case.

On the chilly morning of our departure, I feel a swift pang of affection and nostalgia for the shelter, and for Malcolm, who tried so hard to make it a place of comfort for me. I thought I was ready to leave. I felt in my bones that I needed to leave, but it hurts to watch the fire on the hearth go out. It feels like the end of something. I reach to make sure the blue ribbons are secure with their cargo of pearls around my neck and remember another end, another loss, the loss that is driving this one. But no, that isn't fair. Surely I could not have stayed here forever, even had I held no other obligations.

I look up at the sharp angles of Malcolm's face, wondering what this end means for us. By the time he kissed me, over two months after I lost my family, I was so lonely and so empty I didn't care where comfort came from, as long as it came. I took the human contact I needed, but I never returned his words of love. I couldn't. I might regret my behavior did I not know he was using me as much as I was using him. Loneliness and grief and ever-present danger do not equal love, and I think we both know that. But I will be sorry to lose his warm presence, his breath on my cheek, his hands on my body.

I reach my hand for his as we leave the shelter, trying to preserve some of what happened here, but soon the exertion of movement catches up with me, and I have to let go. Malcolm carries the musket and rifle across his back in a large X and is also loaded down with the cartridge box and his heavy game bag. I have slung the pistol under my left arm and tucked my kitchen knife under the waistband of my overskirt, my jackknife in my pocket.

We make slow progress, staying off the main trails to avoid being seen. We are a week into our journey when we hear the first screams. The deep forest is so dark with no fire, and no moon on this night. The Cherokee have caught someone, a scout or a trader or a settler. Someone on their land who shouldn't have been, someone who was warned away. They are probably burning him alive, which is the most common method of execution among the Cherokee.

Father used to tell us about executions. Once, when he was a young boy, he'd seen a man drawn and quartered in the public square. Mother didn't like him to speak of it, regarding execution gaping as a pastime far beneath us, but from Father's point of view it kept three bloodthirsty children entertained even better than the violence of the Old Testament. Years later, Mark told me that when the Cherokee burn a man to death, they scalp him first and then cover his skull with clay so he will live long enough to suffer the burning, just as European executioners work to keep men alive while their insides are dismantled.

I don't realize I'm crying until Malcolm leans into me and smudges the tears away with his thumbs.

"Sound carries in the mountains," he says. "It echoes, so it seems worse than it is. It's far away from here." But he gathers me to his chest and covers my ears, all the same.

20.

April 13, 1760

Morning

We almost reach Fort Loudoun unchallenged. Every passing day leaves me more nervous, more uneasy, more certain we are cheating the last sister of what is hers by right. I test the strength of the blue ribbons around my neck constantly, for I have come to associate them with my life. They have become my shining thread, pulled tight, waiting for the scissors, waiting for the cut to come. I expect it every day, but my thread holds, even when we are captured.

One moment Malcolm and I are moving quietly through the curling underbrush in the hazy dawn. I am yawning, exhausted from a night on the move, longing for sleep. The next moment we are surrounded and disarmed so quickly I have no time to be afraid. By the time I realize our captors do not plan to kill us immediately, that danger has passed.

When they wrenched the firearms from his back, Malcolm snatched my wrist and held on, and now his grip is so tight my hand is tingling. It's a relief when he slides his hand up my arm and pulls me toward him. I hope he doesn't think I'm one of those women who falls to pieces. I do not fall to pieces. I never fall to pieces until it's an affordable luxury. I got Jaime away from Donald Campbell. I fought the catamount. I didn't scream when Malcolm pushed a thick needle through my skin over and over again. I give Malcolm a small smile to let him know I'm all right, and he shifts my body so my back presses against his chest. I know he's thinking of the best way to protect me, but he has left his own back exposed. Unarmed, we are no match for anyone, but I turn my face into his chest anyway, as if I'm seeking comfort. I raise myself on my toes so I can see over his shoulder. We will not be taken by surprise again.

We're surrounded by five men, none particularly old or particularly young. The shade of their skin and their straight dark hair tell me they are Cherokee, but they are not wearing the vermillion paint of a war party, and this gives me hope. These men are dressed in the typical garb of the back-country, shoes of deer hide leather and dark trade pants and shirts.

Their leader circles us silently, inspecting us for more weapons. They took the kitchen knife at my belt, but my jackknife remains in my pocket, concealed by heavy layers of fabric. The man looks to be near my father's age, and his face is marred by old smallpox scars. As he directs his men, distributing our goods among them, his voice is low and calm, and I recognize something else of my father in it. Curiosity. He is interested in us. He finds us some sort of anomaly and wants to explain our presence to himself.

His measured voice comes from behind my back. His English is perfect, and it's a small relief to know we will be able to communicate clearly.

"You are either very stupid or very reckless. Do you not know the life of any English man or woman who sets foot on Cherokee land is forfeit? You have been warned many times. Why have you not fled east with the rest of your people?"

But we are not dead yet, and there is kindness in this man's voice, which is perhaps our only hope. And he is like my father, which means I must keep him searching for answers. I lower my heels to the ground and turn to face him, grateful for Malcolm's hands on my shoulders and his reassuring presence behind me. The man addressed himself to Malcolm, not to me, and I have to hope my speaking first does not offend him. I am the one with the odder story, the one who can keep him guessing.

"I am safer in the mountains than I would be in the east," I answer. Nothing is stranger than the truth. "We are bound for Fort Loudoun to report a crime to the commandant there."

The man stops before me, his legs planted apart, one hand on his chin. No doubt this is something he hasn't heard before.

"It's a curious tale," I continue, hoping to tempt him. "A white man killed my family. He and his men dressed like Cherokee to do it, hoping to conceal their crime by blaming the murders on the Cherokee. This man wants me dead, too, so there will be no witnesses, and if I go east, he may find me. Before my elder brother died, he advised me to seek safety and justice from the garrison at Fort Loudoun. I promised him I would."

Malcolm's hands are steady on my shoulders, and his thumbs move in gentle circles over the muscles between my shoulder blades. I am so tired of telling this story, and I know I will have to tell it many more times. I blink back tears, but tears are a good thing now. They may win me sympathy.

A wave of pity flows into the man's brown eyes, and he sighs. "That tale is so odd I cannot help but think it must be true. A promise to the dead is a sacred thing, especially in this terrible war."

He appears to be the only member of the party who speaks English. He turns to one of the others and says something in the Cherokee language that sends the man off through the trees.

"You must come with me," says the leader, turning back to us. He sighs, his hands out. "I confess, I do not know what to do with you."

He signals to another man, who steps forward and ties our hands in front of us with a thick cord. This man pulls me away from Malcolm and into position near the front of a single file line. My captor is not rough with me, but there is a knife at his belt, and I know I have been placed in front of Malcolm as a warning. If he tries anything, my scalp will be earning a French bounty.

We have been up for hours already, trying to move in the night, and I am dizzy with exhaustion. I have to pay attention, though, because the trails are really not wide enough for even one person, and my skirts keep snagging. Several times, I believe I truly cannot go on, but then I take another look at the knife in my keeper's belt and manage to keep moving.

The sun indicates it's nearly noon by the time we reach another party of Cherokee. We appear to be in some sort of camp. There are more men here, and evidence of cook fires. Gesturing, my keeper offers me water from a skin bag. I gulp it gratefully as he tips it to my mouth. Water splashes over my chin, but I can't wipe it away because my hands are still tied.

Mercifully, Malcolm is allowed to come to me, and though our hands are still bound, he takes mine. Working his fingers around my wrists, he manages to loosen the rope a little, revealing raw skin underneath. Malcolm is still holding my hands, and I am trying not to cry, because his kindness tears so at my heart and because I am so afraid I will lose him, when a very tall Cherokee man approaches. His chest is bare but for a band of cloth that drapes from one shoulder to the opposite hip, and he has made his already long face longer by shaving the forward lock of his hair back to his ears. From the way the other men defer and the decorations on his body, I can tell he is of no little significance.

The Cherokee man stares down at us. "Do you have any idea who I am?" he asks. He seems amused. For the first time in my life, I have reason to be embarrassed by my appearance. To him, I must look like one of the filthy backcountry children my mother guarded me from.

I know my blank stare does little to improve the man's opinion of me, but Malcolm answers calmly, "You are Kanagatucko, a headman among the Cherokee. We have met before."

Malcolm releases my hands and straightens to stare up at the man he calls Kanagatucko. "Do you not recognize me?"

Kanagatucko's gaze flickers over Malcolm's face. "You look like many Englishmen. Why should I recognize you?"

I barely recognize Malcolm after two weeks on the move. He hasn't shaved since we left the mountain shelter, and though he doesn't have a thick beard, it's enough to shadow the bottom of his face.

"You knew me in Chota nearly two years ago. You and I have borne arms together against enemies. You were there when Connecorte granted me permission to live among you or to live alone in the mountains as I chose."

"Connecorte was old and he is dead," says Kanagatucko, lifting his brows. "I have succeeded him as headman of the Overhills, and I do not share his sympathy for warriors lost far from home. They should have stayed home. Our nations are at war, and you are trespassers. Armed trespassers. Tell me why I should not turn you over to be burned."

I see Malcolm's throat tighten as he swallows.

"You will remember I acquitted myself well defending the women and children of the Lower Towns when they were most vulnerable to attack from English settlers. You will also remember that I am not English."

Kanagatucko pinches Malcolm's chin in his fingers and turns Malcolm's face from side to side.

I am thinking rapidly. Somehow, Malcolm knows the leader of the Cherokee, or at least of the Overhills. And the Cherokee headman knows him. He called Malcolm a warrior far from home. He knows exactly who and what Malcolm is.

Kanagatucko releases Malcolm's chin, apparently satisfied, and turns to me. A prickle of fear runs up the sides of my skull, but I stand as straight as I can, humiliated to be seen in this bedraggled state by a leader of men.

"But who is this? There was no woman with you before."

Because Malcolm's hands are still bound, he has to turn his whole body toward me to take my fingers in his. "This is my wife. Her parents and brothers were murdered by a white man of her own people. She seeks the shelter of Fort Loudoun, where she intends to report this man's crime so he can be brought to justice."

I know Malcolm called me his wife in the hope of placing me under whatever protection he carries, but Kanagatucko unsheathes a blade from the scabbard at his waist with a swiftness that causes my fingers to convulse around Malcolm's. He circles us slowly, pointing the knife, so close I can see the dried blood on the sharp edge. Blood has soaked into the metal. It will never come out, no matter how hard he scrubs.

"Wives of white men are the problem," he says. "The Frenchmen come alone and trade with us and die here or leave. The English bring their wives, and their wives bear children. So many children. Children who need more and more land. When will it stop? The wives," he muses. "They are the reason I am inclined to ally with the French. There are some who say we must kill every Englishwoman we can, even more than we kill the men."

He points the knife to my throat, and I feel my jaw clench with fear as he slips the blade under my blue ribbons. He catches the ribbons on the flat, pulling them taut. I feel a tug at the back of my neck and wait for the cut to come, seeing in my mind the blood and pearls spilling away from my body.

"For without the women, the men are not a threat. The English do not realize how powerful their women are, which is their great mistake."

He quickly pulls the blade away from my throat and sheathes it. "But I have no stomach for killing women, and you, young warrior, I remember your agreement with Connecorte, and I respect your wife for her courage in seeking the blood vengeance on the murderer of her family. It speaks well of her, and I think the two of you are more use to me alive than dead, anyway."

He smiles at me, reassuring, and I see how much of his behavior has been a performance for his men. They will look to him to see how they should treat us.

"Here is my proposal. I will escort your wife to Fort Loudoun myself. You may be sure none will harm her while she is under my care. You will seek a new wife from among the Cherokee women and join us."

My breath catches in my throat, and I feel as if a hand is gripping my neck, choking out the air. A moment ago, fear had crowded out every other feeling, leaving me with no emotion left to consider how I feel about being claimed as Malcolm's wife. But now that it seems relatively certain I am not going to die in the next few minutes, the thought of him leaving me for another woman fills me with anger and jealousy and sadness.

Malcolm's fingers tighten around mine. "I have no wish to leave my wife."

"And I have no wish for your wife to bear more white children," says Kanagatucko, but his eyes soften. "Walk with me, young warrior."

He leads Malcolm away from me, under the trees where I can't hear their conversation, but my mind races over the possibilities. Kanagatucko knows Malcolm. He must know Malcolm is a deserter. If Malcolm chooses to stay with me, Kanagatucko may tell the company at Fort Loudoun the truth, and then Malcolm will certainly face the firing squad. And it will be my fault. I couldn't bear that. I'd rather he left me.

But Kanagatucko returns laughing. "Your husband has convinced me to let you both go to Fort Loudoun. I have ensured he knows just what he sacrifices by choosing to stay with you, and what he risks, but still he chooses to share your fate."

He shrugs. "It will make little enough difference in the end, and we are very close to the end now. I see you as a gift. The war disrupted the autumn hunt, and my people have gone a winter hungry. I think I will ransom you to Fort Loudoun. Forty pounds of salt beef each? Is that too high a price? Do you think they will pay it?"

The Cherokee commander sends a messenger ahead, and a short time later, he and a cohort of men march us from the cover of the trees onto open ground, where one calls up to the fort walls, indicating they have come for the parley. It's not until we are standing in front of the log palisade of Fort Loudoun that I understand the full import of Kanagatucko's words. Ruined outbuildings, burned and pillaged, have collapsed over their foundations. Garden plots are scorched black. The silence outside the walls is heavy as death. Fort Loudoun is under siege.

PART 3

THE SIEGE

21.

April 13, 1760

Noon

The log palisade of Fort Loudoun looms over us, a solid line of tree trunks lodged in the ground at the bottom and sharpened to points at the top. The walls lean outward at an angle meant to make them impossible to scale. A thicket of locust bushes, their thorns inches long and tangled, surrounds the structure, and the black mouths of cannon gape from the bastions. Far to my right, the stripped trunk that serves as a flagpole towers above the rest. The British flag flaps occasionally in the light breeze, and just beyond, the river curves behind the fort. I squint at the sun's reflection off the water as the small door of the sally port opens, releasing a party of soldiers.

The man in the center is tall and broad, with a great mass of bushy red-blond hair he has tried to control with only a little success. Strands of hair frizz out of his queue and around his sunburned face, which is topped by a black tricorn hat with white trim and a black cockade. This must be the man Mark spoke of, Captain John Stuart. His hair is famous, as is his diplomacy in Cherokee affairs. He wears the buff and blue uniform of the provincial militia and is accompanied by two younger men whose plainer uniforms indicate lower rank. Three other men wear the red coats of British regulars. Their commanding officer is shorter, younger, and more smartly arrayed than the provincial captain. Under his tricorn, his dark hair shines with the tallow that keeps it smoothly queued away from his face.

When the men reach us, the escorts fall back to stand at attention behind the two commanding officers.

The provincial captain regards Kanagatucko. Both men are smiling slightly, as though they will enjoy this, as though it is all an elaborate performance put on for an invisible audience. Wrinkles bunch around the provincial captain's eyes as he nods toward Malcolm and me. If I had to guess, I would say he's nearing forty, old in a place where men die young. He surveys us as if we're a pair of horses he's considering for purchase. When he speaks, the cadence of his words is familiar. He is a highlander, or he was once.

"What have you brought me this time?" he asks, jutting his chin at Kanagatucko. "It's common enough to find a man so foolish as to try to traverse this wilderness, but a woman?"

A ball of fear sizzles at the base of my spine, sending flames licking up my back and down my thighs. Kanagatucko doesn't know me. He has no idea who I am; he thinks only that I am Malcolm's wife. But he knows who Malcolm is. He knows where he came from. Numbness follows the flames down my legs, and because my hands are still bound, I lean against Malcolm's chest to steady myself, all the while making up lies, thinking of ways to take their attention away from him. The Cherokee commander holds Malcolm's life in his hands. He could kill Malcolm with a word.

Instead, he nods toward me.

"The woman is weakening, Stuart," Kanagatucko observes. "But I daresay she will live. Unlike the last one I delivered to you, she suffers only from exhaustion."

This is good. They are watching me. I arrange my face into lines of piteous weakness, trying to keep their attention. Truthfully, it isn't hard to look exhausted and upset. I blink, hoping for tears.

Stuart regards me for a long moment and nods. "The other had been beaten before you brought her to us. She died soon after."

Kanagatucko's tone is clipped. "I cannot control all of my warriors any more than you can control all of yours. They know white women bear children, as yours know Cherokee women do the same. Perhaps we all think if we can destroy the women we will end the war."

Captain Stuart makes a little noise of agreement in his throat before he speaks. "Why aren't these two dead yet?" he asks. "You caught them. Why haven't your warriors killed them? Enough people have died in these mountains in recent months. Why spare these?"

I try to swallow, but my throat has turned to stone. The only reason Kanagatucko spared us is Malcolm's agreement with the dead headman, Connecorte.

Kanagatucko regards Stuart and the British captain critically. "My own desire is for peace, though I do not expect to see it. They are lucky they were not caught by those who desire war."

Stuart raises a hand to shield his eyes from the sun and squeezes his forehead between his thumb and forefinger. "I also desire peace, God knows." He drops his hand and looks pointedly at the Cherokee commander. "You know it, too, Kanagatucko."

Kanagatucko nods and shrugs. "Fort Loudoun belongs to the Cherokee. It was paid for in blood by our service to the British in the north. We have spoken of this many times before. Surrender the fort, and you may have peace. Do not surrender, and you and everyone inside will die."

At this, the regular captain speaks for the first time. His tone is tight, as if the words are being squeezed out of his throat. "I will hear no more," he spits. "I will not surrender this fort, whatever John Stuart's advice, whatever his savage sympathies. This is a British fort, an extension of the Crown itself. It cannot fall. It will not fall."

Kanagatucko glances at the regular officer as if he is a pest, a mosquito to be brushed away before it bites. Stuart interrupts, his tone as calm as his brother officer's is agitated. I see why he is the spokesman of the party.

"What's your price for these two?" he asks, sweeping the conversation back to the pertinent question of Malcolm and me.

Kanagatucko repeats the price he quoted earlier. "Forty pounds of salt beef. Each."

"Twenty," Stuart counters. "Forty is out of the question."

"My people are hungry. The war disrupted the autumn hunt." Kanagatucko's gaze skirts over us and returns to Stuart. "I am not obligated to give them up to you at all. Plenty of young warriors would be glad of two more English scalps."

The tongues of flame flare again in my spine. If I weren't leaning into Malcolm, the trembling in my limbs would be evident to everyone, but his body holds me steady as the men negotiate, settling on a final price of sixty pounds of salt beef for the two of us.

"We will keep their weapons and other goods," Kanagatucko adds, inclining his head toward his own escort party, who brought our belongings to the parley.

That shocks the fear out of me. The rifle is all I have left of Mark.

"Oh, no," I say. "Please. Please don't."

Malcolm's hands are still bound, but he snatches the back of my gown and holds on.

"Oh, they keep their arms and anything else they're carrying," says Stuart coolly. "At the price you managed to get for them, it's still a bargain for you."

Kanagatucko laughs and nods. "Very well. We will keep their powder as their arms are useless without it, but beyond that, they may take what is theirs. It will not matter in the end."

Stuart nods and flicks two fingers at his escorts, who reenter the fort and return carrying a large wooden case of salt beef between them.

As he unwinds the rope from Malcolm's wrists, Kanagatucko leans close. "You made a mistake, young warrior," he whispers. "You should have come with us when you had the chance."

In a louder voice, he adds, "Fort Loudoun will not stand forever."

Ignoring the regular officer's sputtering, Kanagatucko turns to Stuart. "Keep them out of the mountains. They will not be so lucky a second time. And keep your people inside the fort. Anyone who tries to leave will be killed. You know the terms of siege, and you also know I always honor my word."

22.

April 13, 1760

Noon

In another few moments, we are through the sally port. Inside, I realize muskets were trained on us the entire time Kanagatucko and Captain Stuart were bartering, aimed through small square holes cut in the palisade. Carrying their arms, men scramble down from ladders propped against the walls. The noontime sun beats down, and the walls block the breeze, making it seem warmer inside the fort than outside. There are masses of people, mostly men wearing some semblance of the buff and blue of Captain Stuart's South Carolina Provincials or the deep red and popinjay green of the Independent Company of South Carolina, but I see some civilians, too. There are also a few women, and children playing quietly or resting in the scarce shade. It is the children who strike fear into me. They are not behaving as children should. They are so quiet, so sluggish in their movements. How long has Fort Loudoun been under siege?

Captain Stuart's large hand rests lightly on my arm. "You go on, lass," he says. "Your intended is waiting for you. I couldn't tell you before because I didn't want Kanagatucko to realize you were anything more than a wanderer and raise your price. He's a shrewd bargainer, that one."

I look up at Captain Stuart, my mind a mass of confusion. I am acutely conscious of the weight of Malcolm's hand in mine. I look down, taking in the bruises on our wrists, the skin rubbed raw. "I don't understand," I say, faltering, suddenly woozy in the heat. "I don't have . . . an intended."

Captain Stuart clucks sympathetically as he pats my shoulder. "Well, I daresay you're quite bewildered."

"Catie!" My old name echoes around me, and though the fort is crowded and busy, the world shrinks to a tunnel as Malcolm releases my hand. At the other end of the tunnel, moving rapidly toward me, is a tall, lean man with thick blond hair in a neat queue. He wears a blue-checkered shirt over dark brown breeches and stockings and black shoes.

The man reaches me and pulls me into an embrace before I quite know what is happening. All I can think is that his shirt seems familiar. He kisses me softly, briefly, warmly on the lips, and then he pulls away to the sound of a few tired cheers and claps I dimly understand must be for us. I feel as self-conscious as I did before Kanagatucko, and not only because Owen and I are now the center of the fort's attention, poised at the top of a hill where nearly everyone can see us. I can only imagine what I must look like, how dirty I must be, how thin and weatherbeaten.

"You look beautiful," Owen says. "Really," he adds, at my withering look. My hat has fallen back, and his fingers brush under my cap. He pulls out a few strands of dark blond hair that is still too short to braid, and a frown crosses his face.

"Catie, have you been ill?" The concern in his voice rings like an accusation. I had forgotten how considerate he is. One side of his mouth turns up in an endearingly lopsided smile. I had forgotten that, too, and the recognition tears at my heart. I forgot so much about him in our months apart. Indeed, I tried to forget, so deeply afraid was I that he might be dead, too. I did not let myself hope.

I laugh shakily, leaning into Owen's chest, trying to hide. "Intended?" I ask. "Are you sure?"

"Oh, Catie." He smiles and shakes his head, and I see the boy who told me of the pharaohs. "I told Captain Stuart we were promised to convince him to ransom you. I think he would have done it, anyway, but he wasn't at all sure the fort could afford it. I had to do something."

He looks down to where his hands are planted firmly on my waist, and his words come out in a rush. "I planned to ask you, anyway. I was going to ask you on your birthday. You knew that, didn't you?"

We fall silent, remembering my birthday, now marked forever by blood. I pull away and look up, squinting into the sun. "Donald Campbell," I say. "Have you told them?"

The smile on Owen's face flickers and fades. He turns away and takes my arm, drawing it through his. "Let's not talk about Donald Campbell right now. I won't let him spoil a happy moment."

But he has, I think. He already has spoiled all of it. He spoiled my birthday, he spoiled Owen's proposal, he spoiled Christmas and New Year's, he spoiled everything.

"It's not a happy moment," I insist. A trapped sob escapes my throat. "I haven't told you about Mark and Jaime yet."

Owen turns to me, his eyes bright in the sun, the popinjay green of the regulars' facings. "Oh, Catie." Neither of us has to say more. My eyes tell Owen all he needs to know.

I feel very tired, and the sun feels very hot. I look around, but Malcolm has disappeared. My legs sway beneath me.

"Is there somewhere I can rest?" I ask faintly.

Owen's arm circles my shoulders. "How stupid of me," he says. "Of course. You must be exhausted." He lifts my hands. "And your poor wrists. I'd take you to the surgery, but this doesn't look too bad, and I'm sure you'd prefer the company of another woman. We'll talk when you feel better."

Owen leads me past a few buildings, down the steep hill that divides the fort almost in half, past a cold oven and bake house. "Barracks," he says, indicating several buildings on our left. At the bottom of the hill are several white marquis tents. He calls at the flap of one of these, and a dark-haired young woman in a floral print gown comes out.

"Hush, Owen," she whispers. "The children are napping. It's the best thing for them in the heat of the day, especially now, with the rationing the way it is."

"Amelia," says Owen. "This is Catie. This is my Catie." His hand presses against the small of my back, warm and protective. He sounds so happy. Sharp, visceral pain stabs my stomach. "Catie, this is Amelia Williamson. She's married to one of the provincial officers."

Amelia Williamson's small face flushes with pleasure, revealing the beauty behind the pinched, dry skin. She's only a few years older than I, perhaps as old as Mark. Swift grief punctures my throat again. As old as Mark will ever be.

"Oh, what a happy thing," Amelia says, clasping my hands in hers. "Owen said when he came that you were supposed to meet him here, but when you didn't make it by the first snows, we all gave you up for lost. What a happy thing," she repeats. "We'll take as many happy things as we can get here."

"The fort has been under siege since February," Owen explains. "It's been—difficult. Amelia, do you think you could take Catie in for a little while? I'm sure Captain Demere will want to talk to her soon, but she needs to rest first."

"Of course," says Amelia, stroking her hand up my arm. "You poor thing. It's as comfortable as I can make it in here."

Her words are kindly meant, but I can't speak because kindness has gotten the better of me again, and she makes me think of Mark, and if I speak, I may sob. I want to be in the shade of the tent, out of the burning sun and out from under Owen's gaze. I cannot explain it even to myself, but all I want right now is for Owen to go away and leave me alone, and this is so unfair that I am repulsed by my own feelings.

23.

April 13, 1760

Afternoon

A very young provincial private who appears to have followed Owen and me hands my basket and rifle to Amelia Williamson. She takes them, dismissing the boy with a polite smile, and stoops to reenter the tent, beckoning me to follow. She deposits my things in one corner and holds a finger to her lips.

"If you wouldn't mind being very quiet for the children," she says. I nod, glancing down at a pallet that holds two children so little I can't tell if they are boys or girls. They are tangled together in sleep, white-blond hair clinging to their damp, flushed faces.

"One of each," she says, in response to the question I haven't asked. "Twins."

"Are they well?" They look like they might be sick.

"Over warm," she says, with a smile that stretches the skin over her jaw. "And underfed, like all of us." So she knows her children are sick.

Amelia Williamson motions toward a small cot in the corner of the tent. "You are most welcome to rest as long as you like. I imagine Captain Demere will have the quartermaster make some arrangement for you by tonight."

She presses the flat of one hand against her apron, the other against her stomach. "Before the siege, we lived in a house outside the walls. It's been destroyed, of course. I miss it. During the winter, we were all crowded into the barracks. Many of the men, officers and rank and file, were willing to give up their places to the men with families, but I prefer the tent, to be honest. The weather is warm during the day now, and soon it will be hot. The tent feels cleaner than the barracks, too. Sickness spreads so quickly in cramped quarters."

She is chattering, which doesn't appear to be in her nature. The notion of illness worries her. My hand moves to the short locks of hair escaping from under my cap.

"My fever came from an injury," I tell her. "I've been quite cured of it for three months. I'm afraid my hair will be the last thing to heal."

I smile slightly, intending it for a joke. Amelia Williamson smiles, too, a smile of relief. She smoothes the tan blanket on the cot with a thin hand. "My husband will be out for several hours. If you'd rest better in fewer clothes, it's quite all right to undress."

Grateful for her kindness, I lay down my straw hat and remove my outer gown and neckerchief, dismayed at the rings of sweat stains under the arms of the wool gown and the griminess of the neckerchief. My mother always managed to keep her linens spotless. I wish I had been able to keep my clothes clean, but once Malcolm and I were out of the shelter, washing wasn't a priority, and it was impossible to keep my clothes from staining. My overskirt is made of the same dark wool as the outer gown and is just as hot. I step out of it and inspect the bottom, which is caked with dirt. I slip off the shreds of my shoes and loosen my stays. I know Amelia Williamson notices the bloodstains, but she says nothing. Perhaps bloodstains are expected here.

I lie on the cot, and I do try to sleep, but I can't. Amelia Williamson has settled herself beside her children on the pallet, where she is trying to cool their flushed faces with a wide decorative fan painted with wild birds.

"Mrs. Williamson?" I whisper.

She looks up, her wide blue eyes large in her small, heart-shaped face. "Amelia," she says. "Please."

"Amelia, then. How long has Fort Loudoun been under siege? What's happening here?"

She studies me closely, curiously.

"Owen said your families were attacked just before Christmas. He arrived in early January, before the snow. Where have you been that you don't know what's happening? Who was that man with you?"

Fear for Malcolm strikes me, swift and sudden. "He was an indentured servant," I lie, remembering our plan to fabricate a history and hoping my lies will match his. "The family he was indentured to was killed."

I sit up, dangling my legs over the side of the cot. I inspect my under petticoat. Except for the ring of dirt around the bottom, it's still fairly clean. Being neither an innermost nor an outermost layer of clothing has protected it.

"So he ran away?" asks Amelia. She's poking too close to the truth.

"He didn't know where he was running," I lie. "The frontier is dangerous everywhere. More than usual, I mean, what with the war. He was trying to get somewhere safe." I have to draw her mind away from Malcolm. I hook my fingers through my blue ribbons.

"Owen was supposed to meet me the day after our families were killed, so we could set out together for Fort Loudoun," I say. "He didn't, and I had no choice but to leave on my own, to keep myself and my little brother alive."

This wakes a nagging question. All these months, I have assumed Owen didn't meet me at Fish Falls because he couldn't, because he was blocked or delayed. I knew he was still alive when Donald Campbell killed Sam Murray, but after that I had no way of knowing. But now I know he reached Fort Loudoun within a couple of weeks after the attack. Did he try to wait for me, to find me? Or did he imagine a woman and a little boy would slow him down?

Amelia continues to fan her children, but her head is tilted to listen.

"Just before the turn of the year, while we were trying to get here, my brother and I were attacked by a catamount. The beast killed my brother and badly injured me. That's what happened to my hair. The fever that came after. Malcolm found me. He saved my life."

Amelia's eyes widen. "That's one I haven't heard. Do be careful, Catie. I saw him when you were brought in. He's no indentured servant, anyone could tell that. He holds himself like a soldier."

In answer, I tug away my stays and pull down the neckline of my shift, exposing the thick scars that hold my torn breast together. Amelia's breath shrieks between her teeth.

"Oh, my God," she says, putting an end to my hope that perhaps it doesn't look quite as bad as I thought.

"Many types of people earn their passage to America by working for a time for someone who will pay for their travel," I say quietly. "Being born wealthy doesn't mean you stay that way. And men stand like soldiers for many years after their discharge."

Amelia is quiet for a few moments.

"They killed the Cherokee hostages at Fort Prince George," she says at last. "The peace delegation Governor Lyttleton took prisoner. In the middle of February. Captain Demere says the hostages were going to poison the well, but I can't believe it. Where would they have gotten poison? The hostages were being held in a small building in the middle of the fort, and Captain Stuart believes they were shot through the roof. He says it would be like Lieutenant Coytmore, though Coytmore was killed the same day, shot outside the fort by Cherokee. We had seen some hostilities before, shots fired here and there by both sides, but that was when we fell under a true siege. Demere keeps telling us the British army will send relief, but who knows when that will be?"

She shakes her head. "I'm not stupid. I know we don't matter to the war with the French. Whether Fort Loudoun stands or falls, it won't make any difference to the fate of the continent."

Her voice lowers and she looks around quickly, as though she expects to be overheard. "My husband says we could surrender the fort to the Cherokee and bargain for an escort back to Fort Prince George and from there to the frontier line. But Captain Demere is determined not to lose the fort. He doesn't want to be the first commandant to surrender a British fort to a native force."

The children are quiet now, in a true sleep at last. Amelia glances down at the decorative fan. "I don't know why I brought this. It looks so out of place here, and yet it's useful."

I swallow hard. "Have you named the children yet?"

Amelia shakes her head. "No. They're so little."

Neither of us says what we're thinking, that it's silly to give names to children under three when it's so unlikely they will see that birthday. It's bad luck, as well. Tempting the last sister, who is so eager with her scissors.

Breaking the strained silence, Amelia reaches for the clothes I draped over the end of the cot and finds distraction from her worries. "My goodness, is that gown wool? You must have been sweltering, or you soon will be. Let me see if I can find something of mine for you to wear."

Amelia rises and opens the trunk that sits beside the cot. She pulls out a lightweight gown and overskirt printed with a pattern of thin green stripes.

"Would you like a clean shift?" she asks, glancing at the jagged stitches that hold the stained cloth together.

"If you can spare it," I answer, so grateful for her offer that it drives everything else out of my head for a moment.

Amelia closes the tent flaps and turns away as I pull my shift over my head and replace it with hers. After I pull my petticoat back on, she helps me secure the overskirt around my waist and shrug into the gown. "I must have another neckerchief and pair of stockings in here somewhere," she mutters. She glances at my shoes, which have been patched and mended with cloth and hide so many times that very little of the original leather is left. "You might be able to beg another pair of shoes off the quartermaster," she says. "They're men's shoes, of course, but you might find a pair to fit, or you can stuff them with cloth or paper, whatever you can find."

Amelia pulls a fresh cap decorated with a thin green ribbon out of her trunk. She settles it on my head and pulls a few strands of my hair out to curl around my face. She steps back to inspect her work. "You look very nice," she says. Charitably, I think. "The gown is a bit large for you, but then it would be a bit large on me now, too." The top of her gown gapes over her collarbones, and I can see down to the silk ribbons on her stays. "I'd wager we've both lost a bit of weight in recent months."

24.

April 13, 1760

Evening

After I spend a couple of hours in much-needed sleep, Amelia and I use the remaining daylight to fit her overskirt and gown to me. It's amazing the difference clean stockings and a clean neckerchief make to my mood. Despite Fort Loudoun's desperate situation, I feel almost reborn. I hadn't realized how heavily the wool dress had begun to hang until I put on the lighter linen one. As the sun goes down, the stuffy heat of the fort gives way to a chill, and I am forced to pull my cloak on, despite its filth. Amelia and I brushed my old clothes clean as well as we could, but she said there was little chance of getting water for washing either my own body or my dirty clothing.

"Water is for tending the sick or drinking," she says, smiling wryly. "Or for shaving the men for Captain Demere's reviews. If you want a bath, you'll have to bring that fever back. No one wants the well to run dry."

Dusk is falling when Amelia's husband enters the tent, ready to get a few hours sleep before his duty begins tonight. I'd guess he is near thirty, between five and ten years older than Amelia. He's a big man, like Captain Stuart, but his blond hair is much tamer than the Captain's wild mop. He nods to me, kisses Amelia on the cheek, and looks with concern at the twins, who have fallen back into a restless sleep after waking for a time in the afternoon. I try to remember the brief lives of the siblings between me and Jaime, to recall what they were like just before they died, to compare them with the Williamson children, but in truth they all run together in my mind.

"Have you seen the man who was brought in with me?" I ask Amelia's husband. "His name is Malcolm Craig. I'd like to speak with him, to make sure he is well. Out of courtesy."

Courtesy. I feel warmth flood my face and hope it goes unnoticed.

Amelia's husband nods. "I believe he's encamped with the militia. He asked to be bunked with them instead of the regulars. Scottish, isn't he? Highlander? I imagine he's like Captain Stuart and doesn't like too much reminding of the British army."

You have no idea, I think.

I know I must move quickly if I want to find Malcolm tonight. My life in the backcountry has made me more cautious and more aware of the many sources of danger than my more elegant counterparts, and I know better than to get caught among the rank and file when the sun goes down. I should be reporting to the commandant right now, but I need to find Malcolm first. I didn't like the coldness that washed over me when he dropped my hand.

I pull my cloak around my shoulders against the chill, check to make sure my jackknife is in my pocket, and hurry across the empty parade ground. I ask after Malcolm among a group of militiamen engaged in a card game behind the barracks, but I get only a lot of tastelessly good-natured comments about how he hasn't been around a day yet and already gets all the attention.

One middle-aged soldier with a week's worth of scruff finally takes pity on me.

"I believe I heard he's in the surgery, miss, for now."

"Is he injured?" I ask, trying to seem patient.

"Not that I know, miss. We lost our surgeon some days ago. I heard this man has some little skill. Captain told him to go in there and see what he could make of it."

He points. "Surgery's at the end of the barracks, miss, at the top of the hill. By the powder magazine."

I climb the steep hill that divides the fort and up the steps to the door of the surgery. The ground beyond is covered with the turned earth of new graves. I rap on the open door and enter. It takes my eyes a moment to adjust to the near darkness inside. By the light of a flickering candle set on one side of the fireplace, I find Malcolm lying on a bunk with his eyes closed. I glance around quickly and determine that the other bunks are empty, so I am careful not to let the door swing shut. I don't know the rules here.

"Good evening," I say. Malcolm opens his eyes slowly, and at first I think he doesn't recognize me because I have changed clothes and stand in partial shadow. I remain still beside the door, uncertain of my welcome.

"Have you come to invite me to your wedding?" Malcolm asks roughly.

I draw a deep breath. "Don't be cruel."

Malcolm swings his legs off the bunk and stands. He is cleanshaven for the first time since we left the shelter. He wears a clean red-checkered shirt and has gotten tallow from somewhere to smooth his curly hair, which is clubbed back and tied with black tape. Without the softening effect his hair usually has, his face looks older, more like a soldier's, less familiar. I cast my gaze downward. He's wearing his old leggings, but he has traded his winter boots for deer hide buskins that tie around his ankles.

He crosses his arms. "I could say the same to you. You might have told me you were promised."

I swallow. "I didn't . . . I wasn't, until today. I don't think I am now. Owen is an old friend, and his family was attacked at the same time as mine, by the same people. He told Captain Stuart I was promised to him to make sure the fort would pay our ransom. Food is priceless to a fort on siege rations."

"He kissed you. He seemed pretty familiar with kissing you."

My spine stiffens. "Maybe he's more than an old friend," I say, suddenly furious with Malcolm, desiring to hurt him. "What business is it of yours?" Malcolm has no right to my memories of Owen, whatever has happened between us.

"Malcolm, I thought he was dead," I say quietly. "I assumed he was dead. So many people are."

Malcolm crosses to the instrument table by the window and picks up a small item with a wooden handle that holds a long stem of hooked metal.

"So he's the one you were raving about when you were under the fever. Something about a fifth cut—you didn't have a fifth cut. You hoped that meant he was alive."

I spread my hands before me. "Of course I hoped he was alive."

"His family was attacked at the same time as yours? Yet you never mentioned him. You might have done that. How quickly you forget people, Catriona."

"That's not true," I spit. "I don't forget people quickly at all." I kissed Malcolm, at least a few times, to help me forget Owen, to help me forget my family, to quiet some of the raging pain. I might feel guilty if I didn't know he was doing the same thing, using me to forget his botched translations and his lost home.

"What are you doing in the surgery?" I ask, changing the subject. "You aren't sick or injured."

"I wasn't busy swooning in anyone's arms, so I reported directly to the commandant. The surgeon was killed two weeks ago, and I told the commandant I had some skill with a needle."

He laughs, that harsh bark I recognize from early days in the winter shelter, and flips the instrument in his hands. "This is a tenaculum needle. For pulling arteries out to tie off when you have to amputate. As an indentured servant, you pick up all sorts of things. It's guaranteed me a decent bunk, anyway."

I sigh deeply. "I said you were an indentured servant. At least we both remembered to say the same thing."

Malcolm shrugs. "It's obviously the best cover. No one's going to go looking for a master anytime soon."

"I said your master was dead. Killed in the attacks along the frontier."

Malcolm returns the tenaculum needle to the table and moves toward me. He takes my hands and circles his fingers gently around my bruised wrists, stroking and squeezing. He guides me over to catch the fading light from the window.

"No breaks in the bone," he says. "No swelling, either. That's lucky. The redness and bruising don't seem serious. They'll go away in a few days."

What I fear will not go away is the way his touch on my wrists makes me want to lock the surgery door and blind the window.

"Malcolm?" I venture. "Why would you risk angering me? You know I could tell them who you really are at any moment." It's cruel to press my advantage like this, but the words he spoke when I arrived cut me to the bone.

He draws closer, so close I can see small flakes of blood on his freshly shaven jaw. He must have shaved without water. He takes my chin in his hand and tilts it up.

"You can threaten all you like, Catriona. I know you'll never do it."

I laugh weakly, and it's my bad luck that at that moment a shadow darkens the door.

"Catie?" says Owen's voice. "I've been looking everywhere for you. I heard you were looking for that highlander who was brought in with you."

Malcolm's hand moves from my chin back to my wrists as Owen steps into the room. "I see you've found him." He looks Malcolm over with ill-concealed distaste. "Though I'm not sure why you needed to. The commandant wants to see you, if you feel well enough." He smiles. "Amelia found you a new dress, I see. She's quite the miracle worker. I knew she'd take care of you."

Annoyance with Owen surges through me. He and an officer's wife call each other by their first names, like intimate friends, and he has the nerve to question my desire to see Malcolm.

"I can go with you to the commandant," Malcolm says. He looks at me, ignoring Owen. I am extremely conscious of the light pressure of his thumbs on the insides of my wrists.

I feel Owen stiffen beside me. "I will escort Miss Blair," he says.

Malcolm smiles, unconcerned. "Of course. As I said, Miss Blair, you have nothing to worry about from the injury to your wrists. The bruises will be tender for several days, but beyond that, they're harmless enough."

He releases my hands before I can pull them away. With a curt nod to Malcolm, Owen takes my elbow and pulls my arm through his. With a grim set to his mouth, he steers me down the steps and across the high ground to the door of the commandant's house.

25.

April 13, 1760

Evening

When Owen and I enter, the two men who parleyed with Kanagatucko this morning are seated together across a small field desk. A single candle casts a circle of light over the desk, and the rest of the room takes light from a small fire. When Captain Stuart and Captain Demere stand, I am impressed again by how different they are. Stuart's bulk seems to fill the room. Demere looks like a small man compared to Stuart, but he's probably of an average size. The stress of recent months appears to have had little effect on his neat appearance. He does not look like the commandant of a fort under siege.

Owen salutes smartly, and the two captains return it. As we made our way to the commandant's house, Owen informed me that everyone at Fort Loudoun is subject to military discipline and law and that while Stuart and Demere share a rank, practically Demere outranks Stuart because he is regular army and Stuart is only militia.

Owen lifts my hand. "May I present my betrothed, Miss Catherine Blair?"

My stomach goes hot with nerves. Betrothed. Catherine.

"Miss Blair, Captain John Stuart of the South Carolina Provincial Militia and Captain Paul Demere of the Independent Company of South Carolina."

I curtsy, dipping as low as I judge is warranted for a captain in the British army. Captain Demere bows over my hand as genteelly as if we were in a Charlestown drawing room. It's warm in the close room, and his fingers are clammy, but he is a handsome man, and he knows it. Captain Stuart pulls out a chair for me, indicating that we should sit.

When we are clustered around the field desk, Captain Demere speaks. "Welcome to Fort Loudoun, Miss Blair. I am afraid you do not find us at our best. These damnable savages have us surrounded right now, but I am confident we shall win through. Relief will shortly be coming in the form of

His Majesty's troops from New York. We need hold out only another month or so, and then the savages will see how British regulars fight."

His words sound rehearsed, like a speech given many times before. I smile politely and refrain from pointing out that there is a whole company of British regulars here, and they haven't broken the siege yet.

From under his thick brows, Stuart casts a look of tired pity at Demere. He turns to me.

"Perhaps you'd be so good as to tell us of your experiences, Miss Blair," he says. "We would be most appreciative of any news you can bring us from the outside."

"Understand from young Ramsay here you were attacked by the savages," says Demere. "It's too bad. Been happening up and down the frontier. The last we heard, the frontier line had been pushed back a hundred miles."

I hesitate, glancing at Owen. Has he really told them we were attacked by the Cherokee?

"I am afraid I have no news of any significance for you," I say. "My brothers were killed and I was injured shortly after the initial attack on our home. I nearly died in the mountains. I was very sick for a long time." I glance down at my hands. "The man I was with saved my life. I would be dead if he hadn't found me. We were unable to reach Fort Loudoun sooner due to my convalescence and because traveling in winter became too dangerous once the cold became intense."

I'm not looking at Owen. I'll never be able to finish my story if I do.

"But my family was not attacked by the Cherokee," I say. Determination rises in my voice. "We were attacked by a white man—a gang of them, actually—but one man was leading it."

Captain Stuart leans forward at this, his gaze intense and interested. It gives me courage and helps me find the words.

"Please continue, Miss Blair," Stuart urges.

I take a deep breath and plunge in, my confidence growing as I speak.

"The man's name is Donald Campbell. My father, Philip Blair, was a Presbyterian minister. He received his education in Scotland but moved to America to serve a congregation in New Jersey, where I was born. When I was nine years old, my father joined a movement to establish schools and churches along the frontier, which is why we moved to South Carolina. I have reason to believe one of the men in Donald Campbell's gang had confessed information to my father which implicated Campbell and the rest of them in unlawful violence against the Cherokee Lower Towns."

My hands twist in my lap, gripping each other of their own accord.

"Campbell was never fond of my father," I admit. "I've always heard he lost his property in Scotland, somehow, and I believe he hated all lowlanders and English. My father was a lowland Scot, and my mother was English, so he was against them from the start. Campbell and his men used the war to stage a Cherokee raid to kill my family and pin the blame on the Cherokee."

I can feel Captain Demere's impatience and Owen's anger, but I focus on Captain Stuart's kind eyes and concerned demeanor. He is listening to me. The other men are not.

Demere's fingers tap the desk. "If this is true, why didn't young Ramsay tell us?"

I turn to Owen. "Did you not see it?" I ask. "Mark told me you saw them kill your family. You were the one who warned him."

Owen shakes his head. "Catie, I can't be sure of what I saw. I thought at first—but it seems so unlikely. The Cherokee were attacking up and down the frontier. Isn't it more likely that's what happened?"

My voice trembles with anger and a fresh wave of grief. "I am sure of my own eyes. I will never forget what I saw that morning. I will never forget that Donald Campbell murdered my brother."

Owen tries to place a hand on my arm, but I fling it off.

Captain Demere shakes his head. "I daresay it was the Cherokee who attacked your family, Miss Blair. It's likely you saw it wrong. Great stress can do that to a person, especially a woman. Probably your neighbors were attempting to come to your aid, and in your hysteria, you ran from them."

His voice is kind, but I look down at my lap and shake my head, recalling the flash of the knife that sliced Mark's scalp from his skull. That memory will never fade, no matter how much time I put between myself and it. I remember Campbell's grimace as he tried to stop the bleeding from his thigh. I remember I could have shot him then. I should have. I never should have given him a chance to get away. I feel sick with guilt that I did.

Captain Demere attempts to be helpful. "Well, whatever happened, it makes no difference now."

He tries to continue, but Captain Stuart interrupts. "I believe it makes a great deal of difference. These small attacks here and there are what started this war and what are feeding it. It could be this Campbell wants to keep the war going by ensuring the attacks continue. There are advantages to be found in war, for those who take them. He wouldn't be the first to do so.

And General Amherst is none too pleased about diverting troops from the drive on French Montreal to aid South Carolina in her war with the Cherokee. He wants this war over. He would be interested in the names of any who are prolonging hostilities, and we should be, on his behalf."

Captain Demere dismisses Captain Stuart's interpretation with a wave of his hand.

"But why did you come to Fort Loudoun?" Demere asks. "Many settlers do seek safety here, but surely it is very far from your home. Why did you not go east with the other refugees from the frontier, or if you sought the protection of the army, to Fort Prince George?"

I swallow, recalling Mark's words. "Donald Campbell wanted no witnesses. He expected us to flee east, but he searched for my younger brother and me in Cherokee territory, anyway, in case he was wrong. There was a smallpox outbreak at Fort Prince George, and a Lieutenant Richard Coytmore was the commandant there. My elder brother said if there was mischief afoot, Coytmore would be in on it, and in any case, he didn't want me near the Fort Prince George garrison."

"Your brother was a wise man," sighs Captain Stuart. "The Prince George garrison got us into this mess, killing the Cherokee hostages like they did."

"I understand Coytmore is also dead," I say. "May I ask what you intend to do with the information I have given you?"

Demere laughs. "I can't do much of anything with it, Miss Blair. I am as sorry as anyone for your troubles, but as you can well see, we're stranded here until General Amherst's relief arrives. Perhaps when we are relieved we can address the issue of Donald Campbell."

Demere smiles indulgently. I am a child to him, an amusing diversion he is beginning to tire of.

I pretend I haven't noticed and press on. "When do you expect to be relieved?"

"Within two months, at most," he says. "One of our scouts got through with a dispatch that says Amherst has ordered a Colonel Montgomery with the 77th Regiment of Foot to sail for Charlestown. Once in the colony, Montgomery will subdue the Cherokee Lower Towns. From there, Montgomery's forces will reach Fort Prince George, and then the 77th will cut a swath through the Cherokee nation to Fort Loudoun."

Captain Stuart sighs and rests his forehead in his hands. A thought strikes me.

"Let me go and meet Colonel Montgomery at Fort Prince George," I say. "If you cannot help me, then surely he must, especially if he is actually in the colony, near the site of the attacks. Once he arrives here, it may be too late. He may be ordered to return to the war in the north."

Captain Demere laughs outright, and even Captain Stuart shakes his head.

"It's impossible," Stuart says kindly. "Very few of even the best scouts can get through the mountains right now. You would have no chance. Kanagatucko meant what he said. It would mean your death. It's out of the question."

"Meanwhile," says Demere. "An unmarried woman with no family is a bit of a nuisance. Causes a deal of trouble, if you take my meaning." He glances from me to Owen. "I can have you married tonight, though I can't offer you much of a wedding night. You might be able to coax a family out of its tent or some soldiers out of a barracks, but I rather doubt it."

My stomach feels like it's been poured with molten lead. My reunion with Owen has been less perfect than I hoped. I don't know this man. I don't know why he has chosen to forget what he saw. He is a stranger to me, yet I could be his wife within the hour.

"No." All three men appear taken aback by my forcefulness. "I mean, I've had a very difficult time. It would be too much. Please, let me stay with my friend Amelia Williamson tonight and think it over tomorrow."

Captain Demere defers to Captain Stuart, I suppose because the Williamsons are under provincial command. Stuart gives me a nod. "Williamson is the duty officer tonight, anyway. Take all the time you need, Miss Blair. You've been through quite an ordeal."

As the door of the commandant's house closes behind us, Owen grips my arm and leads me down the steps, out of earshot of the sentry. I can feel the thick fog of confusion and misunderstanding between us, as heavy as the still air inside the fort. He pulls me into the shadows behind the guard house and spins me around. His hands find my shoulders and force me back against the planked wall. Instinct pushes my hand into my pocket, where I grip my jackknife. I can flip it open with one hand if I must.

"How could you do that to me, Catie? Humiliate me twice in one night."

I look up, marking the lines of Owen's face, so familiar and yet so foreign. Was it only last fall I dreamed of him? My anger is tempered by incredulity, but my voice trembles, anyway. "How could you pretend our families were killed by Cherokee raiders when you know it was Donald Campbell?"

"Catie." His voice is sad, and his hands drop from my shoulders. "We don't know what happened that day, not really."

"I know. I know Donald Campbell killed my brother. He killed Mark, Owen." *And I didn't shoot him. I didn't shoot him when I had the chance.*

Owen looks down at me, sympathy clear in his eyes, and I drop my jack-knife and slip my hand out of my pocket. "Catie, I know it was horrible. I'm so sorry you had to go through that, and then you had to escape with Jaime all by yourself, and spend all those months with that highlander. Did he—did he do anything to you?"

My voice is a loud whisper, a hiss. "Owen! How can you even ask me that? He saved my life. I was so sick for several weeks after the attack that I nearly died of fever, and my injuries weren't fully healed until we left to come here. And Malcolm isn't like that. He didn't do anything to me."

I feel my face flush. Nothing I didn't encourage, anyway. I am glad of the shadows.

It doesn't help that Owen's anger has clearly abated. He looks stricken. "What attack?" he asks. "You were injured? What happened?"

"Jamie was killed by a catamount," I say. "It wounded me when I tried to fight it off. I don't want to talk about it. I'm all right now."

Owen grips me to his chest so quickly and firmly that the wounds that have not actively ached in weeks set off tears in my eyes. He doesn't know to be careful. He doesn't know because I haven't told him, and I don't want to.

Tears swim in Owen's green eyes as he pulls back to look at me. Both of us are crying, from different kinds of pain. He shoved me against a wall, and I nearly pulled a knife on him. What has happened to us? What else has Donald Campbell done?

"Catie, I came to Fort Loudoun to find you," says Owen. "I hoped I'd meet you here, and when you didn't come I thought you were dead. I didn't bring up Donald Campbell because these poor people have enough to handle just trying to stay alive from day to day, and there's nothing we can do about him now. There is nothing to be gained from pursuing this."

He takes my hand, and his tone softens further. "Catie, he may already be dead, and even if he isn't, do you really think we could find him? You're being irrational. Lots of people have lost their families, their homes. The best thing you and I can do is move forward with our lives."

"And how are we supposed to do that?" I ask, running a hand over my face to clear away the tears this pitched battle brought to my eyes.

Owen's fists are clenched around my folded hands.

"We can get married. You heard Captain Demere. The siege won't last forever, and neither will the war. We can make a fresh start. We'll go home, or if you'd prefer, we can go somewhere else. You always seemed homesick for New Jersey."

Sudden laughter catches on a sob. That was Jaime's plan, that Owen and I would take him to New Jersey.

"I can't, Owen," I say. "I'm sorry. I can't move on until I've brought Donald Campbell to the gallows or died trying. I can't marry you or anyone else until I've done that. If you still want to marry me, you'll help me."

26.

April 13, 1760

Night

Amelia's babies are sicker than they were when I left her earlier this evening. Even with the tent flaps tied open in front and back to allow fresh air to pass through, the small space reeks of sour milk and soiled linen, all the smells of a sick room. The first wave of it makes me want to retch, but after a time the stench becomes bearable. I am glad of the chill of mountain night, but I know the heat of morning will bring the smell back to the boil.

"I won't lie, I'm glad you're back," Amelia says, wiping a sweat-soaked lock of dark hair back from her forehead and tucking it under her cap.

"Sit down and rest a minute," I tell her, looking from her flushed, damp face to those of her children. A lantern's light gives their skin a pale yellow cast. "You'll come down with it next if you don't. Has anyone else been sick?"

I think of the new graves behind the surgery.

Amelia nods as she sinks onto the cot. "A few people, here and there. I'm surprised it hasn't been worse, the way we're all packed in here together." She shivers as her body cools.

"It was winter," I remind her. "That's why. Contagion can't live in the cold."

But now it is spring, heading into summer, when there will be little relief from the relentless heat, and madness and fever will run rampant.

The boy baby begins making horrid noises, a gurgle like he wants to scream but can't get the air for it. I take off my cloak, knowing that caring for the children will soon warm me. I settle on the pallet and pick the boy up. His little shift is soaked through with sweat, and I whip it off, leaving him in only his nappy. I cuddle him to try to quiet him, but I can feel the heat of his small body through my clothes. I try to put him down so the fever will have an easier time leaving his body, but every time I do, he makes that awful noise, a scream without the strength of a scream, and works himself into a greater frenzy.

"The sun has been down for some time," I say to Amelia. "It's quite cool, and there's a bit of a breeze. Do you want to try taking them outside?"

Amelia nods and sits up. She hands me my cloak, and I pull it on as she does the same with her own.

I take the boy baby, and Amelia takes the girl. We sit on the ground in front of the tent. I cross my legs under me, making a cradle of my skirt. We are at the bottom of the hill, at the edge of the parade ground. High above, I see the light of a candle shining in the commandant's house. The silhouette of a big man crosses in front of a window. Demere and Stuart are up still, discussing who knows what. I hope they are debating letting me meet Montgomery at Fort Prince George.

The child crawls toward my neck, and his little hands grab furiously at my breasts, setting off jolts of pain from the catamount's wounds, which are already tender from Owen's crushing embrace.

"You won't get anything there," I tell him, pulling his hands away because the pain is bad enough, but the thought of the wounds opening and bleeding again makes my stomach turn.

"Give him to me," says Amelia, and we trade babies. "I'll try to feed him, but they haven't kept much down for days, the few times they have been able to eat. And what with the rationing, I don't have much milk to give them."

Amelia carries her son inside the tent, and I hold the girl baby. Illness has made her quiet and tearful where it has made her brother furious. I try to remember the lullabies my mother sang to me and my younger siblings, but all that comes to mind are the stories in my father's books. Horror stories of vengeful gods and wicked men and monsters. I think again of the final fate who cuts the threads, and I imagine I can hear the three sisters cackling wildly in the skies around Fort Loudoun. Whose thread is being measured now, being made ready for the slash of the last sister's shining scissors?

The girl baby catches at the blue ribbons around my throat. I know they are pretty and tempting for small hands, but the sudden attention paid to them makes me uneasy.

I try to sing several children's chants, but they all stop in my throat as soon as I start.

Ring around the roses. The Great Mortality that killed half of Europe four hundred years ago and struck again in the last century.

Mistress Mary, quite contrary. Mary, Queen of Scots, her head lopped off.

Humpty Dumpty. The Civil War, in which Mother's great-great-grandfather rode as a Cavalier for Charles I, the king whose own head was lopped off in turn.

I fall silent at last, wondering why all the songs we sing to children are about death.

I settle for humming along with a tune I hear coming from the open door of one of the barracks. I am fairly certain the words include a few choice terms for the French, but I can't hear them clearly. By the time Amelia comes back, the baby is quiet in my lap. Her breathing is labored, but she is taking breath, which is something.

"He couldn't swallow at all," says Amelia, frowning. "I've got to get something down him, but he can't swallow." She sits beside me, tucking her skirt under her body and resting the baby on her lap.

"Amelia," I say, struck by a thought. "Do you think I'll ever be able to nurse from this breast? The injured one, I mean."

She shakes her head. "I couldn't say. But I suppose, unless you have twins, one is enough."

The thought makes us laugh a little, though it isn't really funny.

"Owen has missed you," Amelia says gently. "He has grieved terribly for you. I rather thought you'd marry him tonight. It wouldn't be unusual."

I draw a deep breath, wondering if I can explain to Amelia about the rabbit trapped in the thicket on the morning of my birthday, about how much Fort Loudoun is starting to feel like a snare. She has been here longer than I. Surely the fort feels like a trap to her, too. But for me it has become a snare with a double noose.

"It's just that so much has happened to me since I last saw Owen that I don't know who I am anymore. I've lost my entire family. I've been badly injured. He doesn't know how badly, he hasn't seen it. My hair is the least of it, and my hair will grow back."

Amelia lays a hand on my knee in sympathy. "That won't matter to him if he loves you."

My voice shakes. "Perhaps not. But he has to know. And he has to know about Malcolm. The truth is that we were alone together in the mountains for a long time. Months. And some—things—did happen. And now I don't know what to do."

And I don't know how far I can trust Amelia. Loneliness for the company of another woman makes me want to talk to her the way I used to be able to talk to my mother, and to Alice, Owen's young stepmother. But Amelia is clearly very close to Owen, and she has known me less than a day. Her loyalty is probably to him.

Amelia sweeps her gaze more critically over my body. "I see. Are you with child? I can give you something that might take care of it, depending on how far along you are. It will be messy, but we can pass if off as any other illness. I can say it's a woman's complaint, and they'll leave us well enough alone."

I look into her eyes. She means it. She would help me, if that were the kind of help I needed. It's not a light offer, the offer of her own stores and time, the risk of my death if her treatments were off by a bit.

I shake my head. "No. There's no danger of that. Under such circumstances, I wouldn't risk it, and Malcolm wouldn't force me to. As I told Owen, I can't marry anyone yet."

I draw a deep breath. I have trusted her this far. I think I could tell her anything about myself, and she would still try to think the best of me. So maybe I can find a way to tell her about the guilt that has weighed on me for months.

"There's a part of this I don't think Owen has told you, and a part of it he doesn't know," I say, and I tell her about Donald Campbell and my cowardice.

Amelia's eyebrows are still up, her mind still on the point at hand, as though I have not just told her how I failed to protect my brothers. "If you're not carrying a baby, then I don't see why Owen has to know anything more about your relationship with Malcolm than he does. This isn't Charlestown, where your reputation would be a wasteland by now. The frontier plays by its own rules. Which typically means it doesn't play by any rules at all."

I have to whip my mind back to the present to answer. "I don't like keeping secrets from Owen. He trusts me."

Her mouth twitches. "Most couples have a few secrets. This seems like a relatively minor one to me."

"There's another reason I can't marry Owen right now," I admit. "It's not entirely about Malcolm. Not even entirely about Donald Campbell." I tell her of Owen's view that the only way we can recover from the loss of our families is to move forward. "And the thing is, I can't. I can't move forward. I can't marry him or anyone. I couldn't have prevented my parents' deaths, but I could have saved my brothers. If I had shot Campbell when I had the chance, Mark might have lived, which means Jaime might have lived, too. Mark told me to take care of Jaime, and after I let him die, I failed at that. I failed at taking care of the one person I have always taken care of."

I look at the baby in my lap.

"Marriage leads to children, and I don't trust myself to care for them now. I didn't kill Donald Campbell, and the two people I loved most in the world died. Before I let myself have another family, I have to make sure he can't hurt them."

"Owen feels like a stranger to me," I finish. "I never expected him to feel this way. How can he move on with his life while Campbell goes free? How can he even want to?"

Tiny needles stab behind my eyes.

Amelia considers, sympathy clear on her face. "Owen is practical," she says finally. "You want that in a husband. If there's nothing to be done, there's nothing to be done. And remember, his experience of the attack was different from yours. Did he actually see Campbell kill his family, or did he just cobble together information from what he did see? I doubt he feels as threatened as you do."

"I have to do something," I insist. I tell her how Montgomery's relief forces will pass through Fort Prince George, how I need to meet Montgomery there, near the site of Campbell's attack, in case he is recalled north before I can approach him. "I think Captain Stuart would let me go, if he could."

"He's right not to let you. He's right that it would likely mean your death. But I have a sense you are determined to do it anyway, and in that case, I'd rather you had a guard and a guide. There may be a way to change Captain Stuart's mind. I'll speak to Susannah Emory when next she comes."

"Who's Susannah Emory?" I ask.

Amelia turns to me, and a brief, conspiratorial grin flits across her anxious face. "Captain Stuart's Cherokee wife."

27.

April 14, 1760

Before Dawn

Amelia and I catch snatches of sleep between caring for the sick children, but when a grunting noise wakes me, I look down and realize the baby boy's breathing is more labored than ever. I lay my ear against his chest and hear the congestion. If nothing changes, I don't think he'll live through the night. There's only one thing to be done.

I shake Amelia awake to tell her where I'm going. She shakes her head. "Doctor Anderson is dead," she says. "He was caught outside the fort two weeks ago and killed."

"I'm going to the surgery anyway," I whisper.

I skirt around the parade ground and up the hill, hoping no one will notice me in the dark. The fort is quiet. Those who can sleep are sleeping. The door of the surgery is half open to allow air in, so I slip through quietly. I am filled with relief to find Malcolm's sturdy form on one of the cots. I tiptoe across the room and look into his sleeping face for a moment, glad I have not had to go this night without it. That is a dangerous feeling, I tell myself. I have gotten too used to Malcolm, and we are no longer in the dream world of the mountain shelter. I sit on the edge of the cot, put my hand on his shoulder, and shake him awake.

Malcolm blinks as his eyes focus, and then he reaches a hand to my cheek. "Pleased as I am to see you, Catriona, you can't be here at this time of night. Your intended wouldn't like it, to say nothing of the rest of the garrison."

I have seen enough of Fort Loudoun today to know the inhabitants don't have much energy left to spend on the virtue of one woman. I am filled with sudden fury. I have slept in Malcolm's arms every night for nearly two months, absorbing the comfort I so desperately need, and now, because we're in this outpost of British civilization, we are forcibly separated.

"I've come to get you," I say. "Amelia Williamson's babies are very sick, Malcolm, and I thought you might be able to help."

"Who's Amelia Williamson?" he asks, sitting up and yawning as he reaches for his buskins. He's slept in his clothes, as usual.

"She's a friend of mine. This is her dress."

"You do know this is the first decent night's sleep I've gotten in weeks?"

"Yes. I'm sorry."

He smiles, and I hope it means he has forgiven me. "You make friends fast. What's wrong with the bairns?"

The way he says *bairns* makes me smile, ridiculously. "High fever, vomiting, chest congestion. The symptoms of a thousand sicknesses."

"Catriona, you know I probably can't do anything you couldn't do yourself," he says. "I'm all right with wounds because that's a good skill to have on the battlefield and I've gotten a lot of practice. I don't know how much use I'll be with sick babies."

"You did so well with me," I explain. "And I'd feel better if you would come. Please. I don't think her little boy is going to live through the night."

Malcolm smoothes his hair back and ties it.

"Oh, while you're here." He reaches under the bunk and pulls out a pair of buskins like the ones he wears. He holds them out by the laces.

"These are for you. I'm not sure when I'll have another chance to give them to you."

I take the shoes in my hands. "Where did you get these?" I should thank him, but I'm quite struck that he thought about my feet what with all that happened today and the uncertain nature of our relationship.

"There's a leather worker who makes them. I traded my pistol for them," he glances down, shy, the way he was in the cold of deep winter. "It's all right. A pistol isn't much use to me. I still have my musket."

We are alone, and I can think of several interesting ways to thank him, but his shyness has made me shy, too, and in any case, Amelia cannot wait. Malcolm turns away from me, studies the instrument table for a moment, and chooses a lancet and a bleeding bowl.

"Do you know how to use that?" I ask. I've seen people bled before. I've been bled myself. But there is something terrifying about slicing into perfectly healthy skin and letting the life force out.

In answer, Malcolm only nods. We both know bleeding can go terribly wrong.

When Malcolm and I enter the Williamsons' tent, Amelia stands with a low cry and clutches my arm.

"Catie, thank God you're back. I don't think he's breathing. If he is, he's not breathing much."

I take the baby from Amelia's arms and lay him flat on the cot. I put my hand on her shoulder and briefly introduce her to Malcolm.

Malcolm kneels by the cot and puts an ear to the baby's mouth. "He is breathing, barely. We have to loosen his lungs and then work to bring the fever down." Malcolm looks up at Amelia. "Has he ever been bled?"

Amelia shakes her head, her face so white it looks like she's been bled to death herself. Malcolm's voice remains steady. I know that tone. I've heard it. He's trying to calm Amelia, to keep her from making the situation more difficult than it is. "Ma'am, if you can look to your other child, Catriona and I will do our best to loosen this one's lungs."

Amelia doesn't even notice that Malcolm calls me by a different name. She just nods and picks up the girl baby and carries her outside.

Malcolm sends me first to the well to get water and then to the black-smith shop to boil it. I have to do some fast talking to get water drawn and boiled at this time of night, so it takes longer than it should. The night goes by in a haze of exhaustion and frustration through which images rise like bubbles in boiling water. The baby coughing wetly as Malcolm holds him over the water, trying to get his lungs to give up their deadly cargo. The strip of cloth tied around the tiny wrist as a last resort. My own hands uncurling the baby's fingers and gripping his forearm as the lancet makes its cut. The crimson splash of blood against the walls of the pewter bleeding bowl in a final attempt to purge the illness from the tiny body.

When the sun rises, Malcolm and I are facing each other across the cot, which now holds the body of a dead child. Exhausted, Malcolm leaves by the back of the tent and returns to the surgery. I clean the baby as best I can, swaddle him in his small blanket, and lay him on the cot. Then I go to find his mother, who is sitting outside the tent, rocking the living.

"I know," Amelia says quietly. "I've known for some time now. There was a point where you two stopped talking to each other and started moving more slowly, less urgently. I could tell the battle was over and you had lost."

"I'm sorry, Amelia," I say. "We did everything we could."

She nods. "I know you did."

She stands, still holding her baby girl close. "I must go and find Adam," she says. "I don't want someone else to tell him first."

Amelia takes a few halting steps away from me before she turns. She smiles sadly.

"I understand why you didn't want to marry Owen last night, Catie," she says. "It's because you're in love with that highlander."

28.

May 11, 1760

Morning

Many times during the weeks we pass within the walls of Fort Loudoun, I have reason to long for the mountain shelter I shared with Malcolm. It is not only Malcolm's company I miss, though the duties Captains Demere and Stuart dole out keep us busy and well away from each other. Malcolm is established in the surgery, and I am engaged with the rest of the women in tending the small garden plots we hope will yield food. The soldiers of both companies continue to drill on the parade ground and to engage in reviews, just as if they were simply garrisoning the fort. That seems to be Demere and Stuart's strategy. Keep the over two hundred people trapped inside as busy as possible so we don't have time to sit and think about the doom that surrounds us. Death was with us in the mountain shelter, but I didn't feel it as I do here. At least there we had charge over our own lives, for as long as they lasted, instead of living according to the bidding of the army.

The steep hill that divides Fort Loudoun in half also tilts the fort on the side of the mountain. This placement was intentional, for it allowed the Cherokee to see inside the fort when they were Britain's allies. Now it allows Cherokee scouts to track our every movement. Kanagatucko is close to Captain Stuart. They have been cordial acquaintances in happier times, if not friends. Captain Stuart tells us he does not believe Kanagatucko will order an attack, but the Cherokee commander intends to hold the siege tight, and he has warned Captain Stuart that any British ally caught outside the fort will be killed. So those who sneak over the walls, thinking to escape or simply to try to join the Cherokee, have fair warning. Kanagatucko allows for the recovery of their bodies, and that is the only time anyone gets to see the horizon. But I know some do make it through, because their bodies are never found, and this gives me hope.

As I have made it clear I have no intention of marrying anyone anytime soon, I am allowed a small campaign tent behind the Williamsons' larger one. I am regarded as a member of their family, and Adam Williamson has agreed to count me as one of his household. I miss the freedom the mountains gave me, the knowledge that, while my life was in peril every day, I wasn't caught like a rabbit in a snare. As the weeks go by, the daytime heat steadily increasing, I feel more and more that Fort Loudoun is nothing but a giant snare for the people trapped inside, and that whenever Kanagatucko wishes, he will tighten the noose. Already, rations have been reduced to a half-pint of corn per person per day and a small chew of salted meat. I am hungry all the time. I have to tighten my stays around my ribs, and the green-striped gown I borrowed from Amelia hangs on me.

Amelia's daughter follows her brother to the grave some days later, along with several others taken by illness born of weakened bodies and close quarters. Amelia takes it stoically, as she has begun to take everything, as though none of this is real, as though Fort Loudoun is a nightmare from which none of us will ever wake. For me, it is not a nightmare of horror, not like the ones in which Donald Campbell chases me through endless flames, which continue to visit me. It is a nightmare of tedium, in which every day is exactly like the last, and there is no end to them in sight.

The only events that break the monotony of the days are the visits of the Cherokee wives of the Fort Loudoun garrison. Kanagatucko and Stuart and Demere allow them to visit their husbands to bring food and to trade with other inhabitants. The extra dried pumpkin, venison, and other foods that come from these trades are what keep us going. I have nothing of value to trade but my brother's rifle and my mother's necklace, and though each would likely fetch a high price, I would rather go hungry than lose them. I feel the same way about my kitchen basket and knife, and the few other small items I carried into the woods on my birthday morning. Sometimes I look into the basket and wonder what I would have done had I known I was leaving my childhood home for good, what else I would have taken with me. I think of a few things—trinkets, and my father's books—but I know in the end I am practical, and I would have filled the basket with food.

Amelia is good enough to share what she gets with me, insisting she's not hungry, but sometimes I wonder if she's trying to starve herself to death. Even Malcolm sometimes seeks me out to share our portions and anything else he can manage to get. Since the night I refused to marry him, Owen has treated me with a cool indifference that breaks my heart when I remember the pharaohs. Sometimes I feel the crowded fort is filled to bursting with just the two of us and the vastness of our misunderstanding.

Sweating in the midmorning heat, Amelia and I are hauling a heavy bucket from the well to water a pitiful row of summer corn when the sally port opens and a group of Cherokee women enters, all of them laden with heavy baskets. Most of them wear long dark skirts and light-colored shirts. Except for the slightly darker shade of their skin and their straight black hair, they don't look so very different from most of the women of Fort Loudoun.

Amelia watches the women closely, and finally she nods and says, "There's our chance." She indicates one of the women, a girl with a long black braid who looks younger than I am. "That's Susannah Emory."

We lower the bucket to the ground beside the garden, careful not to let the water slosh out, and Amelia straightens, wincing as she stretches the muscles in her back.

"Susannah!" she calls, waving her arm.

The girl waves back and reaches for the hand of the child beside her. He's a little boy, just walking, and he toddles unsteadily as they descend the hill and cross the parade ground. Even from a distance, I can see the resemblance to his father in the bushy hair that sprouts from his head.

When Susannah Emory reaches us, Amelia gives her a quick hug and then introduces me.

"I know you don't have much time, Susannah, so I'll be quick," Amelia says. "We need you to talk to your husband."

Amelia sketches out a brief history of my family's murder and my arrival at Fort Loudoun. It's odd to hear it in another's voice, but I am relieved not to have to tell the story again.

Susannah Emory smiles sadly up at me. "I'm so sorry about your family," she says. She strokes her child's hair. His face is buried in her skirts, his little hands gripping bunches of cloth. "We have seen very little of my husband since the war started, and now that Fort Loudoun is under siege, even less."

Amelia glances up the hill to the commandant's house. "Captain Stuart seems to be in conference," she says. "Perhaps I'll just wait until he's available and let him know you're here?"

Susannah thanks her, and Amelia leaves us. My mouth is dry. Convincing this woman to convince her husband to let me meet Montgomery's troops at Fort Prince George may be my only hope of getting out of this trap and getting someone to listen to me. I break the silence with the first thought that comes into my mind.

"This is the strangest siege I've ever heard of. The Cherokee are besieging the fort. Why are Cherokee women allowed in? To bring food, no less?"

Susannah shrugs. "This is a strange war. These are strange times. The British and the Cherokee have been close allies for decades. Kanagatucko is a hard man, but a fair one, and he doesn't like to split up families. Besides, his aim is to immobilize the fort, not to destroy it. He knows Fort Loudoun will fall eventually. It's deep in Cherokee territory, completely cut off from all sources of aid. He is patient."

I look down at the coppery head of the little boy and at the woman in front of me. "Are you really a Cherokee?" I ask.

Susannah looks surprised. "I am," she answers. "But my father was a white trader who married my mother according to the customs of her people. I miss him very much, as I suppose you must miss your father."

"Yes," I answer. I do miss him, terribly, but a rush of anger floods my brain as well. I hate him, too, for bringing us south, for putting my family into danger we didn't have to enter.

Susannah looks curiously up at me, reading my face. "Let's sit somewhere quiet," she suggests. I follow her into the shade cast by the west wall of the palisade, where she sits and gathers her little boy into her lap. She indicates a place for me to sit beside her on the grass.

"Are you really married to Captain Stuart?" I ask. My mother would wring my neck for my bluntness. I've done nothing but badger this woman with personal questions since I met her.

But Susannah laughs. "Yes, I am. I like you, Catie Blair. You ask questions other people are too polite to. I know they all look at me and wonder, but you actually ask."

I grimace. "I'm not sure that's a compliment."

"I married Captain Stuart three years ago, when he was living among the Cherokee," she explains. "Because he's married to me, he's technically a Cherokee, too, which gives him quite a bit of protection and influence here. Of course, he also has a white wife, in Charlestown."

I'm staggered by this, but I remember my mother's admonitions to show no astonishment, no matter what I am told. Astonishment is impolite. "He has two wives? Is that legal?"

"His marriage to me is legal here, and his marriage to her is legal there, so I suppose they both are."

"And you don't mind that he has another wife?"

Susannah shrugs. "I'm happy for the times we can be together. And besides," she adds, "Who says he's the only one who's allowed to have more than one spouse?" She smiles. "Do I shock you?"

I laugh. "Once, maybe, you would have. So very little shocks me anymore."

I answer Susannah's questions about the attack on my family and my situation here. She leans back against a support and pulls her baby's hands away from an ants' nest and back onto her lap.

"My husband is right, you know. It's much too dangerous for you to try to get through." She shakes her head. "The Cherokee headmen try to control the young warriors, but there's not much they can do with people who are out of their sight, and the French are offering huge bounties for English scalps. I'd like to say they wouldn't attack a woman, but I know it's not the truth. My life and the lives of the other women who come here are threatened, even. Honestly, I don't think you can get through, but . . ." She hesitates. "If it were my family, I'd want to try. And for my own sake, I want you to try, because I hate this stupid war. It keeps my husband away from me and my son away from his father. I'll speak to John for you. He'll listen to me."

I hear the certainty in her voice, the knowledge of the strength of their bond. I can't deny that the idea of Captain Stuart's two marriages makes me uncomfortable, but it seems to work for Susannah Emory, so maybe my judgments are out of place here. If their relationship can endure everything it has had to face, they must have a deep well of love and resolve. If I ever do get married, I know I don't want what I see between Adam and Amelia, a willingness to keep secrets, a respect for the duty of marriage. I want something with the kind of certainty I hear in Susannah's voice.

29.

May 13, 1760

Morning

Two days later, Captain Stuart searches me out.

"Miss Blair?" he says, tipping his hand to the side of his tricorn.

I rise from weeding my garden patch and drop a short bob of a curtsy, though keeping to social conventions in the increasing mania of a fort under siege is beginning to seem very stupid.

"May I speak with you? Perhaps we could take a walk around the parade ground?"

Captain Stuart draws my arm through his as formally as if we were on the streets of Charlestown. The bright sun gives no quarter, and I'm glad of the wide-brimmed straw hat that protects my face from burning.

Stuart cuts his gaze sideways at me. "So you are determined to do this mad thing?"

I don't have to ask what he means.

"I am," I answer. Given confidence by the resignation in his voice, I continue. "I always have been. I must. I'll never have any peace if I don't. I cannot consign my family to their graves without doing all in my power to bring their murderer to justice, to make sure he never does it again."

Captain Stuart sighs. "The Cherokee observe the law of blood vengeance. If people from one clan are killed, the family members have the right to kill an equal number from the killer's clan."

Blood vengeance. I recall Kanagatucko's words. He said he respected me for seeking blood vengeance, but I didn't know until now exactly what he meant.

"But that's terrible," I protest. "How unfair."

Captain Stuart smiles and gives a bit of a laugh. "Oh, it's not as terrible as you'd think. It keeps things under control so well that it's rarely needed. You see, the killer knows his own people will give him no quarter if they know they'll have to give up an innocent instead of a guilty party to do so. For their part, the wronged clan has the responsibility of pursuing the killer. The law keeps things from escalating into an all out war. Usually. In this case, the law of blood vengeance ran right up against the British way of punishing no one unless you can catch the guilty party. These border conflicts. White settlers and Cherokee killing each other, and the British authorities insisting on having the guilty party whether the Cherokee could find him or not. In their turn, the Cherokee headmen not understanding why the royal governor couldn't turn over anyone if he couldn't find his own guilty party." He shrugs. "A difference in custom, but it led us here."

"I don't want blood vengeance, then," I say. "Punishing anyone else would not bring me peace. Donald Campbell is the one with blood on his hands."

Captain Stuart stops and turns to me. "How long will you search? Even if you meet Montgomery at Fort Prince George, even if he listens to you, what are the chances you could find this man? It's unlikely you will find him. He has probably pulled back east with the other settlers."

I think of Campbell's thirst for land, the way he always wanted more of it, and still more. He would never give it up. He would die first. His blood would soak the ground, and his ghost would haunt it.

"If anything, he is only in hiding," I respond. "Captain Demere says a British force will march for Fort Prince George from Charlestown. I feel sure Campbell will show himself once they reach the backcountry. He will press his claim to the land he farmed before the war started, and if I am not much mistaken, to any other land he can beg, borrow, or steal."

Stuart shakes his head. "Captain Demere is a fool if he really thinks relief will ever reach us." He smiles sadly. "Don't tell anyone I said that."

He takes my arm again, and we walk on. "Very well. If you are determined, and if you truly understand that your life is absolutely forfeit once you leave these walls, I will try to convince Captain Demere to let you go."

30.

May 14, 1760

Afternoon

"Absolutely not." Demere clicks his heels smartly together and turns to face me and Captain Stuart. I am sitting in one of the chairs by Demere's desk, and Captain Stuart stands beside me. A man I don't recognize is seated by the chimney corner, silently smoking a pipe. He has the lean, weathered look of one who has spent many years on the frontier. We have not been introduced, and I wonder why on earth Demere and Stuart have seen fit to make a stranger party to my pleas.

Demere leans wearily against the chimneypiece, his fingers pinching the bridge of his nose. "Miss Blair, there is no point in this mad expedition. Colonel Montgomery will arrive here shortly, in any case, to relieve our garrison. If you cease badgering me, I will make sure you are able to speak to him then. Stuart, I cannot believe you are party to this madness. May I ask what possessed you? Was it that little savage trollop of yours? You had your senses well enough about you before she arrived."

Stuart's face darkens. Demere has made a critical error. Captain Stuart will do anything to help me now.

"Miss Blair is aware of the danger. She is determined, and it'll be one less mouth to feed. Two, because we can't send her without a guide."

Captain Demere leans over his desk, his clenched fists taking the weight of his body. "Are you suggesting we send an unmarried woman into the wilderness with a man? A guide? Unchaperoned, because I won't send another woman with her."

I cast my eyes down into my lap. I am no less married now than when I arrived at Fort Loudoun in a man's company. I wonder vaguely what Demere must think of me, but I can't find it in myself to care. I'm too concerned with the outcome of this conference.

Captain Stuart pulls at his short beard. "It's her decision."

"How are we even to get them out of the fort? Every man who's tried to get out, either as a scout or as a deserter, for the past month, has been slaughtered." Demere looks at me. "You've seen the bodies when they're recovered? Riddled with shot, blood pouring from their scalps. The scalp bleeds, Miss Blair. That's what will happen to you."

My stomach rolls at Demere's description, but I swallow the burning bile that rises in my throat. I have grown stronger in the months since I watched my elder brother die.

An apologetic smile fleets across Demere's face. "I'm sorry to be so indelicate, but you must have all the facts."

"I have all the facts I need," I answer steadily. "I'm not an idiot, Captain. If I were, I would have tried to get out of the fort without asking for your help. I know what could happen to me. I also know some men have made it through."

"All you know is that they made it past the immediate vicinity of Fort Loudoun. You don't know what happened to them after that."

"I know some dispatches get through, which means some people are still able to pass through the mountains," I insist. "It's my life, and I can do what I like with it. If you won't let me go, I'll go anyway. You have no power to hold me here. And I won't go alone. I'll take Owen Ramsay with me. His family was killed by the same man, and he deserves satisfaction as much as I do."

"But he isn't determined to have it. He's willing to allow that his interpretation of events may not be correct," says Captain Demere. "He's a sensible young man."

My heart twists in my chest. I'm not sure I'm glad Captain Demere approves of Owen so heartily. I'm not sure why I thought threatening to take Owen with me would sway him.

"Paul," says Stuart quietly. His tone, and the use of his brother officer's Christian name, cause Demere and I both to look up. "Paul, someone has to go. You know as well as I do that Montgomery can't possibly understand how desperate our situation is here. Someone has to meet him at Fort Prince George and insist he push through the mountains. Miss Blair is volunteering. Look at it that way."

Stuart lowers himself into the chair beside mine and leans toward Demere.

"She's volunteering for dangerous duty, and she knows that. I agree with you that all odds are she'll never make it to Fort Prince George. It's a duty no one wants, and we'd be hard pressed to get another volunteer from the garrison. Think about it. There's a chance—and I know it's just a chance—that a woman could live through the mission. I don't say she'd be unharmed, but she'd be alive. And a woman pleading for us might have more influence with Montgomery than one of our dirty soldiers."

The three of us are silent, staring at each other. I am gripping the wooden arm of the chair.

The stranger speaks at last, breaking our strained silence. "I can get her through," he says, offhand, as if he speaks of nothing more difficult than crossing the parade ground.

Demere's voice is sharp. "Swan. We have heard your news already. This is none of your concern."

Stuart raises a hand. "I asked Gabriel to sit in with us. I think he could help."

The man belonging to the voice unfolds himself from the chair by the fireplace. "Sounds to me like the young lady's got a score to settle. She's got the right to do that."

The man holds his hand out to me, and I take it. His skin is weathered to the color of old leather, softened like old leather by much use, rather than callused as I expect to find it. He stands taller than Demere and leaner than Stuart, and his black hair is streaked with gray and smoothed away from his forehead and plaited into a long braid down his back.

"Name's Gabriel Swan," he says. He winks. "And before you ask, yes, I'm half Cherokee, on my mother's side, of course."

He regards Captain Demere. "Since you've heard my news, you know General Amherst didn't order Montgomery to save Fort Loudoun. The truth is, you're not in Amherst's good books right now."

"Of course he did," Demere insists. "Amherst knows we are surrounded, cut off."

Gabriel Swan taps his pipe against his palm. "And why should Amherst care about one fort set far inside Cherokee territory? Territory he's not concerned with. You're not the only one I carry dispatches for. Amherst needs all the forces he can get for the drive on French Montreal, and Montgomery's only orders are to push hard enough so the Cherokee will sue for peace and then scurry on back to New York as quick as may be. He'll relieve Fort Loudoun if he can, but Montgomery's a cautious man, and he's already itching to get back up north. He doesn't want to miss the drive on Montreal, either. He's none too pleased to be here."

Swan falls silent for a moment, allowing this to sink in, and Stuart speaks.

"I think Swan agrees with me that it couldn't hurt to have someone on the ground at Fort Prince George who could do a little persuading if Montgomery needs it. Miss Blair and her party might do that. You think you could do that, Miss Blair? Make sure Montgomery understands that without relief Fort Loudoun will fall? Convince Montgomery to push through?"

"I can try," I say, disbelieving that after a month of badgering, Demere and Stuart are actually going to help me. The exchange is so easy. They help me get to Montgomery, and I make Montgomery see that he must push through to Fort Loudoun before he returns north.

"Montgomery's encamped at the Congaree River, about halfway between Fort Prince George and Charlestown," says Swan. "From there, he'll push to Ninety Six and then on to Fort Prince George, which he plans to use as a staging ground. If we leave in the next couple days, we should be able to reach Prince George about the same time as he does."

He looks pointedly at Demere. "And you know I can't make your plea for you because Montgomery's too cautious to trust me. I may not live among them, but I look like a Cherokee, and he'll suspect a trap."

Demere looks around, finds himself outnumbered. He throws up his hands. "All right, Swan, if you're so tired of being cooped up here after a single day that you want to risk your life again, I won't stop you. You and Miss Blair make your plans. I assume she'll insist on taking Ramsay with her."

I stare back at Captain Demere. Heat rushes into my face, but I try to keep my words calm and steady. "I'd like to take Malcolm Craig, my former traveling companion, with me, too," I say. "He's been very helpful so far, and he knows the mountains well."

"That is out of the question," snaps Captain Demere. "Your intended is another provincial mouth to feed, miss, but Malcolm Craig is the nearest thing we've had to a surgeon since Lieutenant Anderson was killed."

"You have no control over him," I say. "He can do what he likes."

Demere steps around his desk, closer to me.

"I have every control," he says steadily. "I can commandeer his services for the good of this fort as I would commandeer a horse for the transport of the army. Besides, I'm not entirely convinced by his little indentured servant story."

I take his words like a blow to the chest, but I know I cannot react. A reaction would be a giveaway.

Captain Stuart comes to my rescue. "Until we figure out how to get Miss Blair safely out of this fort, there's no point in arguing about who's going with her."

Demere turns to Stuart. "You would send her out in the company of two men, unchaperoned? I won't do it, Miss Blair. If you must leave, I'll have you married to Ramsay first."

I can't control that reaction. "You won't." My voice falters. "You can't. Please understand. I can't marry anyone until I've resolved this. I have to bring Donald Campbell to justice first. I can't even think of anything else until I've done that. What kind of life would I have, always looking over my shoulder? Always wondering if he's coming for me or my children?"

Demere's face is nearly as red as his uniform. "I repeat my earlier order, Miss Blair. Under no circumstances does Malcolm Craig go. I need him here."

Demere pushes past me and out into the sunlight. Stuart and Swan remain, Stuart busying his fingers with the tie of a leather satchel on the desk. My presence feels suddenly superfluous, and I feel old and worn. It occurs to me that perhaps I should appreciate the feeling, as it's unlikely I will ever be old. It's not a morbid thought, only a fact. So few people have the luxury of years.

"Thank you," I say quietly.

Stuart looks up. "I'm afraid you owe me no thanks, Miss Blair. I've done you no favors. There are several thousand Cherokee between us and Fort Prince George, guarding every pass, ensuring we stay completely cut off from all help."

He looks pointedly at Swan. "One man alone is lucky to get through. I'm not bothered about the danger to your reputation, Miss Blair, because I don't think it will ever make the least difference. I don't expect you to live more than two days after you leave Fort Loudoun. If that long."

He picks up the satchel and goes after Demere.

I turn to Gabriel Swan. I am grateful for his help, but I don't understand why he has given it. "Why are you doing this?"

"I'm a trader in time of peace," he answers. "Carrying dispatches doesn't pay nearly as well. I want this war over as quick as may be so I can get back to my business. If, as he seems to be, this Donald Campbell is acting to prolong it, I want him taken care of. I've no particular loyalty to Demere or Kanagatucko, but I do hate seeing all these people here like sitting ducks because Demere is too proud and too stubborn to know when he's been beaten."

Swan sticks his pipe in the corner of his mouth and talks around it.

"Mainly, I'm doing it for you. I like you, Miss Blair. You've got spirit, and as I said, you've got a right to fight in the way you see fit. Anything you do on behalf of Fort Loudoun, you'll do on your own. I'll get you as far as Fort Prince George, and then I'll slip away and you'll never see me again."

31.

May 15, 1760

Morning

"Demere won't let you go," I say to Malcolm. I am standing in the open doorway of the surgery, pulled back into shadow in the hope Owen won't spot me. Malcolm picks up a thick bite stick covered with the tooth marks of many men in horrifying pain. He rolls it slowly between his palms.

"I don't see what say Demere has in the matter."

"He says he can commandeer your services the way he would commandeer those of a horse."

Malcolm grins. "As long as he doesn't make me pull carts. Demere's an idiot. I probably don't know much more than most people here. I suppose I shouldn't have made myself so useful."

"Demere thinks you're valuable. He's decided you are, anyway. He had a need and decided you were going to fill it. There's little changing his mind when it's made up. I've seen that."

Malcolm replaces the bite stick among the other instruments and draws nearer to me. He takes my hand and pulls me closer, and though there's plenty of air in the open doorway, suddenly I can't breathe.

"What about you?" he asks, searching my face. "Do you think I'm valuable? I think you must, or you would have married Ramsay by now."

I look down, studying the grain in the floor planks. "I have my own reasons for not marrying Owen. But I want you to come with me to Fort Prince George. I've missed you."

Malcolm runs a finger down my jaw line and tilts my chin up. He's so close I'm sure he is going to kiss me, and I am planning to let him, because his kisses have always been so good at making me forget.

But then I hear shouts and screams that shock both of us out of forgetting anything. I flatten myself against the surgery door as two men drag another, stumbling and sobbing, up the steps. The wounded man's face is blackened with powder, and the blue coat of his militia uniform is soaked with blood over the right side of his chest.

"Get him on the table," Malcolm orders, and the two men lift the third onto the wooden board that serves as a table for examining and operating.

"What happened?" Malcolm asks.

"He was trying to get to some of the old garden plots outside, to see if there was anything left we could use for seed. We're running out. He was hit, but he was able to get back inside before they could finish him off."

Malcolm looks up. "Catriona, I need you," he says. "Here, quickly."

I move to the table as Malcolm says, "Water, as much as you can carry," to the second man. "Build up the fire, too," he adds.

"Pull back his clothes so I can see the wound," Malcolm tells me. "Here, use these." He hands me a large pair of scissors. I slip my fingers through the holes, trying to get a grip on them, to get ready to cut.

My fingers fumble at first, finding the best way to tear and cut the coat and waistcoat and shirt away from the man's chest. I've always thought women's clothes more complicated than men's, but this changes my opinion. The wounded man's blood is slippery on my fingers, and it's hard for me to get a good grip on the scissors. His chest expels more blood every other second, and his breathing rattles like a bee in a closed room. Dimly, I see the first man return with water, which Malcolm instructs the men to boil over the fire. Rags appear, and I press them onto the man's chest until they are soaked, doing my best to clear away the blood. Illogically, I think that the blood is such a beautiful shade, like roses in June. I slowly realize I am the only one still moving, and Malcolm's hand has been on my arm for a long time.

"You can stop now, Catriona," he says, his voice a whisper in my ear.

"But it's doing some good," I insist. "There's less blood now. You see?"

Malcolm's voice is firm. "There's less blood because he's dead, sweet."

I look into the man's face and see the pink blood bubbles on his lips. The blood mixed with the gunpowder makes him look like a fiend of hell. Then I look more closely. I soak a clean rag in water and wipe away the gunpowder, revealing a face I recognize too well.

"We were almost there," I whisper. "We almost saved him."

Malcolm's arms are around me, and I cling to him, not caring that our hands are bloody, or that the two men who brought the dead man to us are still here.

"No, sweet, we didn't," says Malcolm. "The ball punctured his lung. There's nothing we could have done."

"Oh, Malcolm," I whisper, pressing my forehead into his chest. "This is Adam Williamson. This is Amelia's husband."

32.

May 15, 1760

Morning

I take off my bloody apron and scrub my hands as clean as I can before I go to find Amelia. I am especially careful to try to get the blood off my borrowed clothes, though I know the stains never will come out. I find Amelia in her tent, where she takes the news quietly. I am relieved to be spared an exhibition.

"I always knew we'd never make it out of here alive," she says. She looks around the small tent, which has become heavy with the evidence of her lost family. So many threads cut in such a short time. I remember the feel of the scissors in my hands, cutting away her husband's clothes, and I curl my fingers into my lap to hide the thin red lines that border my nails.

"You're leaving, too, aren't you?" she asks. "Off on your mad chase."

"Yes," I answer. "As soon as I can."

Amelia sighs and brushes a hand across her eyes. She takes a good look around the tent. "I'd like to come with you."

33.

May 20, 1760

Night

We leave Fort Loudoun under cover of night. Though we must be weighed down by heavy weapons, we travel as lightly as we can. Owen carries Mark's rifle across his back, and Gabriel Swan carries his own. The glint of metal is hidden under their cloaks. Amelia and I carry knives at our belts, and all four of us carry bundles of supplies for our journey. Mine is wrapped in a blanket in my basket. Though it might be easier for Amelia and me to move in men's clothes, we wear our own in the shallow hope that our sex may protect us from death in the event of capture. Sometimes, women die in the same way as their men; sometimes, they suffer much worse things before death, in the way that the rage of enemies will fall upon women. But sometimes, women are spared and taken prisoner, made slaves or wives. It is all chance. It all depends on whose decision it is.

Fort Loudoun is risking its own life to get us free tonight. Captain Stuart admits, and Captain Demere knows, too, that Colonel Montgomery's forces are Fort Loudoun's only hope. Without his aid, the fort will fall before summer is out. This is our trade, that in exchange for their help to get free, I do my level best to convince Montgomery to push through the mountains. As Gabriel Swan leads us rapidly toward the tree line, I hear the crack of musket and rifle fire coming from the fort, and the louder report as a cannon fires from a bastion. The small explosions that come with every shot light my eyes. Fort Loudoun is attempting to break the siege on the far side of the fort. I'm worried though, afraid Kanagatucko will realize Demere's mad attack is a diversion.

Our only chance is that the Cherokee who surround the fort don't think we'd be stupid enough to leave it. The first challenge is to get past the immediate vicinity of Fort Loudoun without being seen. I fear my life will be over the second we run into the Cherokee warriors in the woods, but we do not run into them. Swan has not run this blockade many times for nothing. I have no idea where he is leading us, but it must be a way only he knows. I stare at Swan's back and listen to Amelia's faint breath behind me. Owen is behind her, covering our rear.

Before us is the oblivion of the woods and mountains, a darker silhouette against a dark sky. Behind us are the light and noise of the skirmish around the fort. All I can think about as we make the relative safety of the trees is the man I was forced to leave behind and may never see again. For so long after I lost my family, I did not care if I lived or died, and that made me brave. And now that death is so close and so likely, I desperately want to live, if only long enough to see Malcolm again and know he is safe.

In the darkness that consumes us as we move farther and farther away from Fort Loudoun, my mind fills with him.

I said goodbye earlier tonight, before we left. For the first time since Amelia's little girl died, Malcolm came to her tent, where the two of us were silently making our preparations to leave. Amelia made some excuse and left us alone for a few minutes.

There seemed to be so little left for us to say to each other, and I recalled the long winter nights in the shelter and how we filled them with conversation, marveling at our silence and the impassable distance between us now.

"You haven't married Ramsay," said Malcolm.

"No."

"Will you? Once you've faced Donald Campbell and the war is over?"

I turned away from him, inhaling deeply and pressing my hands against the hollow of my stomach.

"I don't know, Malcolm, if I'll ever marry anyone. I may never find Donald Campbell. I may die hunting him."

Men are dying tonight at Fort Loudoun, men of the garrison, men of the Cherokee siege party. Perhaps women, too. Perhaps children. Because of me and what Amelia called my mad chase. For the first time, it occurs to me that I have brought the lives of others into danger, for myself, for my own grim satisfaction, for my own fears. I thought anything was better than the tedious living death of Fort Loudoun as it waited to fall, but perhaps I was wrong. Perhaps I am not the only one who desperately wants to live.

I felt Malcolm approach me from behind, felt the warmth of his chest against my back as he circled his arms around me and turned me to face him. For a moment I thought about asking him to come with me, to leave Fort Loudoun as he left his regiment. But then he kissed me for one long, aching moment, slipping his fingers under my cap and into my hair, which is still shorter than a man's.

He pulled away from me and, his hands cupping the sides of my face, he whispered, "I hope you find him."

Gabriel Swan urges us onward, ever on, forcing us through the black night until it seems this night is all that will ever be, and all I can do is wonder that I am still here, my heart still beating, my feet still moving, my back and arms still carrying the burdens I brought from the doomed fort. Malcolm will be in the surgery now, busy with the wounded and dying. Will he know we got though? When he doesn't see our bodies, will he know?

Or perhaps we are all dead already, but our souls don't know it, and we will haunt these hills forever, wanderers in the night. The thought makes me shiver, and I look into the darkness for the last sister, look to see if she is wielding her terrible scissors and waving my own fragile thread.

He pressed his forehead gently to mine, and then he was gone and Amelia was back, telling me we had to leave.

I didn't even manage to get a lock of his hair to remember him by. I have only the memories of it shining in the firelight of the shelter, dark rivers between my fingers, like blood.

34.

May 21, 1760

Morning

The black night is lifting by the time Gabriel Swan holds up a hand, signaling us to stop.

"We'll camp here," he says, indicating a depression edged by high ridges and concealed by thick foliage. "I'll take the first watch. The rest of you try to sleep for a few hours."

I am so tired that I barely register Owen's and Amelia's faces. I notice only the gray circles under their eyes and the pallor of their skin in the scant light. I know I must look as haunted. I set my basket on the ground and lie down beside Amelia. I claim a few hours of restless sleep, despite the calling of waking birds and the incessant biting of the small insects that invade my clothing. The hazards of spring are different from those of winter.

The sun is high when I wake. I stretch and feel my limbs tremble with weariness. I want to go back to sleep. I want to lie down and sleep forever. But I hear movement in the trees, and I am wide awake. I lay my hand on the knife in my waistband, wondering how quickly I can get to a rifle without attracting attention.

In an instant, the man is upon us, and I start up, disbelieving, wondering if I am looking at a ghost or the figment of my own tortured imagination. I do not dare believe my eyes are telling the truth.

"Malcolm," I whisper. He is there before me, and I look to the ground to see if I am still asleep and dreaming. I need to touch him to be sure of his presence. When he holds me, his flesh is warm enough, his cheek rough on mine, and the muscles of his upper arms hard under my palms.

"I didn't think I'd see you again." My voice cracks from trying to hold too long.

He presses my head to his chest, tangling his fingers in the hair that curls from under my cap, and his breath is warm in my ear.

"Did you really think I'd let Demere keep me there?" he whispers. "Like a horse, for his use?"

"Oh, but Malcolm," I say, pulling back, struck again by the seriousness of the danger I've inflicted on others. "They have no surgeon now."

"They didn't have one in me," he says. "Just a man with a little experience. Between the rest of them, they know as much as I do. Demere was determined to have a surgeon, so he made me into one, just like he's pretending Fort Loudoun can stand. I wasn't going to let you go alone."

I start to point out that I am not alone, but I don't because I understand his meaning. Without him. And it's true that until he stepped through the trees, I felt very much alone.

Owen and Amelia are beginning to stir, and I hear Swan approaching through the trees. I pull reluctantly away from Malcolm.

"I thought I'd let you make your greetings without a witness," says Swan. A grin seams his face.

Over our scant breakfast of salt beef, Malcolm tells us how he escaped Fort Loudoun.

"There was a bit of a skirmish outside the walls," he says. "I got myself involved in it, and instead of pulling back into the fort, I pushed forward. I had an idea of the way Swan would be leading you."

He and Gabriel Swan share another grin. I wonder how long they've had this plan.

"There were four of our men down when I left," Malcolm continues. "And about as many Cherokee."

I rest my head on my hands. "This is all my fault," I whisper. More threads cut. More blood on my hands.

Swan pats me on the back. "Don't you feel that way, young lady," he says. "Fort Loudoun's got to do something. Anything's better than sitting there quietly starving to death and waiting on help that isn't coming. That plan let Stuart see how Kanagatucko would react to an attack, gave him an indication of how many men Kanagatucko has. He can use that."

Owen stands, brushing bracken from his clothes. "That was a damned stupid idea, Craig. You could have gotten yourself killed for no reason. We have no need of you here."

"Owen," I say, trying to calm him.

"No, Catie. I've let this go on too long. If you prefer him to me, you should come out and say it and not string me along. But if you don't, you should have the decency to tell him so." He glares at me. "Your behavior is shameful."

Amelia's face goes red, as I know mine does, and Swan coughs hard into his hand.

I stand, too, ready for a fight, but I consider our circumstances and lay a hand on Owen's arm.

"Owen," I say again. My words are iron. "You forget yourself. Malcolm saved my life."

I stand staring into Owen's green eyes for an impossible moment, frozen until Gabriel Swan wins my eternal gratitude by telling Owen to stop behaving like an ass and prepare to move.

"We've got to be quiet, too," he says. "So work out your problems once we reach Fort Prince George. We've got enough to deal with for now."

The quiet as we move through the deep mountain passes only Gabriel Swan knows gives me too much time to think. I have loved Owen so long, but I have loved Malcolm so intensely. I think of what Susannah Emory said about having more than one husband, and I am swamped with regret that my life will not be long enough to love them both.

35.

June 3, 1760

Morning

Gabriel Swan loses his life when we are only two days away, by his estimation, from Fort Prince George. That morning, we camp near a small spring. Owen accompanies me when I go for water, armed with Mark's rifle in case enemies lie in wait for those who must come to drink. I am trying to be kind to Owen, trying to keep him calm and reasonable at least until we get to Fort Prince George and are out of the constant danger of the open. And truthfully, until I have time and rest enough to work out my own feelings.

"Catie," he says quietly, when I come up from bathing my face in the water. He sounds so unlike the Owen of the past few days, so much more like the boy I knew, that I look up, expectant, overwhelmed with the knowledge of how sad I will be to lose the boy who spoke to me of pharaohs.

I stand, and he holds out a hand for me. I take it, and he pulls me toward him. I don't resist. Sorrow and loss are in his face, not passion, and this is the clinging together of two people who are all that is left of a world and a life that are forever gone. Owen knows me, I think, closing my eyes and breathing in the familiar scent of him. He knows me in a way no one else ever will, and if I lose him, I will lose that part of myself, too. I realize now that he is the last person left who knew me when I was a child, and I feel tears hovering on the edges of my eyes.

"I love you, Catie," he whispers. "I've always loved you, ever since I met you, ever since we were children."

The tears leave my eyes and trickle down my face. This is such a strange farewell. I have waited so long to hear those words, have shed so many tears when they did not come, and now I fear they have come too late.

"You might have said," I say. "Sometime, in all those years when you were acting like I was a bothersome wasp, you might have said."

I'm not being fair, and I know that. This confession would have come months ago, on my birthday, if it hadn't been for Donald Campbell. I would have been happy, thrilled, and our families would have celebrated. It would have been a perfect day, my mother's pearls around my neck, my ever so longed for intended by my side. I would have lived my whole life with Owen Ramsay, and we would have been happy, because I never would have known there was anything more. For a moment that life flashes before my eyes, and I see all I will lose. I hate Donald Campbell for that, and for a moment I hate Malcolm, too, for interrupting with the intensity of sudden passion feelings that have simmered for half my life.

Owen's arms tighten, choking a sob out of me.

"Is it really too late, Catie?" he asks. "You can't know your own feelings now. Too much has happened too quickly." His hand runs down my back. "I'll give you as much time as you need."

I look up at him, hating myself for what I'm about to ask.

"Owen." Sobs stick in my throat. "Were you really going to let Donald Campbell get away with it?"

His face hardens. "Is that what this is about, Catie? Are you punishing me for that?"

"You didn't try. You wouldn't have tried, if I hadn't shown up at Fort Loudoun." I know the hopelessness in my voice is my answer.

Owen pulls away from me, sliding his hands down my arms to take my fingers in his.

"Catie," he says. "The best thing we can do, the best way we can heal, is to move on. That's what our families would have wanted for us. Your parents wanted you to marry me, you know. I'd already asked your father. He and your mother were delighted. Can't you give them that? Don't you think they would be mortified if they knew how you were carrying on just to avenge them? They'd want you to move on, Catie."

My face burns. "I loved my parents," I say. "I didn't always understand them, but I loved them. I would like to think I managed to please my mother, especially, at last. And once that might have been enough for me."

Owen's hands tighten around mine and his green eyes burn into mine. "Why isn't it still?"

"Because I have to move on with my life, not theirs. If they wanted me to behave like a proper English lady, they shouldn't have brought me to the backcountry. If I had behaved like a proper English lady out here, I'd be dead many times over. Mark would tell me to be myself, to live my own life. He always did."

Owen's face clouds.

"So you're going to marry that highlander? Do you know what your mother would say to that? She'd rather see you married to a Cherokee."

"Owen," I say sharply. But that's all I can say, because I know it's true. Neither a Cherokee nor a highlander would make an acceptable match for me, in my mother's view. A lowlander or, preferably, a good Englishman. She married a lowlander, after all, and look where it got her.

"Are you my intended or not, Catie? That's what I really want to know."

I pull away, straightening my arms by my sides. "I am no one's intended right now. I have to take care of Campbell first, and then perhaps I'll be able to think things through." I grit my teeth. "And my name isn't Catherine. It's Catriona. I'm named for my father's grandmother, who came from a highland clan." I draw in my breath. "Would you have wanted to marry me if you'd known?"

Owen looks staggered, but I don't have time to reflect on that because I hear Amelia's high-pitched scream coming from the camp.

36.

June 3, 1760

Morning

"Give me the rifle," I say to Owen. "Don't argue. I've always been a better shot than you."

I wish I could leave him the illusion of protecting me, but our lives are more important. Owen and I drop to the ground and crawl up the bank. When we reach the top, I look down at the scene before me. It happened so fast it's nearly over. Gabriel Swan and a vermillion-painted Cherokee warrior are both lifeless and bloody on the ground. The handle of a hatchet protrudes from Swan's breast; the blade appears to have cleaved his ribs. The dead Cherokee has been shot, also in the chest. Amelia is struggling to free herself from the grip of another Cherokee, whose arm circles her neck. Her feet scrabble for purchase on the ground and her dark hair swirls out of her cap and over her face. Malcolm is reloading Swan's rifle. Quickly, but not quickly enough to suit me.

I angle Mark's rifle on the rising ground in front of me, praying I don't miss my shot and hit Amelia instead of the Cherokee warrior, and thinking of the scissors I used to cut away Adam Williamson's clothes and the curiously similar feeling of the trigger. I fire before I can think any further. Every time I hold the rifle, I am so conscious of Mark's words in my head. *You wait too long to fire and lose your nerve and your aim.*

The Cherokee holding Amelia goes down, hit in the side. And then Owen's body slams into mine, knocking me down the bank. Owen screams, and blood spurts in a crimson arc over our heads as we tumble toward the spring. I hear the crack of another rifle and hope it is Malcolm's. I land on my back and turn my head toward Owen, who is lying on the ground, his face pale as death, his lips turning blue. I crawl over and take him by the shoulders. His eyes show he's still conscious, and I shake him.

"Owen, stay awake," I order, struggling with the tie of my apron.

Blood is pouring from his forearm. His shirtsleeve is already drenched with it.

"All right," I say, shushing him, though he isn't talking. "You're going to be all right."

I don't try to take off Owen's shirt. Instead, I wrap my apron around the wound and pull the cloth tight. I want to call for Malcolm and Amelia, but I don't know if it's safe to make a sound. I don't know if they're still alive. I don't know if it's safe for me to stay in the open like this. I know only that I can't leave Owen here alone. I know only that Owen cannot leave me, too, like everyone else.

Every bit of strength I have is in my hands, holding Owen's arm together, willing the bleeding to stop. It seems a long time later when Malcolm appears on the bank above me. He hovers there for a moment, but when he sees what is happening, he rushes down.

"Where's Amelia?" I ask, fearful.

"She's all right," he says. "Just a little shaken."

I wipe a hand across my mouth and taste Owen's blood. My palms are red with it where it has seeped through the cloth of my apron.

"Do you know what hit him?" I ask, hearing the tremor in my voice. "He blocked something. He put his arm in front of me, and now I can't get the bleeding to stop."

"We have to stop it," says Malcolm. "Soon. Even if this doesn't kill him, he's already lost enough blood to make him too weak to travel, and we can't stay here. We'll have to start with a tourniquet."

"He'll lose his arm," I protest.

"Better than losing his life. We've got to get the bleeding stopped. Get Amelia and bring her down here. It may take all three of us to hold him, and we'll have to start a fire."

I look at Malcolm. "No," I say. "It's too dangerous."

"I saw it save a man's life once," he insists. "There's a risk of inflammation after, but there always is. Firing the wound will stop the bleeding enough for us to remove the tourniquet, and he'll be dead shortly if we don't do it."

I nod. Fire is dangerous, but there is less chance Owen will lose his arm this way. I scramble up the bank and find Amelia checking the four bodies for signs of life. She kneels by the Cherokee who held her, the one I shot. A dark bruise spreads over his torso from where the ball entered.

"I don't think he would have killed me," she says quietly.

"I couldn't take the chance," I answer.

I go to Gabriel Swan's body, fluttering my eyelids down to keep from looking at the wound in his chest. I take his rifle from where it fell beside him.

Amelia stares into the face of the man I killed.

"He lived for a little while after you shot him. He said the English came in the night, attacking the towns, killing the warriors, the women and children. He said they came in the night like demons. Malcolm told him that, in his experience, the British army would do that. What did he mean, Catie?"

"I don't know," I lie. Still holding Swan's rifle, I kneel beside her and put my arm around her shoulders. "Amelia, Owen has been badly hurt. We're going to fire the wound. We don't have any choice. We can't stop the bleeding."

That snaps her out of her daydream, and for the first time in many days, she looks like the Amelia I knew before her husband and children died.

"What can I do?" she asks.

I keep my arm around her as we stand. I'm not sure if I am helping her or if she is supporting me.

"Can you build a fire? Just a small one that won't smoke much. Use the flint from one of the rifles."

Amelia and I make our way down the bank to the spring. At the top of the ridge, I catch sight of the hatchet that split Owen's arm open. The blood on it has dried black, but the blood on my apron remains fresh, constantly replenished.

Malcolm has already fashioned a tourniquet from strips of cloth cut from a blanket and the ramrod from his musket. Amelia builds a small fire while Malcolm holds Owen by the upper arm and wrist and I use my jackknife to saw away what remains of my apron and Owen's shirt. With the cloth removed and the bleeding temporarily stopped, I can see that the gash runs along the back of Owen's arm almost the full length of wrist to elbow.

I know I have to work fast if I want to save Owen's arm, not to speak of his life. I bite open a cartridge, spitting at the taste of the powder, and pour the powder into the split in Owen's arm.

"Not too much," Malcolm cautions. "Amelia, help me hold him."

"Is it going to hurt him?" I ask.

"If he were conscious, terribly. He's out, though."

I take a small lit twig from the fire. Malcolm shifts so that he is lying over most of Owen's body, and Amelia holds Owen's head. I touch the fire to the line of powder, and flame shoots out of Owen's arm. It's a good thing Malcolm is lying on top of him, because the pain brings him back and sets him roaring. But when the flame dies, the bleeding has stopped, though the flesh around the original wound is burned.

"It needs a poultice," says Amelia. She speaks softly, though Owen is past hearing us, lost again to a netherworld of pain. "He needs to be covered and kept warm. Bring me all the blankets."

She unties her own apron and folds it, then soaks it in the cold spring. She comes back with it dripping and ties it around the blackened flesh of Owen's arm. She sits and rests his head on her lap. "It's probably best if he sleeps as long as possible," she says. "Weren't we making camp, anyway? You two can do whatever else needs to be done. I'll stay with him."

37.

June 3–7, 1760

Owen sleeps through the day and far into the night, moaning and shifting when Amelia removes the cold poultice to replace it with another. His injury notwithstanding, we cannot linger here. The danger of another attack is too high, as is the danger to Owen should greater inflammation take hold.

I know the pain of the charred flesh of Owen's arm must be terrible, but he says, almost cheerfully, to Amelia, "At least it wasn't my leg. Then you'd have to carry me." Though Malcolm strips a sturdy tree limb for him to use as a walking stick, Owen's weakness slows us, and he leans heavily on Amelia's narrow shoulders from time to time.

The best thing we can do for Owen, and for our own safety, is to get to Fort Prince George as quickly as possible. Owen's arm is bound in bandages that Amelia changes frequently to keep cold water on the burn, strips of cloth she insists on cutting from her own petticoat. She washes her apron the best she can and ties it into a sling for Owen's arm. Though no one mentions it, we all know if the arm becomes inflamed, it will have to come off, and we have no chance of operating successfully in the wilderness. I think of the hooked tenaculum needle Malcolm showed me at Fort Loudoun and push myself to move faster.

On our fourth day of painfully slow travel, we finally come within sight of Fort Prince George, and I have never been so glad to see the flag of Britain as I am when I see it flying over the bastions. I remember the last time I looked down onto the diamond shape of the tiny fort, when I feared it, when Mark had warned me away, when Jaime was still alive.

Owen is faint, so he and Amelia stop to rest as Malcolm and I push forward to judge the lay of the land around the fort. Surrounding tiny Fort Prince George, so much smaller than Fort Loudoun, the 77th Regiment of Foot is bivouacked, their campaign tents dotting the green like a field of white flowers. Men in short red jackets move among them, men wearing blue tams and dark plaid kilts. And then I remember where I have heard Montgomery's name before. The 77th Regiment of Foot. Montgomery's regiment. Montgomery's highlanders. I don't know why it has taken me so long to work it out. I remember reading about them in old Charlestown newspapers that made their way to our settlement, but I didn't make the connection until I saw their regimental number, their uniforms. Three highland regiments landed in America in 1757, but only one of them landed in Carolina. And Malcolm headed for Carolina when he deserted.

"Oh, Malcolm," I say, looking up at him, stricken with terrible, sickening fear. He is not safe in the woods. He will not be safe in the fort.

"That can't possibly be the entire regiment. I don't think my company is here," he says, scanning the encampment. He spreads his arms, indicating his frontier garb and the short beard he has grown in the fortnight since we left Fort Loudoun. "Look at them. Look at me. Unless they look right at me, unless they're looking for me, they'll never suspect. I'm sure I've been listed among the missing since Fort Duquesne. They probably count me as dead. Don't worry. I can be inconspicuous when I need to be."

I grab his wrist. "You're an indentured servant," I say. "You're my indentured servant."

He nods. "If it will make you feel better. Will that work for Ramsay?"

"He doesn't know what you really are. And for God's sake, he doesn't want you dead, Malcolm. You just saved his life."

We return for Owen and Amelia, and the four of us make our way through the encampment by the mercy of a friendly sergeant who tells us he is heartsick at our troubles. We present ourselves at the guard house just in time, for Owen is in no shape to expose anyone's true identity. Amelia is half holding him up, in the end, and I can tell she must be much stronger than she looks. But when we receive permission to enter the fort, I step back and grab Malcolm's arm, for the man who almost runs into us coming out of the gate is none other than Donald Campbell.

PART 4

THE HIGHLANDERS

38.

June 7, 1760

Afternoon

Donald Campbell's broad, florid face is just as horrid as I remember it in my dreams, but for a moment it blanches with shock. He didn't expect to see me alive ever again. He pauses as I take a small, startled step back, and the mixture of hatred and contempt in his eyes is a simple exaggeration of what I've seen for half my life. He never liked my family. I was right about that. We were always lowland trespassers to him.

Campbell is quick. The surprise vanishes from his face in an instant, and he grabs me by the shoulders, swinging me away from Malcolm and placing himself between me and my companions.

"Catie! Catie Blair. It is you, isn't it?" His hands press my shoulders down as he stoops to look in my face. "Bless your heart, lass, we thought we'd lost you. When we found your parents and your brother, we thought the savages had taken you and little Jaime. We got up a search party. We looked everywhere."

His words ring with sincerity, as if I truly am a miracle. Catie Blair, back from the dead.

Demere's voice clangs in my ears. *Probably you saw it wrong. Great stress can do that to a person, especially a woman. Probably your neighbors were attempting to come to your aid, and in your hysteria, you ran from them.*

Owen's reluctance to pursue Campbell comes to mind. Is it possible? Is it possible I've been wrong all this time?

"But where's wee Jaime?" Campbell asks. "We never found his body. Did the savages take him, too?"

His words drive the air from my lungs.

"He died." My own words take the last of my breath.

Campbell touches his hand to his hat, a gesture of respect.

"Poor lass," he says. "You've lost all your family. You'll come with me, won't you, Catie-girl? No need to stay here with a mess of old soldiers when I can carry you back with me. A lot of us are holed up at Ninety Six, in the courthouse, holding the savages off from there. We can raid quite as well as they can."

He means that to be taken for a joke on the Cherokee, but I know it is meant for me. The man is so clever. Doubt leaves my mind. Of course he sounds genuine. Donald Campbell is a fine actor, even without his vermillion stage paint.

"We buried your parents and your brother. I'll take you to see their graves. You'll want to pay your respects."

He buried their bodies. Of course he did. It was the final scene in his play of the grieving neighbor. It's an insult, a slap. I will not weep over my brother's grave with this man by my side.

"Do come," he says. "Come with me. All the old neighbors—well, all the ones left, to be sure—will praise God to see you alive."

Campbell's fingers are tight around my wrists. If he gets me alone, he will kill me. But he can't get me alone without my consent. He can't very well carry a screaming, clawing woman through the camp, and my jackknife is in my pocket.

I don't want to call attention to Malcolm. And I want Campbell to understand he has not fooled me. I know him for the monster he is.

"Owen," I say steadily. "Owen, help me." I turn to the one person who owes Donald Campbell as great a measure of vengeance as I do, and the only one of my companions who would recognize him. Owen's face is drained of color and pinched with pain. He has little enough breath left for speech, and none for a pursuit. But he tries.

"Tell me, Campbell," Owen says. "Did you bury my family, too?"

Campbell peers beyond me, past Malcolm, at Owen's face. "Ramsay?" he says. "Well, isn't this a day of miracles? I nearly didn't recognize you, man." He takes in Owen's bandaged arm. "You'll come with us, of course."

He does not see either of us as a threat. A woman and a cripple. He thinks we'll be easy to take out.

My best help comes from where I did not think to look. Amelia's voice is as insistent as I have ever heard it, which is saying something.

"No one is going anywhere except into this fort. We need to get Owen to the surgeon."

Owen's good arm is still slung around Amelia's shoulders, and she looks as drained and pale as he does. I look at the clumsy dressing on Owen's wound. Blood in various stages of drying has stained Amelia's apron in all the shades from pink to black, and I wonder if the original wound has opened again or if the burn itself is bleeding now. Owen is greatly weakened. Campbell could easily overpower him.

"Catie must stay with me," Amelia adds. She looks up at Campbell. "I ask your pardon, but I will not be a woman alone among all these soldiers. Perhaps at a later time, you would be good enough to return for Miss Blair and Mr. Ramsay, should they wish it. For now, I'm afraid they must stop here."

Campbell knows he cannot force us to accompany him, and I can see frustration bubbling under his skin. But he smiles.

"A later time. Of course. It's so good to see you both well and returned to us." He catches my eye and smiles. "A later time."

I watch Campbell make his way through the highlanders' camp. His pace is calm and unhurried, while my heart races with rage and frustration. Of all the things I could have said, could have done. I let him threaten me, mock me, and get away. Again.

I turn back to the others. "I'll make our report to the commandant. Amelia, see if you can get someone to take Owen to the surgery right away. They won't stand on ceremony for a wound like that."

Malcolm moves to accompany me to the guardhouse, but I stop him. "Make yourself scarce." I soften the blow with a hand on his chest. "You promised me."

The news travelers bring is valuable, so after I deposit most of what I'm carrying in the guardhouse, I don't have to wait long to be admitted to the commandant's quarters. I drop a curtsy to the man who stands before me in the small wooden box of a house. Colonel Montgomery isn't as old as I expected. He's a big man in his late thirties, thickset in the way that tends to turn men obese in later years. His dark hair is smoothed with tallow and queued under a blue tam. His eyes, though they are warm enough, have a sort of hard glint to them that says he's used to getting what he wants.

His short red coat bears the green facings of his regiment, which match the green in the plaid of his kilt. Red and white checkered stockings are tied with red ribbon around his calves. His stature and elaborately decorated officer's uniform make him seem very grand, despite the bare knees that would mark him in my mother's book as a savage, and I am intensely conscious of my own bedraggled state. My skin is burned and chapped by sun and wind. My hair is still not long enough to dress, and my clothes are stained with mud and blood, though I have done my best to make myself presentable. I wipe my palms down the sides of my overskirt, regretting the loss of my apron.

But I am not about to let something as petty as my appearance stop me now. I could be neat and pretty and dead, but I am none of those. My blemishes mar a living body, and I am proud to be alive.

"Colonel Montgomery," I begin. "My name is Catriona Blair."

Having found my voice at last, I try to go on, but he waves me to silence.

"I am not Colonel Montgomery," he says. "I am acting Lieutenant-Colonel James Grant, Colonel Montgomery's second-in-command." He bows crisply over my hand. "Colonel Montgomery is unwell—it's this damnable climate—and as we have just marched sixty miles from Ninety Six with no sleep and razed the Cherokee Lower Towns in the process, he is recovering. Hence, I am acting commandant."

I draw a deep breath and remind myself of my mother's society lessons, the lessons I thought I would be unlikely ever to use. Lieutenant-Colonel Grant doesn't look like a man who has just done what he says he has, exactly what Captain Demere insisted Montgomery's forces would do. He looks as though he would be equally at home in a London drawing room as in a minor fort on the Carolina frontier. A nagging begins in my brain, a wondering at why his name sounds so familiar.

"May I offer you some refreshment?" he asks. "Tea, perhaps?"

It's been ages since I tasted tea, and I think with a pang of the precious little tin Mother kept on a shelf by the hearth. Tea is a rare luxury in the backcountry, among the luxuries Mother refused to do without. Grant reads my face and dispatches his silent aide-de-camp, a man who has been standing still enough to be taken for a piece of the spare furnishings, to fetch the tea.

"Do sit, Miss Blair." Grant indicates a chair in front of his desk and rounds the desk to seat himself.

As I sit, I say, "You are angry. I hope I do not trouble you." All these formalities, so pointless and so necessary.

Grant laughs bitterly. "Yes, Miss Blair, I am angry, but have no fear. My anger is not at you."

Then I put my finger on what bothers me about Grant, what seems so familiar. He's like Malcolm, with that slow undercurrent of anger, not at me but at the way the world is, that sense that nothing ever will come right. *Grant,* I think again, starting as I remember how I know his name. Major James Grant led the doomed attack on Fort Duquesne in the Pennsylvania wilderness, the attack where Malcolm lost his language and decided he could not lead men into certain death.

But Malcolm told me Grant was taken prisoner, and I'm sure I remember that from the newspaper accounts. What is he doing here?

I draw a breath and make my face a mask. Grant must not know I am familiar with his name or his story, for that could put Malcolm in great danger. I hold out the dispatch case with the letters from Captain Demere and Captain Stuart.

"If I do not trouble you, then please allow me to present you with the contents of this case from Fort Loudoun. My party and I left there a fortnight ago with these messages."

Grant opens the case, breaks the seals on the letters, and scans the pages. He looks up sharply. "You come from Fort Loudoun? How did you ever get through the mountains? I didn't think anyone would escape that godforsaken place, and it appears the situation is more dire than I feared."

I think of the people I left behind in Fort Loudoun, trapped between Demere's pride and a superior Cherokee force. I think of the increasing desperation, the decreasing rations. This man may be their only hope.

"You must forgive me, Lieutenant-Colonel Grant, when I say it is not God who has forsaken Fort Loudoun. It is the British army. You must know your regiment is Fort Loudoun's only hope of relief. I have been sent here to plead with you to press on through Cherokee territory, to break the siege on Fort Loudoun and relieve the garrison there."

Grant gives me that sharp, bitter bark of a laugh again. "Trust these colonials to send a woman to plead for them." He stands and leans across the desk. "You don't know what you're asking, miss. I didn't cross an ocean to fight women and children, but that's what I've been forced to do in the last weeks."

I think of the Cherokee warrior who held Amelia, the one I shot. Someday, perhaps, I will have to acknowledge that I killed a man, that my hands are no cleaner than anyone else's. Now it doesn't seem real, but I remember the man's dying words. He said the English came in the night like demons, but it appears it wasn't the English, after all. It was the Scottish.

"What happened in the Lower Towns?" I ask. "You said they were razed."

Grant tilts his head and laughs. "Are you an angel sent to judge me, Miss Blair?"

He begins to pace restlessly. "Very well. My orders were to teach the Cherokee a lesson, to strike them hard enough to make them sue for peace, but not so hard there was no chance of their ever allying with Britain again.

I came to this beastly continent to fight the French, and instead, after being held as their honored guest until my prisoner exchange, I'm here, sorting out a squabble in a colony that, frankly, is more trouble than it's worth. Like as not, I'll miss the drive on Montreal, and with it the chance to distinguish myself."

Grant's pacing takes him to the wall, where he turns sharply.

"Night marches are difficult under the best of circumstances. We were supposed to burn the cornfields in order to damage the enemy's food supply, to force them to come to terms. There weren't supposed to be any warriors in the Lower Towns, but there were. I don't know who fired first. I only know that as we approached Little Keowee, I heard a dog bark, and then the firing started. We razed Little Keowee, Estatoe, Qualatchee, and Toxaway. I nearly had my men under control by the time we reached Coonasatchee, but there we found the body of a white man still tied to the stake where he had been burned. There was no controlling them after that. We broke the light siege on Fort Prince George easily. The Cherokee retreated into the western forest."

Grant's tone has been growing stronger and angrier, but the aide who sets the tea tray on the desk seems to recall him to himself, and he sits and pours the tea with as great a grace as if he were hosting the king himself.

When it is offered, I take the hot pewter cup by its wooden handle. My fingertips sting as I balance the cup, but I keep my hold.

"So you will not relieve Fort Loudoun?" I ask.

Grant shakes his head. "Of course. Of course we will try. The people there are our countrymen, of a sort. However little I care for the methods of colonials, what choice do I have? Please, drink your tea, Miss Blair. I ask your apologies for speaking so strongly."

I sip, relishing the strong, bitter flavor. Relishing, too, the chance to feel normal again, to be treated as a guest in a civilized home, even if that home is only the commandant's house at Fort Prince George. But I let myself relax for only a moment.

"There's something else I must tell you," I say. I nod at the letters. "You're being less than fair to Captain Demere. He did not simply send a woman to plead for him. He didn't want to let me come at all. I insisted. You see, I've been trying to report a serious crime to the British authorities for nearly six months now, and I've battled obstacles at every turn. The more I consider it, the more pertinent I think it must be to the course of the war and to relations between the Carolina settlers and the Cherokee."

Grant leans back in his chair, leaving his tea untouched on the desk. He crosses his arms and clears his throat. "Go on."

I sketch the events of that December morning, the days that followed, and the conversation I overheard between Donald Campbell and Sam Murray that ended in Murray's death.

"I think it must matter to the war," I say. "Because Donald Campbell did something, something he wanted to make sure no one knew about, so he silenced my father and the rest of my family. I imagine he killed the Ramsays because they were close to us, and to make the raid look more authentic. He has been here, in this very fort. I saw him this morning. He tried to persuade me to leave with him."

Grant nods, his face pensive, his tea cooling in its cup. "Yes, he came to introduce himself. He's been trying to catch us all the way from Ninety Six, so he said, to offer his services and allegiance, though what use he thinks we have for him I couldn't say."

"He doesn't care what use you have for him," I say. "That's a ploy. He cares what use he has for you. He's glad to see you. He wants you to strike the Cherokee hard. He wants anything that will allow him to beg, borrow, or steal more land. He hopes your presence means he'll soon be able to return to his former land in safety. He hopes the war will push the legal treaty line west, leaving him with more open land."

Grant's fingers tap a tattoo on the desk. "Miss Blair. I am certainly extremely interested in any behaviors that would serve to increase or prolong the state of war between the colony of South Carolina and the Cherokee nation. I find this war abhorrent in every particular and consider it my great misfortune to be forced to participate in it. But all I have is your word, and all the other witnesses are dead. It is unlikely anyone would believe the word of a—forgive me—a woman who had just witnessed the murder of her family and was likely hysterical against that of a clearheaded man."

For a moment, my stomach rises in anger. Donald Campbell is the furthest thing from clearheaded. "But that's not true," I say. "There's another witness, and he's here with me. His name is Owen Ramsay. He survived the attack on his family and sought shelter at Fort Loudoun, as I did. He isn't with me now because he was injured several days ago in an encounter with the Cherokee. I don't believe he is in immediate danger, but he is greatly weakened. I came to you also to beg him the care of your surgeon."

"By all means," says Grant. "When he is strong enough, I would love to hear his witness. Together, your words corroborated by his, you might have enough for me to act."

After all this time, all these travels, and so many disappointments, I am reluctant to believe this man can help me any more than the others could.

"Do you really have the authority to move against Donald Campbell?" I am wary.

Grant smiles. It's a handsome smile, but behind it is something like a cat with a juicy bird. "Miss Blair, the royal governor has abandoned South Carolina for his new post in Jamaica. The acting governor cowers in Charlestown. Save the Ninety Six courthouse, there is not a building left standing west of the Congaree River. I have just broken the Cherokee hold on this area and stripped the corrupt officers of this fort of their honors. My own commanding officer is indisposed. I am the authority in this little backwater of the world. It would be my great pleasure to move against those who perpetuate a state of unjust war with the Cherokee nation and keep His Majesty's forces from their nobler aims."

"I feel the same," I answer, trembling a little at the feel of the power behind Grant's words, at the prospect of at last making Donald Campbell accountable for his crimes. "And I want justice for my family's deaths at the hands of a man who is not a soldier, but a cold-blooded murderer."

"My actions on your behalf must be subordinate to the needs of the military, of course," says Grant. "But I think I can promise you Donald Campbell will pull no wool over my eyes."

I stand to go, realizing the interview is at an end. At last I remember to ask about my own accommodation. For a moment Grant's eyes flicker over my body, and I fear his help may come at a higher price than I am prepared to pay, but at last I secure a tent for Amelia and me to share. In case it is needed, Grant writes a pass for Owen to be taken to the surgeon. Afraid I will make Malcolm conspicuous by not mentioning him, I tell Grant another man traveled with us from Fort Loudoun and hear he can bed wherever he can find a place.

As I prepare to leave, Grant lifts my hand to his lips. "We must be sure of our course," he says sadly. "So often it is hard to tell the hands of a soldier from those of a cold-blooded murderer." He sighs. "After the march through the Lower Towns, I fear I cannot tell the difference myself."

39.

June 7, 1760

Night

The quartermaster allots Amelia and me a small space for a tent against one of the fort's inner walls. As I prepare to sleep, feeling reasonably safe for the first time in a long while, I realize Amelia's visible exhaustion has more to do with the grief she's trying to outrun than with our escape from Fort Loudoun and subsequent days in Cherokee territory. Lying on my borrowed bedroll, I listen to her sob in her sleep until I can't bear it any longer.

I sit up, pulling off my cap and running a hand through my tangled hair. I will be so glad when it's long enough to braid.

"I'm not asleep, Amelia," I whisper. "We can talk about it, if you like."

Amelia rolls toward me. She raises herself up, pressing her fingers to her eyes, flicking away tears. "I'm sorry I woke you," she says. "You must think very little of me. I know I must have slowed you down on the way here, but after what happened I couldn't spend one more minute at Fort Loudoun without running completely mad."

I fluff the top of my shift, trying to get air down to my skin. The air is close in the tent, and the summer night is warm and heavy.

"You didn't slow us down at all," I say. "We were lucky you were there when Owen was hurt. And you stood up to Donald Campbell today, which is more than I've done."

Amelia pulls her knees to her chest and presses her forehead into them. In the dark, her white cap and shift stand out starkly, their purity marred by the spill of her dark braid down her back. Her breath rattles in her chest, a choking kind of sob.

"I'm not like you, Catie. I'm not strong like you. I wasn't made for the frontier, and I never should have been here. I never would have been if I hadn't married a militia officer. I thought Adam would be fairly safe, the war being in the north, and the regular army so disdainful of the colonial militia.

I thought he'd just drill and march around home. I never thought he'd go to war. And Fort Loudoun—Fort Loudoun shouldn't have been at war. They were only supposed to garrison a fort. Adam wanted me to stay home, and I should have, but I couldn't stand to think of him going off and never coming back and waiting and waiting and never knowing whether he was alive or dead. That's what happens to so many men. They cross the treaty line, and they never come back. And now my children are dead because I had to go with him. Because I couldn't let any of them go, I've lost them all."

Slowly, the fragmented threads in my head weave themselves together. My confusion about my parents shakes itself out, and things I never understood before become clear. I crawl over to Amelia and put my arms around her. Her shoulder blades are sharp against my chest.

"I think you are strong, Amelia. You're strong in the way my mother was strong. She hated it here, but she loved my father, and that's why she came with him. She couldn't stand the thought of sitting comfortably somewhere far away while he was living on the edge of the world."

I swallow over the lump that rises in my throat, thinking of my poor parents, so out of place, so unable to comprehend the two children the frontier had claimed. No wonder they loved Jaime so much.

"I know a little of what you're going through, because I lost my whole family almost at once, too."

I smooth a lock of damp hair away from her forehead. "But I've never lost a husband or a child, so I don't know what that's like."

We sit in silence for several minutes, both lost in a world of memory where the dead live on, and then Amelia laughs through a sob. "Why are we still alive, Catie? When you first told me about your plan, I thought you were a fool. I grieved for you because I believed you'd never make it to Fort Prince George. And then I envied you, because you lost your family, but you could fight back. You knew who killed them. How could I fight against illness or against an entire war? I wanted to come with you because I was quite sure we were all going to die. And now I'm still alive, but my life feels over."

She looks down, smoothing the corner of the rough army blanket between her fingers. "Poor Gabriel Swan," she says. "That poor man."

My arms tighten around Amelia. "I think it will get better for you," I say. "When my parents and Mark were killed, I had to keep going for Jaime's sake, but after he died, I felt I really had no reason to live any longer. I didn't want to, because the pain was so bad I couldn't stand it. But now—I don't know how to say it—the pain isn't better, exactly, but I'm more used to it. I can go through my days without it distracting me at every turn."

I put a hand to my throat, and my fingers find the edge of the scar that pokes over the neckline of my shift. "I think it's like a scar. I'll always have these scars. My body will always be marred, and sometimes it still hurts, but I don't think about it all the time. Once I'm dressed, I often forget the scars are there until something reminds me. And then I remember, and it hurts. The grief is like that. I carry it with me everywhere, but sometimes I keep it covered up. There will always be a time before and a time after. It's one of the great dividing lines of my life. But I'm starting to feel my life will go on. And yours will, too."

Amelia gives me half a sad smile through her tears.

"You're stronger than I am, though, really." I disentangle my body from hers and return to my own bedroll. "At least you're able to face it, to cry. I haven't been able to, not really, not yet."

Because my tears are biding their time, waiting until I can bring Donald Campbell low, more patient, now that I know he is near, and his destruction a possibility.

40.

June 8, 1760

Before Dawn

I don't know how long I've been asleep when the hand clamped over my mouth wakes me. The palm is thick and meaty, smelling of sour sweat, and I gnash my teeth, tasting salt and skin. My eyes dart to Amelia's bedroll, but she is gone. I thrash wildly, making as much noise as I can with the hand sealing my mouth and nose shut, until the flash of a knife above my head shocks me into silence.

As the knife strikes, the tent's front flap lifts, spilling moonlight. A shadowy form I recognize as Malcolm's silhouette appears, swearing in Erse at the man whose knife just sliced the skin at my hairline. The silver dirk is in his hand, ready for fighting in close quarters. My attacker turns me loose and tries to escape out the back of the tent, but Malcolm is too quick for him, and in a second the man is pinned to the ground under his knee. The dirk presses into the fleshy throat. I don't have to look to know it is

Donald Campbell, come to finish off the last of the Blairs before she can expose him.

"Would you kill a woman in her sleep?" Malcolm spits.

I grope under the bedroll for my own knife and then wrap the blanket around my body. Donald Campbell is not going to get the pleasure of viewing me in my shift any longer than I can help it.

"He slaughtered two families," I say. "I doubt he has any qualms about killing a woman in her sleep."

Campbell's eyes dart about the tent.

"Where's Amelia?" I ask.

"Gone to the necessary," he says, with a kind of exaggerated courtesy. "I waited for her to leave. I have no wish to bother killing those who don't need to die."

Malcolm's blade presses into Campbell's throat. A red line appears, thin as thread. My hand goes to my own throat, to my blue ribbons.

"Malcolm," I warn.

"Listen to your little lover," says Campbell. "Kill me and you'll hang."

Malcolm leans harder on Campbell's chest, forcing a cough. "You tried to kill Catriona. Shouldn't you be the one hanging?"

Campbell smiles indulgently, as if we are intolerably stupid. "The regiment thinks itself safe since they have driven the Cherokee back. They think the encampment around the fort is enough of a guard, enough to deter their enemies. The guards are tired, and it is late. Men fall asleep. What a shame that a Cherokee slipped through and killed a woman, then left without a trace."

He laughs. "So your real name is Catriona? Your poor mother, passing you off as a Catherine all those years."

I cut a strip of cloth from my blanket and press it to the new wound on my forehead, which is bleeding freely, the blood wet and warm on my face.

"Catriona, I know this man," says Malcolm. "And I would see him hang as gladly for his other deeds as I would for your sake. We should take him to Grant."

Campbell's eyes flicker up to meet mine. "I think Miss Blair knows that would be a bad idea," he says. "Her word against mine—a hysterical woman against an upstanding citizen trying to bring peace." His eyes cut back to Malcolm. "Isn't it lucky I knew the area and was here to protect her? Unless you'd like to come with us?"

There's a terrible threat in Campbell's voice, and I have a dreadful feeling I know what it is. I'm beginning to feel lightheaded. I need to lie down and get the bleeding to stop.

The threat in Campbell's voice makes my decision easy. I cannot get him to Grant on my own. I cannot let Malcolm come with me, nor can I draw the attention of the regiment with Malcolm here. If we kill him now, at least one of us will hang for murder, and if Malcolm is recognized, he will be shot for desertion. But there are a few things I need to know before I am forced to let Campbell go.

"Why?" I ask. "Why did you kill my family? And the Ramsays? How did you get our neighbors to help you?"

Campbell grunts a laugh. "Didn't you ever realize you weren't welcome here?" he asks. "Your lowlander father with his learning and his books. Your English mother with her silks and her snobbery. Thought you were a bit too good for us, didn't you all, even that dandy little brother of yours and he just a child? Good as a missionary to the heathen, your father was, bringing the word of God to the savage backcountry."

I have no reply because I know Campbell speaks truth. Father did see himself that way. Mother was more than a little haughty. Jaime was weak.

"Oh, but he put the savage heathen of the mountains before us, did your father. Quite a one for rule of law, for not pushing past the borders agreed upon by Britain and her precious Cherokee ally. But your father chose to be here, didn't he? He didn't have his cottage razed by his own laird, he wasn't chased away from his home like a criminal in the night. He didn't watch his children's bodies fall in the crossfire between his landlord and King George's men."

Malcolm grimaces, but he keeps his hold on Campbell. I recall what he told me of the Forty-Five, of the poor highlanders forced to fight for landowners like his own father and then treated as traitors by the Crown.

"Did they force you to fight in the Forty-Five, Campbell?" I ask. "Is that why you came here? Were you transported to America as a penalty?"

Campbell's body twists, but he does not answer.

"Your father didn't understand that Britain cares more for what those savages can do for her than about her own people. He didn't understand that Britain would never give us the land we deserve, so we had to take it whether the Crown willed it or no."

"You wanted land," I say calmly. "That is reasonable enough. But it doesn't explain why you killed my family. Did you want our land?"

"Your land," he scoffs. "Your land is no good for anything but settling the preacher on."

"Then what did my father know?" I ask.

"What he shouldn't have," says Campbell. "That simpleton, Sam Murray. He told your father about the women of Estatoe."

Estatoe is one of the Cherokee Lower Towns, one Grant confessed to burning in the night. I recall what Mark told me about the attacks on the women of the Lower Towns while the warriors were away fighting the French and their allies. A hard ball of ice forms in my belly at the thought of the Cherokee women left for the wolves, but I manage to hold my voice steady.

"What about the other attacks? Were you responsible for those?"

He shrugs, still laughing. "One or two, perhaps. Certainly not all." He grins nastily. "Did you think when you'd killed me you'd be done with the evil in the world? You won't. There were so many others, there are so many others, who will fight for their right to land. English, highlander, lowlander, Cherokee, it doesn't matter. Did you ever think I might care for my land as much as you care for your family?" His voice falls. "Did you ever think you might be the one who is wrong? Or that your holy father might not be so holy? He never reported what he knew."

"Because you killed him."

"Perhaps. But he had time before that. Months. He was probably—thinking—about what was best to be done. That's what your father was good at—thinking. Not acting."

Campbell is taunting me, thinking he will get me to lower my guard, thinking his words will weaken me. But I knew all this long ago.

"If you think I don't know that about my father, you don't give me much credit. Neither of my parents was suited for the backcountry. They weren't happy, but they always did what they thought was right, and if my father spent too much time thinking when he should have been reporting you to the governor, it was because he had so much to think about."

My voice rises in fury and grief.

"It seems to me you don't think enough. You're one of those who started this war, and it has brought you nothing. It has brought the settlers nothing. You underestimated the Cherokee. The frontier line has been pushed east by a hundred miles, and your countrymen are wasting away at Fort Loudoun. Your land is worthless. Is this what you wanted? Is this what you planned?"

My words appear to have no effect on Campbell. Perhaps the questions are too big, their answers too broad.

"Why the Ramsays?" I ask at last. My voice cracks in spite of me. "Why did you have to kill the Ramsays?"

Campbell twists under Malcolm's weight, which Malcolm takes as an invitation to yank him up and slam him against the ground.

"Answer her," he says.

"You were close to the Ramsays," Campbell says. "You were all outsiders. Your father could easily have let something slip. And a raid on two farms looks more realistic than a raid on one only."

I press the rag harder into the cut on my forehead. I feel like the blood is taking my ability to think with it.

"Let him go, Malcolm," I say. Malcolm looks up, uncertain, and I nod. He climbs off Campbell's chest and lets him stand, keeping the cruel sword-blade of the dirk trained on him.

"Get out," he says. "And if you ever come near Catriona Blair again, I'll kill you, hanging or no."

"You think you know who I am?" Campbell laughs. "I remember you, too, young highlander."

Campbell scrambles out of the tent, anxious to be gone now that his plan has failed. Malcolm sees him well out and rapidly turns.

He takes me by the shoulders. "Did he hurt you, sweet?"

"Not badly." I grimace at the stinging pain of the cut.

"Let me see," he says. "Thank God there's a bit of a moon tonight."

He pulls my fingers and the bloody rag away from the wound. My cap has fallen off somewhere, and despite what just happened, the feel of Malcolm's fingers on my face is enough to make me long for the winter nights in the mountain shelter.

"It's not as bad as I feared," says Malcolm. "It bled a great deal, but it's stopped now. The cut itself is not so deep, and I think it will heal cleanly."

Malcolm grips me to his chest. "I'm sorry I let him get so close to you, sweet," he says. "I saw Amelia leave, and I thought I heard her coming back. I was nodding off."

"You can't be awake all the time," I whisper. "Thank God you were here at all."

A horrifying thought shudders through my brain.

"Owen," I say. "Where is Owen? Malcolm, he's killing off witnesses. Owen isn't safe."

I drop the blanket and fumble for my clothes, pulling my overskirt and gown on quickly and leaving the other articles in a messy pile.

"Owen was seen and released by the surgeon's mate," he says. "They changed the bandage and put a poultice on, but beyond that, there wasn't much they could do. We bedded down with the provincials at first. I felt uneasy about leaving you alone, so I came to keep watch here later in the night."

"Campbell will be looking for him," I say. "Malcolm, we've got to find him."

"Catriona." Malcolm grips my hands. "I'm not leaving you again tonight. I suspected Campbell of something like this."

"We have to warn Owen," I insist. "We'll go together."

Amelia returns, startled to see Malcolm in our tent and a bloody rag on my head. Malcolm waits outside while Amelia discards the blanket she is wrapped in and scrambles quickly into her most necessary articles of clothing, and then the three of us find Owen and wake him and bring him to my and Amelia's tent.

Though Malcolm tells me the men sleep six to a campaign tent like this one, it feels cramped with four of us inside. Owen is still weakened by his wound, and Amelia by her tears, so they fall asleep quickly.

"Malcolm," I whisper, stretching my hand toward his dark form. He rolls toward me, closing the gap between our bodies. I press myself into him, realizing what a relief it is to be against him again, how much it heals.

"What did Campbell mean when he said he knew you?"

Malcolm takes my hand and entwines my fingers with his.

"I told you long ago I took refuge among the Cherokee after Fort Duquesne. That's how I knew Kanagatucko, how I earned permission to live on Cherokee land. I went with some of the warriors to help them defend the Lower Towns. There had been attacks, rapes, killings by a band of settlers, and it seemed this was more of the same. One of the men was Donald Campbell. I thought I recognized him earlier today, but when I saw him up close tonight, I was sure. Even if you had no quarrel with him, I know enough to hang him several times. This was one of the attacks before war was declared, you see. Completely unlawful in every way. And the Cherokee and the colony were trying to keep peace."

My mouth is a tight line as I consider this. "How did he know you were a deserter? Weren't there other white men among the Cherokee? Traders and the like?"

"I don't think he was sure. But he suspected, and our reaction to his threats has been enough to tell him he's right."

So now I have another reason to wish Donald Campbell dead. He is not only the murderer of my family, my own pursuer. He is a threat to Malcolm, too. I need to know we are safe from him. I need to make us safe from him. But now I need to sleep, and I need to know I am not alone. I press as close as I can to Malcolm's warm body, nestling my bloodied forehead against his chest.

41.

June 8, 1760

Dawn

I don't sleep well, despite the comfort of Malcolm's body. I am too alert, too confused, too acutely aware that the desires of my heart have come crashing up against each other, and unlike the ancient slabs of rock that formed the mountain shelter, the two of them supporting each other is not a possibility. Malcolm's account of the attack in my tent, corroborated by my own, might be enough for Grant to arrest Campbell, if he could find him. But Malcolm cannot speak to Grant. The lieutenant-colonel would certainly recognize one of his lieutenants, especially one who was with him at the disastrous attack on Fort Duquesne. The price of holding Donald Campbell last night would have been a musket ball through Malcolm's heart.

I am still dressed in the clothes I pulled on last night, and I sit up and brush my hair with my fingers, tucking it under my cap as best I can, trying to make it appear my hair is only pinned up, not cut short. The air of the tent is close with too many bodies, and I wonder how six fully grown men can ever sleep comfortably in here.

I crawl outside, gulping in the clean air of dawn. Beyond the fort walls, I hear the noises of early morning, the metallic clack of equipment hitting other equipment, the snorting of horses. I stand, staring up at the log palisade of Fort Prince George. I can come and go from this place. It is not in the desperate position of Fort Loudoun. But it's smaller, tighter, and I have the curious feeling of walls closing in, of a snare I didn't expect preparing to capture me.

I sense Malcolm's body block the breeze to my back, as I sensed his presence beside me so often in the darkness of the mountain shelter, and I turn and look up, lifting my hand to brush the dark curls from his face.

"You should leave your hair like this," I say. "It's safer. You look more like a woodsman and less like an officer."

He smiles, but he ties his hair back loosely with an old ribbon. I try to speak, but the words stop in my throat, caught on an old sob I have to cough free.

"You can't stay here, Malcolm," I tell him. "It's too dangerous, and I won't let you. Campbell recognizes you as surely as you recognize him. I don't know if it matters, since you weren't with your regiment when he saw you, but if Grant sees you . . . I won't let you take the risk."

Malcolm raises an eyebrow. "Not even to hang Donald Campbell?"

I shake my head. "I've been thinking about what my mother would say. She always told me all the frontier did was take life. I'm sure she would tell me this isn't worth another life."

Malcolm smiles, sad amusement. "I didn't know you had a habit of listening to your mother."

"I don't. But she'd be right in this case. I'm still going after Donald Campbell, but you can't go with me. Once I report the attack, I think Grant will keep me safe enough. I don't need you to stay."

Malcolm's fingers settle on my temples, and he nudges my cap back to inspect the wound Campbell inflicted last night.

"If you think I'm going to leave you alone when Campbell has already tried to kill you once, in this very fort, surrounded by the regiment, you're madder than he is."

"Malcolm, you can't stay," I insist, gripping his arms. "Not to protect me, not even to bear witness against Campbell. If they find you out, they'll shoot you. I can't watch them shoot you. I can't lose anyone else I . . ."

I trail off. I was about to say *love*, but I can't. There's no point in loving anyone until Donald Campbell is dead. I think of Mark and swallow hard.

"I can't be the reason another person dies."

"Oh," says Malcolm, a bit roughly. "I was beginning to think it was because you cared for me, but it's because you don't want my blood on your conscience."

"I do care for you, Malcolm," I say desperately, not knowing what matters more, that he understands my feelings or that he leaves, that he just gets away from this terrible danger. "I care for you very much, which is why you must leave."

Malcolm gazes over my head, over the walls of the fort to the surrounding tree-covered hills.

"Where would you have me go?" he asks. "The woods are full of Cherokee looking to kill Englishmen. Being a Scot won't save me, especially since a highland regiment just destroyed the Lower Towns."

"I don't know," I answer. "But you can't stay here. It's too dangerous. Do you think Grant won't recognize one of his officers?"

Malcolm shakes his head slowly. "I can hide in the woods," he says. "But that's no safer than taking my chances here, and I don't like the notion of leaving you to Campbell's madness."

"I won't be alone," I say. "I'll tell Grant what happened, and he'll give me a guard. I'm sure of it. He likes me. He doesn't like Campbell, for all Campbell's toadying."

I feel the sting of tears in my eyes. "Please, Malcolm. Please go."

He shakes his head and pulls me forward by the elbows so my arms wrap naturally around the small of his back. My mouth is beside his ear, and I whisper, "I won't be alone, I promise you. I'll have Owen."

When Owen himself approaches me a quarter of an hour later, I am still standing there, gazing with dry eyes toward the small sally port. He looks at my blank face and asks, "Where's the highlander?"

I turn to him, raising my hands, a gesture of surrender. "Gone."

42.

June 8, 1760

Morning

If Owen suspects why Malcolm has left us, he makes no mention of it. When I ask him to accompany me to the commandant's quarters, he comes willingly, without the resistance I sensed in him earlier. Grant sits behind his desk, his large body overwhelming the small room, his fingers impossibly immaculate, the nails manicured to perfection. The same silent aide-de-camp sits to one side, taking down our words.

"I heard from Miss Blair yesterday, Mr. Ramsay," says Grant. "Let us now hear what you have to say."

With a start of shame, I realize I have never asked Owen exactly what happened to his family on the morning of the attack. I have been selfishly consumed with my own grief, obsessed with claiming my revenge and restoring some semblance of safety and order to my life. I never once stopped to listen to Owen's story.

As he speaks quietly, I begin to understand how deep his horror goes and how he has attempted to cope by avoiding the rage rather than by living inside it as I have. I look at Owen with new eyes. Perhaps when he said the only way to move on was to move forward, he was right, for himself, at least. We have been looking past each other, misunderstanding, failing to acknowledge that our paths to healing might be different, each of us knowing and fearing that the day that split our lives in two would have split us apart even if I had never met the lost highlander.

"It was just dawn," Owen says. "I had woken early and gone out to the barn to feed the hogs. It was cold. The first thing I heard was the hatchets hitting the door and then my stepmother screaming and begging them to leave my sister alone."

Owen swallows, his eyes far away. Just dawn. They hit the Ramsays first. I take Owen's hand and squeeze, trying to pass the strength to continue from my skin to his.

"My sister, Agnes, was only seven. I heard her crying and my stepmother screaming, and then the noise—stopped. I never heard my father, so I hoped he might have escaped."

Owen pauses and looks up at Grant, his green eyes empty and broken like shattered glass. "I knew he hadn't. He never would have left them. I caught a glimpse of them as they fired the house. Until that moment, I had assumed it was a Cherokee raid. I was trying to think what to do. It happened so fast I didn't have time to try to fight back."

Owen looks up at us, his eyes pleading for absolution as the aide's quill scratches over the page.

"Something about it didn't look right. I couldn't believe it at first, but I recognized the men. It must have been something in their mannerisms, the way they walked. And then I realized it was Donald Campbell and a group of five or six men I thought had gone east to get away from the war. I knew they'd check the barn next—they'd know to look for me—so I lit out over the fields for the Blairs' place to warn them, but I had to go the longer way round, and by the time I got there it was too late, and they had been attacked, too."

Owen buries his face in his good hand for a long moment before he continues. "I spoke to Mark Blair—Catie's brother—warned him it wasn't the Cherokee. I guess he'd been thinking the same thing I had, that we'd all be safest hiding in the woods until it was over and then we'd better go east."

Owen sucks in his breath, and his hand convulses around mine. "Sometimes people do survive attacks. I've even heard of those few who have survived scalping. Once I had warned the Blairs, I needed to get back to my own family and see what could be done. My brother, Roger—he was a year younger than I am—had left the house with me, but by the time the attack came he was driving the cows to pasture. I thought there was a good chance he had escaped, and I said as much to Mark. I agreed to circle back and meet Mark and Catie and Jaime later that afternoon. Roger was dead. I found him in the pasture. I—was delayed. I had to hide from Campbell's men again when they came back for the livestock. I couldn't get back to the Blairs that day, and there was no one at Fish Falls when I arrived, so I set out for Fort Loudoun on my own, hoping I'd meet the Blairs on the road, but I never did. I thought Catie and Jaime would be safe enough with Mark. I thought even if winter caught them in the mountains, Mark would know how to take care of them. I didn't know until Catie arrived at Fort Loudoun that Mark had been killed, too."

Owen's voice catches, and I realize he lost a dear childhood friend in Mark, even as I lost a brother. I feel tears starting, too, for Roger, the funniest little playmate I ever had, and for dear little Agnes and Patrick and Alice Ramsay. Strange how, all this time, I have not thought of them as among the dead.

"My stepmother wanted to go east," Owen adds. "We planned to leave the next week, just after Christmas. We were waiting."

Owen looks at me. The Ramsays weren't waiting for Christmas. They were waiting for Owen to propose to me and our engagement to be an accepted thing.

Grant remains matter-of-fact, not visibly moved. He must have seen so much death he has become inured to it.

"You were significantly delayed in reaching Fort Loudoun, were you not, Miss Blair?" asks Grant.

"Yes," I answer. "My younger brother, Jaime, and I were attacked by a catamount. Jaime was killed, and I was badly injured."

Grant looks me over, appraisal in his eyes, wondering where and how badly my body is damaged. "And how did you manage to survive your injuries?"

"I wasn't alone," I answer. "A man who was living in the mountains found me and treated my injuries and also sheltered me through the winter."

"And where is this man now?" asks Grant. His voice is so cool. He cannot possibly know the true answer. Perhaps all he sees is a woman whose virtue he cannot harm.

"He accompanied me to Fort Loudoun," I say. "And again to Fort Prince George, as he had great knowledge of the mountains." I'm not lying yet. "But our party from Fort Loudoun was attacked not far from here, no doubt in retaliation for the destruction of the Lower Towns, and he was killed."

"What was this man's name?"

I watch the aide's quill, poised to scribble down my words.

"Gabriel Swan," I answer, avoiding Owen's eyes, praying for his cooperation.

"Is this all the information you have for me?" Grant asks.

"No," I answer. "I hope you won't think me indelicate, but I need you to have a look at my scalp." I stand and pull back my cap. Though the bleeding has stopped, the wound still feels sticky.

Grant leans forward to peer at my scalp. "That's a fresh wound."

"I was attacked last night, in my tent, by Donald Campbell. If you need further proof of his guilt, there it is. He knows I know what he did to my family, and he's trying to make sure no one remains to accuse him."

"I see." Grant rounds the desk, frowning. "May I ask how you managed to fight him off, when you were taken unawares and he is so much larger and stronger?"

My heart starts to race, and my mind is drawn again to the darting eyes of the rabbit caught in the vines. It seems no matter what I do, I will betray Malcolm. I am about to speak when I hear Owen's voice.

"I was keeping a watch on Catie's tent," he says. "We knew Campbell was in the area, and I didn't feel comfortable leaving her alone."

I breathe out, feeling my heart slow. If only it had been Owen who drove Campbell off last night.

Grant tilts his head to one side, regarding Owen's arm. Blood is seeping through the new dressing. "You were able to drive him off in your injured state?"

Owen glances down at the wound. "It's not as bad as it looks. And Catie helped me once she was awake."

"Why did you not take him captive at once, then?"

"We couldn't," I answer. "We had the strength to make him leave but not to hold him."

Grant shakes his head. "Do you have any idea why Campbell might have attacked your families, other than to make it appear that the Cherokee had killed settlers and thus feed the fires of war?"

"I believe I do know," I say. "One of Campbell's men confessed information to my father that implicated Campbell in attacks on the Cherokee. Campbell found out and decided to silence my father. I imagine he thought my father might have shared this information with his family. And then, of course, he had to kill us once he knew we were witnesses to his crime."

Owen's story made me realize something else. Campbell attacked the Ramsays for an entirely different reason.

"The Ramsays were our closest neighbors and friends, and I've been thinking that's why they were attacked."

I turn to Owen. "But didn't you say they came back for the livestock? Owen, your family was quite well off. They stole the livestock. That must be it. They would have pretended they found the animals roaming after the attack, and with none of the family left, anyone could have claimed them."

Grant sighs. "I have been thinking of the best way to handle this, Miss Blair. I'm afraid I have come only to the conclusion that Donald Campbell is a sly fox, and it will be difficult to catch him in the chicken house. Give me time to think on it."

He returns to the desk and scribbles a pass. "You see the surgeon's mate about that wound. It doesn't look too serious, but best to have a look. He can give you a decent bandage, at least. I will summon you to my quarters when I have anything more to tell you."

43.

June 8, 1760

Afternoon

Mercifully, the surgeon's mate decides the slice under my hairline doesn't need stitches. He cleans the wound and covers it with a bandage that winds around my head. Most of the bandage and the wound itself are covered by my cap. Though I expect the question, Owen does not ask why I lied about Malcolm's identity. For the moment, he is taking my word that Malcolm is gone and seems unwilling to upset the fragile peace between us.

Late in the afternoon, Grant calls Owen and me back to his quarters. He stands when we enter and invites us to seat ourselves before his desk.

"I believe I may have an answer," says Grant. "Though it will require some considerable risk for you both. I cannot guarantee you will escape unscathed, or even alive, though in this troubled time and place, that is not a guarantee I could offer anyone."

Grant does not sit. Instead, he paces restlessly behind his desk, his large body graceful, reminding me of the delicate heaviness of the catamount's tread, of the deadly beauty of the animal who split my body open.

"I find myself in an unenviable position in this colony," says Grant. "Though I have no personal quarrel with them, the Cherokee are, naturally, hostile toward the regiment. I have little sympathy with the local settlers, yet I cannot afford to provoke their animosity. Few as they are in number, though the ones who remain are in hiding, we cannot afford the hostility of settlers, too. They will likely return in droves once they hear the Lower Towns have been sacked and the Cherokee driven into the mountains, and I cannot go about arresting them, much less hanging them, on only your word."

Grant pauses, and a great wave of disappointment, anger, and frustration nearly overwhelms me. He will not help me, after all. I thought he would, but he won't. No one will ever help me. Donald Campbell killed my family, and he is going to get away with it. I'm looking at my lap, trying to hide the tears and control the fury, so I nearly miss Grant's next words.

"To accomplish our objective, we will have to catch Campbell in the act of murder or kill him in self defense."

I look up, disbelieving. Catching my confusion, Grant attempts to explain.

"You say Campbell wants you dead, Miss Blair. Well, then, he hasn't left you. He will be waiting for another chance to kill you. We will set a trap, and you will be the bait."

Grant sweeps the contents of his desk to one side with his arm and begins to inscribe a map with his finger.

"We will pretend your party was sent from Fort Loudoun solely to plead for relief. Having heard your plea, I cannot keep you at Fort Prince George, not when I'm preparing to use it as a staging ground to move against the

Middle Towns, so my duty is to get you as far east as the new frontier line. To safety, as it were. Now, as is natural, you desire to stop at your former home, to see it, to search for a memento, perhaps. We will make sure Campbell knows you are leaving the fort and knows the route you will take. I will not send you alone, of course. No, I will give you an escort, and I myself will accompany you, under the guise of exploring the country. It makes sense for me to do that. The regiment will not move on the Middle Towns for some weeks, and Colonel Montgomery is well enough to resume command here. As his second, it makes sense for me to do some light reconnaissance. And it suits me."

Grant points to the invisible map again. "Now, it is doubtful Campbell has enough allies left to risk attacking a large party, so I will make it known our party will divide. I will take the bulk of the men with me, leaving the two of you with a small escort—four men or so—to take you for a brief visit to your former homes. I wager Campbell will keep to his plan of concealing his own misdeeds under the guise of Cherokee attacks, especially in such an inviting scenario. He will take the opportunity to attack a smaller party. You will not know when, so you must be on your guard. There is a risk he will fire upon you from a distance, but that does not follow his typical pattern."

I nod silently, thinking of all the ways this plan could go wrong. All the ways I could die if I follow it. The heat in the room is smotheringly close.

"You have escaped him before," says Grant. "God willing, you will do so again, and end his hold over you. The escort of soldiers I send should be enough to protect you. If Campbell attacks British troops, he will die by British fire."

I swallow over the anxiety that rises in my throat. Until this conversation, it seemed like an easy thing, a thing removed from me, to report Donald Campbell and have him hanged for his crimes. Now it could not seem more complicated. Owen sits beside me, quiet, holding his injured arm with the other.

Grant makes a noise of sympathy in his throat. "If you have no questions for me, then you are free to go. I will take a few days to spread the word, to make sure Campbell hears of our plans, and then we will act."

Grant stands to see us out. Owen steps back to let me go first, but I turn.

"Why are you doing this?" I ask Grant. "I'm very glad you are, but I confess I didn't expect it to be so easy to convince you to help me. Most people would have told me not to risk my own life to avenge my family, especially after all this time." Even Malcolm told me that, months ago.

Grant smiles, again the look of a cat with a bird. "I am not most people. I believe you have the right to risk your life in the ways you see fit, for the causes in which you believe. And I am using you, too. It is not only sympathy that leads me to help you. I believe the war between the Cherokee and South Carolina colony is a great wrong. I abhor my own participation in it. I believe the Cherokee would like to have peace but are unable to get it from the colony, thanks in part to the influence of men like Donald Campbell who would see the end of many innocent lives, British and Cherokee, and watch the mountains burn to gain more land. Great wrong has been done here, and stupid, reckless men have been give charge over matters they do not understand. I have made it my business since I landed at Charlestown to remove these men from power, insofar as I am able. I have relieved Ensign Miln, Coytmore's heir in spirit and in deed, from his command of this fort, and I hope to do the same to Captain Paul Demere, should we reach Fort Loudoun, which, in truth, I do not expect to. If Donald Campbell is one of those settlers who attacked Britain's Cherokee allies in time of peace, then he is guilty of treason as well as murder."

Grant pauses, then finishes simply. "I make it my business to destroy him. If that brings some peace to you, I am glad of it."

I don't know if it will bring me peace, if anything can bring me peace after these long months of loss, of destruction, of the breaking of bonds and the cutting of ties.

Mentally, I count again the scars on my breast. Four. One for Mother. One for Father. One for Mark, the one that tore deep into my flesh, the one that will never quite heal. One small one for Jaime. I touch my fingers to my bandaged forehead. And now another. One small, sharp cut for the man who touched my life so briefly and with such sweet, exquisite pain. Malcolm, whom I will not see again.

44.

June 14–16, 1760

Lieutenant-Colonel Grant is as good as his word. He spreads a rumor that he will send Amelia, Owen, and me east with an escort as far as the relative safety of the new frontier line. A couple of days later, another rumor follows:

the escort party will divide, with the smaller group taking Owen and me by our former homes and the larger one continuing on with Grant to assess the damage to local settlements. The rumors also tell that Grant will rejoin our small band, ostensibly on his way to confer with Lieutenant Governor Bull and to investigate further the state of the backcountry. I know Grant is doing his best to force Donald Campbell to act while Campbell believes I am most vulnerable, and I am both grateful and fearful.

We leave Fort Prince George early in the morning, before the dew has burned off the grass in the heat of the day. Our escort is a platoon of soldiers, about twenty men who fall into formation behind Grant and their lieutenant. It is a journey of several days to the new frontier line, so two horses have been spared to pull a supply wagon behind the platoon. Because Owen is still weakened and unable to move quickly, Grant makes him the driver. To spare the horses, Amelia and I walk alongside the wagon.

No piper or drummer is thought necessary for this rather unofficial journey, so we move to nothing but the music of tramping feet and the clack of shifting equipment. Red dust swirls up and around the men's black shoes, settling on their checkered stockings and the blue and green plaid of their kilts. Most of the men have wrapped rough cloth around their thighs, covering the skin their uniforms leave bare. I think of the many times my clothing has protected me from the thick underbrush that often chokes the narrow paths and understand.

Because the platoon moves without speaking, Amelia and I are silent, too. The silence gives me too much time to think. I wonder if these men know they are as unsafe with me as they would be if they were marching on the Middle Towns. The Cherokee could spring from the trees or the fields at any moment, and God only knows what Donald Campbell has waiting for us. I have no idea how many men Campbell has left, no idea how many he has turned to his twisted thinking. I know the soldiers will try to protect me, but it could come to a firefight between this platoon of regulars and Campbell's men. If I am not mistaken, that is what Grant plans.

By the time we stop to water the horses, it is midmorning, and the air has become hot and sticky, the sun blinding. My thighs ache, and my calves wobble beneath them. Grant joins me by the stream while the men rest, drinking, bathing their faces in the cool water.

Grant offers me a draught from his own canteen, which I take gratefully.

"Why do you not ride?" I ask. I saw him bid his beautiful campaign horse farewell last night. He seemed oddly vulnerable, for such a powerful man.

Grant laughs. "I haven't ridden since we left the Congarees. Only an idiot would go into Cherokee territory mounted. It would be an invitation to shoot me."

He nods toward Owen, who is letting Amelia check the bandage on his arm.

"Your friend there would be an easy mark. Elevated. Alone."

That troubles me. I didn't realize driving the supply wagon would put Owen in further danger.

Grant mops his forehead with a large handkerchief.

"Settlements all through the backcountry were raided in February, around the time Coytmore murdered the Cherokee hostages," he says. "Very little remains. There's barely a building left standing west of the Congarees, as I told you before. You must prepare yourself, Miss Blair."

I thank him for his advice, but inside I give a tired sigh. I slip my fingers under my neckerchief to the scar that crosses my collarbone. If I have learned anything over the past six months, I have learned it is better not to prepare yourself, because you never know exactly what will happen. Preparation becomes a waste of energy.

Still, I am shocked when we pass the razed holdings of families I once knew well. I remind myself that some of the men of these destroyed cabins participated in the raid on mine and banish sympathy from my mind.

Late in the afternoon of the third day, Grant halts the platoon and splits us into two groups.

"Miss Blair," he says. "Mr. Ramsay."

He assigns us a detachment of four men, three privates and a corporal. It occurs to me that only Grant, Owen, and I know our true purpose. From all I can tell, the rest of the men really believe they are seeing us safely to the frontier line and evaluating the war damage as an aside.

"We will rendezvous at Miss Blair's former home by sunset," Grant says. I have given him the instructions he will need to pass in a wide circle and approach my family's cabin from the opposite direction.

"Mrs. Williamson?"

It takes me a moment to realize Grant is talking to Amelia, but Owen looks up quickly enough. I see how much further the journey has weakened him, and guilt sticks in my throat.

"No doubt you would wish to avoid seeing such scenes as may pass before the eyes of your companions." Grant is so graceful. "Would you care to accompany me? You would do us great honor."

Amelia looks startled, and I realize even she does not know the real reason we are here. She thinks we really are heading for the frontier line. The
guilt grows. I have repaid her friendship poorly, especially after all she has
suffered.

"Go with Grant, Amelia." In Owen's voice is the comforting calm I trea-
sured for so many years.

Amelia looks up at Owen, making a little murmur of assent. "Be careful,"
she says. Six of us, Owen and I and the four soldiers, watch Grant's column
move slowly away. I wonder if the lieutenant-colonel wonders what he will
find when he circles back. I hope he doesn't expect to find our bodies. I hope
the men with us know what they're doing. And then I realize they have no
idea.

Grant's party is planning a quick reconnaissance of the surrounding area,
so the supply wagon stays with us. Before we move on, I reach under the seat
and pull out Mark's rifle and slip the cartridge box into my pocket. The rifle
is heavy, but the weight is reassuring in my hands.

The soldiers of the 77th are less formal now that their commanding officer is out of sight, but they still look imposing, armed as they are with muskets, pistols, and dirks. They carry hatchets where their backswords should
be, and I think of Malcolm's comparison of American and Continental warfare. America is changing them. Nothing so elegant as a backsword has any
place in this war.

Not until we reach the stream that leads to Fish Falls do I wonder how
I will handle seeing my home again. Fear of everything I don't know crashes
over me. I don't know what is left after all this time. I don't know if I can
bear to see it. We pass far around Fish Falls by the path that once led to my
family's home, the path where Mark was shot and scalped. When we pass
the spot where he died, I glance up the hill, half expecting to see myself
concealed in the underbrush, holding the rifle, failing to fire.

I look down. The same rifle is heavy in my hands now, but the knife in
my waistband is far better than the kitchen knife I carried then. It's a token
of good fortune from Grant—my good fortune to have a better knife. The
soldiers do not wonder why I am armed, why I chose to carry my rifle once
the larger escort left us. Only an idiot would walk these paths without a
weapon.

Half a year ago, I think. Such a short time. This time last summer, Mark
was away in the mountains, trapping and trading along the rivers of the
Carolinas and Virginia. He returned when the war started, when he learned

Father didn't plan to flee along with the settlers who had sense. Mark shouldn't have been here at all, I think, with another stab of that peculiar guilt I fear will haunt me until I die. Mark never should have stood between me and Donald Campbell.

Donald Campbell. Meeting him now may be my only chance to eliminate the threat that haunts me, to have a chance at moving on. Yet I never imagined it would be like this. I thought I could report him and let someone in authority find him and hang him. I knew I was risking my life by going to Fort Loudoun, and then by leaving it, but I never thought I would have to put myself deliberately in Campbell's way. I finger the blue ribbons at my throat. They look so delicate, but they have proven to be so strong. I wonder if they will hold. I wonder if, now, I want to meet Donald Campbell. But then a vermillion-painted man springs from the trees, and I no longer have a choice.

The first hatchet cracks through the collarbone of the youngest private, a boy near my age, only to be yanked out and buried in his belly. The blood is everywhere, turning his red coat a deeper, blacker shade. He slides off the blade, crashing onto the ground.

The two remaining privates begin to do as they've been taught, dropping to a knee to load their muskets quickly, but the corporal understands something is wrong, something is different, these are not the Cherokee they have fought before. He calls to his men in their own language, something that tells them to run, to scramble, to hide. Owen and I, brought up on the frontier, both disappeared by instinct the minute we sensed danger.

I remember Malcolm's words, remember him telling me the men of the highland regiments *were farmers, cattle and sheep herders mostly, not professional soldiers. If it hadn't been for the sergeants, we would have been completely lost.*

I am off the path, hidden in a hollow beside the road. The man who killed the young soldier will never kill another. A ball from the corporal's pistol drops him where he stands. He lies on the ground, his breath gurgling and his limbs twitching. They are alone on the road, he and the corporal, and the corporal draws his dirk, walks over to the man, and plunges his blade through the man's belly. He didn't have to do that. I recognize the wound. The man would have died soon enough of a ball through the lung, like Adam Williamson.

The dead man cannot have been alone. Donald Campbell would not have sent another man to kill me. He plans to do it himself, I'll give him that. I stay down, hoping any other attackers will approach from across the road, where the first man came from, and miss me. I load my rifle, a tricky business when I'm lying on the ground.

At last, I understand some of what Malcolm's frustration must have been with his role in the army. Grant's soldiers have no chance. They cannot hide against the green and brown landscape. They might conceal themselves in autumn, but never in the summer woods. Their red coats stand out like splashes of what, soon enough, is really blood. *White shirts, Catriona. God help us, it only made us easier to pick off.*

I try to determine where the shots are coming from, an impossible task from my position. It doesn't matter, anyway, because if the riflemen who downed the soldiers are any good, they will have changed positions by the time I figure it out.

I sneak my head up to study the face of the man who fell in the road. Yes, I know him. Michael Ross, the man who held Sam Murray while Campbell killed him. Beneath the vermillion dye is the face of the man who sat at my parents' table so many years ago and asked my father to teach his sons to read. And then, apparently, changed his mind.

Campbell must be near. I remind myself this is a trap. Not a trap for me, a trap for him. I am the bait, and he has taken it. The corporal, the youngest private, and the first of Campbell's men are dead in the road. The other two men from the 77th fell in the woods.

The horses stand calmly before the supply wagon. I wonder why they didn't bolt, but then I remember they are trained not to react. It's quiet now, but I know the stillness will not last. The whole forest is holding its breath. I hope it will keep holding its breath until Grant gets here. He cannot be far away. Surely he heard the shots. Or maybe I am a fool, and I will die here, and the men of the 77th will have sacrificed their lives for nothing.

Owen, I think. *Where is Owen?*

I try to count the shots I heard, but I can't remember with any sort of accuracy. I have not seen Owen since the skirmish began.

The crack of the underbrush is loud in the silence. My rifle is loaded, ready to fire, but I can't fire until I have something to aim at.

I hear an amused laugh, one I know too well.

"I hear you're an excellent shot, Miss Blair. Better than your brother, I hope. And your sometime sweetheart. Difficult to aim when you only have one good arm. So hard to steady the weapon, you see. So the Ramsay boy was easy to kill, in the end."

I lie still on the ground, reaching for the source of the voice. I pull back against the bank that rises to the road, crouching to keep my body hidden. Gripping the rifle, ready to lift it.

Four soldiers are dead, I think. *And Owen. Owen. I am the only one left.*

"What did you think were the chances of a man defending himself with only one good arm?" asks the voice.

Owen. I'm sorry, Owen. Please, please, forgive me. For everything.

The voice is coming closer. It is above me, on the road. I check the load on my rifle. I will have to be fast. I will have to step back, exposing my own body, to fire. He will not give me a second chance. Or, to be more accurate, this is my second chance, and I surely will not live to see a third. I wait, measuring time. I wait.

I slip my fingers over the lock, around the trigger. I will lift the rifle. I know I can. I can hold it to my shoulder long enough to fire. *You wait too long to fire and lose your nerve and your aim.* Not anymore. At last I am sure of what I first suspected the day I cut Adam Williamson's clothes from his body. The feel of the scissors, the feel of the trigger, so similar in my hand.

I know who I am. I think of my dead brothers and sisters, of Jaime and Mark, of Mary, of the twins, and of the two other nameless children who died so long ago. I think of my parents. I am the last of the Blairs, the last child, the last daughter. Mark's face flashes across my mind, smiling at me like my own reflection in water, hazy, gone. I remember him as I last saw him, near this very spot. And I know, more than anything else, I am what I have most feared. I am the last sister.

I stand, turning, lifting my brother's rifle to my shoulder. *Spin.* The butt presses into my scarred shoulder as my left hand slides down the barrel, measuring the weight, gauging the distance. *Measure.* A flash of movement. He sees me move, perhaps he senses he has gone too far, and he hides among the trees. He cannot give up taunting me, but he should know better than to tempt the last sister. Especially when she is the last, when he has left her on her own. It will take only a moment, only the length of a knife's flash. I feel my fingers on the scissors. Donald Campbell's thread is between the blades. *Cut.*

45.

June 16, 1760

Sunset

I am in the open, scrambling across the roadway. I know I am being reckless. I know more of Donald Campbell's men could be hiding in the trees. I don't care. I have done what I came to do. The last sister can do what she likes with my thread now.

Campbell lies on the side of the path, rolled onto his front. I find myself on the ground, shoving his shoulders, trying to turn him over, to look in his dead face, to see the light gone from his eyes. He's too heavy for me. All my strength passed into the single shot that killed him. The back of his head is a bloody mess, his skull blown open. Slick bone shows through the blood. I couldn't take his scalp if I wanted to.

And I can't turn him over, I can't shift him at all. I push and tug at him, finally turning my hands into fists, pummeling his back, his thighs, his upper arms, anywhere I can manage to hit. The tears begin at last, blinding me, and the guttural shrieks I have held back for so many months. I pound the dead man with my fists, jab his body with my elbows, rip his clothing with my hands, scratch his skin with my fingernails. No weapon can do what I want to do to him. No weapon is as close as skin on skin. I want to tear him apart. I want to rend him.

I feel remarkably similar to the way I felt after the catamount's attack, separate from my body, as if it is a thing apart from me. The screams and sobs burn in my throat, mixed with the taste of powder from the rifle cartridge, but it means nothing. My eyes are still clouded with tears and rage when powerful hands hook me under both arms and pull me to my feet. I thrash and kick at the air.

"Go away." It's an order between a shriek and a sob, but the arms don't leave me. They turn my body and tighten around my back and shoulders, pinning me until I have stopped thrashing, until my legs have stopped kicking. I recognize him by scent before I see his face, and the recognition starts the tears again.

My hands ball themselves back into fists and beat Malcolm's chest. "Go away, go away. You have to go away."

In answer, Malcolm tightens his hold and presses his lips into my forehead. "No. I don't."

Necessity brings me back to myself. My sobs slow, but my eyes keep stinging.

"You have to go, Malcolm."

Perhaps it is only my own fear, the thumping of my own heart, but I imagine I hear, far off, the tramp of feet. The sun is low in the sky, and our small party did not reach the cabin. Grant will search for us. He will come here.

I turn back to Malcolm, gathering his shirt in my fists, the way I gripped it in the mountain shelter the night he first kissed me. I wonder if he remembers. His slow, sad smile makes me think he does.

"How did you know I would be here?" I lean against him to prove to myself that he is real and solid. And mortal. To force myself to force him to leave.

Malcolm's hand leaves my back to press my head to his chest.

"Grant's quite a one for spreading a rumor," he says. "I wasn't about to let you face Campbell alone after what he did to you. I've been tracking you since you left Fort Prince George. Grant used you as bait, didn't he? That's his favorite trick. He used it at Fort Duquesne."

Malcolm leans back and pushes up the edge of my cap to inspect the wound on my forehead. For some reason, the action reminds me that, much as I want to, I cannot keep him here.

"It's healing," I insist, twisting to free myself from his arms. "You have to go now, Malcolm. Quickly, before they catch you."

Grant is so cool, so efficient. I am not imagining the tramp of marching feet.

"Go now, Malcolm. Please." I hear the urgency in my voice, a kind of urgency I haven't felt in a long time, not since I begged Mark to let me stay with him and he refused. And died.

Malcolm looks down at me, that sad smile still on his face. "I loved you, Catriona. I really did. You were the best thing that ever happened to me." He runs his thumb under my neckerchief and over the scar it hides. "But I can't offer you anything more than a life on the run, a life in hiding, the life of a wanted man. This is the one thing I can give you, and it's the only thing I really want." He presses his forehead against mine. "I can see you safe."

"I don't need you to do that anymore," I insist, tears threatening. "Campbell is dead. I killed him. Go, Malcolm. Go, please. They can't find you here."

Malcolm kisses me once, gently, with a kind of sweet bitterness. A farewell.

"You're trembling," he says. His hands study the back of my neck, under the hair he cut short all those months ago. "You're feverish. You're not well. I'm not going to leave you alone again, not here, with God knows what dangers in the woods. How long would I last, anyway, Catriona? You said yourself living alone in the mountains is a dangerous business. I've cheated death often enough."

The echo of commands, the tread of marching men, the clank of wood on metal. Grant and the platoon are so close now.

But you will. You will leave me alone.

We must have been standing here, in the middle of the path where my brother died, for a long time, but I've lost all track. This doesn't seem real anymore.

Seeing the destruction, the bodies on the path, Grant halts the platoon and advances toward us alone. The flicker of confusion in his eyes is consumed by a flash of recognition.

"Well, well," he says. "Lieutenant Craig."

46.

June 16, 1760

Dusk

Amelia darts through the crowd of soldiers before anyone thinks to hold her back. In a flash, she takes in the bodies, the blood. That strange strength of hers enables her to do what I cannot. She invites pain as she begins searching for Owen's body. I see her fall to her knees on the other side of the path, but she does not speak or cry out. Instead, she goes to work, checking his old and new wounds, leaning down and listening for breath.

"He's still alive!" she calls. "He's taken a bad blow to the back of the head. It might have killed him, but it didn't."

She must be so strong, I think again, as I watch her turn Owen's body, rolling him so his head is once again in her lap. True, Owen is much lighter than Donald Campbell, but I don't know if I could have turned him so easily.

My fury calmed, I can control the shaking of my limbs, and I see by the glower in Grant's eyes that he wishes me gone. Malcolm is a complication he will have to deal with now. Malcolm's hands brush down the sides of my arms as I leave him, and I know I will feel the tips of his fingers for the rest of my life, however long or short that life turns out to be.

Somehow, I manage to walk down the path, away from Malcolm and Grant. I go to Amelia and Owen. Amelia is right. Owen is not dead, but I understand, by the way his eyes pass over me when he finally comes round, searching for Amelia instead, that he is no longer mine. Though I accepted weeks ago that the life I once planned with Owen Ramsay is not to be, the child I was loved him, and I know I will carry this minor grief through my life, along with the heavier ones.

To hide my tears, I look down the path, to where Grant is personally tying the hands of the man who should be mine to the back of the supply wagon.

There's a reason Grant is a high-ranking officer, despite his evident difficulties in the field. He is calm as he orders men to dig a common grave for their fallen comrades, as he orders another grave dug for Donald Campbell and the single follower who remained with him to the end. He is considerate as he ascertains that I am unhurt, as he briefly interviews me. Commanding as he questions Malcolm about the presence of other locals and learns there is no one nearer than Ninety Six.

Malcolm and I stand so close as Grant questions me that I can feel the heat from his skin, but we might as well be miles apart. I search Malcolm's face for something that will tell me it is all right, that he will be all right. I don't find it, because Malcolm isn't looking at me. He answers Grant's questions in full, but his eyes are fixed faraway, on something I cannot see. On his own death.

Grant's full face burns with controlled anger.

"Walk with me, Lieutenant." He releases Malcolm from the wagon but leaves his hands bound in front. They move down the path, a long way off, and hope surges through me that perhaps this is not the end, perhaps Malcolm can trade his information about Campbell's attacks on the Lower

Towns for his own freedom. But I recall Grant's furious face, and that hope leaves me.

I feel a gentle touch on my arm and realize Amelia has joined me. Owen is sitting up now, resting against a tree and talking to the corporal who was part of our party and also turns out to be only wounded. She slips her arm through mine, and we walk, too, away from Grant and Malcolm, toward the clearing where the ruin of my family's home stands. Amelia somehow knows where I want to go, and her steps follow easily along. I am grateful she does not force me to speak, for I know how close to tears I am.

If only, I think. *If only Malcolm had not accompanied me to Fort Loudoun. If only he had stayed there. If only he had gone when I begged him to. If only I had not been so reckless in my pursuit of Donald Campbell. If only we had stayed forever in the mountain shelter.* I was the reason Mark and Jaime and I left our parents alone. I didn't shoot Campbell before he could kill Mark. I let Jaime be attacked by a catamount, and I left his body. I inspired Gabriel Swan to try to make it to Fort Prince George. I touch my fingers to the neat slice on my forehead. And now I will have another life on my hands.

"Amelia?" My voice cracks over her name.

She makes a small murmur that says she heard.

"I want to go home."

She squeezes my arm in sympathy, and then she lets me go.

I step from the shade of the trees into the circle of cleared land that surrounds the ruin. Tall and smoke-blackened, the chimney towers over the charred and splintered logs that were once my shelter.

The ground is dry and hard under my feet, baked in the heat of the summer sun. It has not rained here for several weeks, I can tell. The red dust settles on my feet and the hem of my skirt as I walk slowly toward the ruin.

I don't expect to find anything, but I cast my eyes over the ground anyway, hoping for something, the dull glint of pewter or the shine of silver.

By the time I reach the cabin, I've nearly forgotten about Donald Campbell because everything is coming back in waves of memories that threaten to drown me. I look up. It is dangerous to enter the ruin, I know that, but I also understand I must do it. I must face the ruin. I must understand that my old life, the only one I have ever truly known, is gone, destroyed, and I have to build a new one from the ashes.

I step over the shattered doorstep and pull myself over a fallen timber, careful of splintering wood, and step onto the remnants of the puncheon floor. I move slowly, carefully, inch by inch, testing the floor with each step to make sure it will hold my weight, avoiding the beams that are black with smoke, mincing onto the boards that look safe. This was the main room. Behind it was a smaller room where my parents slept. Upstairs were two lofts, one for me and one for my brothers. Those are gone now, collapsed into the mess of charred wood. I think I see what might have been the ladder we climbed to reach them.

I reach the hearth and sit. I run my hands over the stones, feeling each one, thankful that stone is hard to destroy and may scorch but not burn away. I search the hearth for something remaining, something that would not burn. Everything of value has been looted. But I glance up and spot one thing, one thing I want to take. Clinging to a bit of timber like a tattered battle flag is a strip of dark green silk. I know that silk. It belonged to my mother's best gown, the one she never had occasion to wear in the back-country, the one she promised would be mine on my wedding day. I stand, determined to somehow reach the silk.

47.

June 16, 1760

Night

We make camp in a large clearing in the woods. The men have been informed of a change in plans. We are heading straight back to Fort Prince George, where Malcolm will be executed for desertion in front of as many people as possible. Malcolm's hands are bound and his body lashed to a tree to prevent his escape. We have not spoken since he pulled me away from Donald Campbell's body this afternoon.

Despite Amelia's calm, measured breathing, I can't sleep. We are sleeping fully dressed in case of attack, and it's too hot. I pull on the leather buskins Malcolm traded his pistol for at Fort Loudoun and poke my head out of the tent, thinking perhaps of going to him. But I see the glow of candlelight through the fabric of Grant's tent, so I follow it, passing the bodies of the men of the escort party, who sleep in the open to avoid the heat.

The sentry stationed outside Grant's tent allows me to pass. Perhaps he is accustomed to not drawing attention to the visits of women to his superior officer's quarters. Grant is sitting up on his bedroll, his coat and waistcoat off but still dressed in his shirtsleeves and kilt. A deck of cards is spread before him. He's playing a solitary game. I sit beside him, tucking my legs under me, and he looks up.

"You couldn't sleep?" I observe. Close up, I can see the fine lines around his eyes.

"What can I do for you, Miss Blair?" he asks. "Normally, I am not averse to young women visiting my quarters in the dead of night, but I sense this is not such a friendly visit. Have you come about Lieutenant Craig?"

"What will happen to him?" I ask.

"The same thing that happens to all deserters," says Grant, collecting his cards. "The whip or the firing squad. Have you ever seen a man lashed to death? I once saw a fellow sentenced to nine hundred ninety-nine lashes for desertion. He didn't even look human by the end."

His mouth curves, but not in a smile. "They don't call us bloodybacks because of the color of our uniforms, Miss Blair."

I try to speak, but my mouth has gone dry.

"It makes an example to the rest," Grant continues. "And God knows I need it. Men have been deserting in droves since we landed at Charlestown. A friendly civilian population of their own countrymen has made it too easy."

I find my voice at last.

"Has it occurred to you that perhaps your men are like you?"

Grant raises his eyebrows, but he doesn't answer.

"Perhaps they, too, dislike fighting the Cherokee. They came to fight the French, after all."

Grant shakes his head. "It doesn't matter. How many of us like doing the things that must be done? Fighting men the Crown tells us are our enemies one moment, our allies the next. Yet it must be so. It is the way of the world, the way of the army."

"Lieutenant Craig gave you information about Donald Campbell," I say, hoping I'm right. "He told you about the early attacks on the Lower Towns, didn't he? The ones he witnessed? Isn't that what you needed to know? Won't it help in the peace talks to know the actions of a madman precipitated the war, at least in part?"

"True as that may be," says Grant, shuffling the cards. "It does not change the fact that he deserted his regiment. Dereliction of duty. And we are nowhere near peace talks yet. This war will last another year, at least."

I think of Malcolm, of the way he reacted the night I forced him to tell me what happened at Fort Duquesne. I lean closer to Grant. "You were taken prisoner at Fort Duquesne. There was such confusion there, so many men killed or missing. How long did it take all of them to rejoin the regiment? How long did it take you?"

I can tell I've hit a nerve because a shudder runs over Grant's body and he drops a hand to the ground to steady himself. "Our forces did capture Fort Duquesne, in the end," he whispers. "I've heard they found the French had put the heads of my men on spikes and tied their kilts below. Like puppets. They had been left like that for months."

Grant's large hand covers mine. His beautiful fingernails reflect the candlelight. "It's Fort Pitt now. Fort Duquesne doesn't exist."

"Except in your mind," I whisper. "And in your reputation. Think how long it took you to rejoin your regiment. Perhaps Mal—Lieutenant Craig was trying to meet up with you. You have no idea what happened."

Grant looks into my eyes, and his mouth curves again. I have given myself away. "Is he your lover?"

The words bring heat into my cheeks. "Not yet," I admit.

A shadow passes over Grant's face, wiping clean the memories and bringing back the smirk I've come to expect. "These young lieutenants," he says. "Such innocents, in so many ways." He runs the back of one finger down my cheek. "All the beauty of the world is theirs."

I take Grant's hand and gently pull it away from my face. A flash of regret crosses his own.

"It's no use, Miss Blair. He admitted his desertion to me. You must let him go. He is ready to die."

"Like you?" I ask.

Grant smiles mirthlessly. "I am a soldier," he says, slowly dealing out the cards between us. "I am always ready to die."

I spread my hand before me, though I have no idea what game we're playing. The face cards, with one head up and one down, make me think of the terrible medieval wheel in my father's book.

"You're a liar," I say. "You're ready to escape the world in which you botched the attack on Fort Duquesne, in which you attacked the Lower Towns without meaning to. But you're not ready to die."

I lay down my cards and lift my hand to Grant's shoulder. "I don't pretend to know what's happening here," I tell him. "This war is too big for me, and there's another war outside it that's bigger still, and I hear there's a war beyond that. Maybe the colony is in the right, maybe the Cherokee. But more and more I think there is no answer. Nothing is simple. Campbell wanted Cherokee land, yes, and the way he went about trying to get it is horrifying, but he had lost something, too. His home in Scotland, perhaps his family. It turned him wicked."

I pause for breath.

"There are dangerous men like Donald Campbell, and mistaken men like Captain Demere, and misguided men like my father."

I think of John Stuart, married to a Cherokee woman, yet leading men at Fort Loudoun, of Susannah Emory, raising her child with a husband present only when he can be spared, of Kanagatucko, unwilling to attack, yet driven to hold Fort Loudoun hostage for the good of his people. My mother, raising her children the best she could in a world she didn't understand, a world that killed her, in the end. My great-great-great-grandfather, who died fighting for a king. Malcolm's father, who died for rebelling against another one.

"I don't know who is right and who is wrong," I repeat. "My experience is that most people are doing the best they can with the cards they've been dealt. I know that's what I'm doing. I think that's what you're doing, too."

I lean in, close to Grant's face, as near as I can get without issuing an unintentional invitation.

"You keep saying the Cherokee want peace but don't know how to get it," I say. "I believe you want to be a good man, but you don't know how. Is helping me kill Donald Campbell enough to wash your hands clean of the destruction of the Lower Towns? Don't you need another good act?"

Grant pulls away, but still I go in for the final attack, the last card I have to play.

"Didn't you get enough men killed at Fort Duquesne?"

When he speaks some minutes later, Grant's voice is dry.

"Tomorrow night, we will camp in a thickly wooded area," he says. "It will be hard to see what is where, who is whom. There may be scattered Cherokee warriors waiting for us. I don't know. It is possible."

He continues, speaking almost to himself. "If I wanted to escape this war, I should go north, into the wilderness of North Carolina." He shakes his head. "It is a lawless place yet, full of renegades and pirates. I would not expect to find safety there for many years. Yet the army has no reason to go there. All forces will soon be turned on Montreal. North Carolina is a good place to be lost."

He smiles that mirthless smile again, and this time I return it.

48.

June 17, 1760

Evening

As Grant promised, our camp is heavily wooded, so it is easy to slip away from Amelia in the gathering dusk and make my way to Malcolm. The guard, a stocky man with a kind face, insists upon staying in sight, though he moves far enough away that our whispers are out of his hearing.

"Are you all right?" I ask, cursing myself for asking such a stupid question. Malcolm has not been allowed to sit since we left the scene of his capture. He has been forced to walk tied behind the supply wagon all day and lashed against a tree at night. He is flushed with the heat, and the dark curls cling to his face. He has not had a shave, either, and his cheek is rough when I lay my hand against it.

"Please, Catriona. Don't touch me," he says, flinching visibly. I pull back, hurt and confused, and he shakes his head. "If I hadn't met you, things would be different."

"Yes," I agree, understanding how much he must blame me for what is happening. "You never would have encountered Grant. You would have been safe, from this, anyway. Malcolm, I'm so sorry."

It's not enough to say that. Those words are so cheap, such an unworthy exchange for a man's life. I can say nothing that would not sound flippant, insulting, and he has asked me not to touch him. There is no way I can say goodbye that will not haunt me for the rest of my life.

"It's not that I don't want you near, Catriona," says Malcolm. "It's only that all this feels so much harder when you touch me. If I were alone in the world, I wouldn't be so sorry to die, but it's hard to leave the world while you're still in it."

The voice of Malcolm's guard comes heavily through the shadows as he returns. Our time is up.

"Say your goodbyes, miss," says the guard, his voice almost sympathetic. "We'll reach Prince George tomorrow, and then there will be little time."

I look up at Malcolm, trembling as my body is torn between needing to touch him and trying to honor his request not to make this any harder than it has to be. His dark blue eyes pierce my heart.

"Goodbye, Catriona," he says gently. "I'll rest easier knowing Donald Campbell won't be able to hurt you anymore."

I will not say it. I give Malcolm a small, sad smile, but as I turn to leave I whisper, "No." I have said enough goodbyes in recent months to last a lifetime.

I always thought I was being smart, letting things go when they were gone, letting life take me where it would, even if that meant standing still. I always thought my mother's deep unhappiness came from her insistence on fighting to keep some of the baronet's youngest daughter alive, to mold the world into a shape she understood. Now, I see that fight as the strongest thing about her, the thing that held her steady when she would otherwise have gone mad.

I thought I learned to fight long ago, to fire a gun, to swing an ax. But that is only fighting in its most obvious form and it, too, is a means of letting go, of letting the world be as it will. I slip my hand into my pocket, where my fingers find the surprisingly strong cloth of my mother's green silk. In her death, my mother taught me to mold the world, to tie its severed threads together again, so that the cloth holds good and keeps out the elements. In her death, my mother taught me to fight for what is worth keeping.

I catch Owen alone and lay my hand on his arm, feeling under my palm all that might have been. A wave of sadness hits me, and I hesitate, but only for a moment.

"I need your help," I tell him. I take him to a far edge of camp and whisper my plan.

Owen's burned arm is still in a sling, but he grips my wrist with his good hand. "Catie, do you understand what you're doing?" he asks. "What you're asking me to do? You'll be a criminal, too, in as much danger from the law as he is."

"So you won't help me?" I ask.

Owen looks down at me. "Was there ever any chance for us, Catie?"

I lay my palm against his cheek. "Yes. There was always a chance for us. But we missed it."

It's true. I know, looking up at him, that if it hadn't been for the morning Donald Campbell cut my life in two, I would have married him. I would probably be married to him already, and I would have been happy my whole life, letting the world be as it would be. But I have learned to fight.

"Take my family's land, Owen, if you can. When the war is over."

"I don't want the land, Catie," he says, taking my hand from his face.

"I want you to have it."

He laughs. "A trade? The land for you?" He does not love me anymore, not in the way he once did, but the memories are strong enough to make him angry, to lead him to lash me with words.

"Will you help me?" I ask again.

At last, he nods. "But I won't take the land as payment. I'll do it, but by God, I'm not going to make it easy for you."

49.

June 18, 1760

Before Dawn

Owen crouches beside me in the dark morning, outside the circle of the camp. I glance over.

"Are you ready?" I ask. "They won't suspect you, you know. They'll never believe you fired with one arm." I steady the musket on the small stand I've built of rocks and branches, and he reaches to make sure he can hold it.

Owen smiles sadly, as if I should know the answer. "To say goodbye to you forever? No. I'll never be ready for that."

"Owen," I say quietly. He turns to face me. "Maybe it's not forever. Maybe it's just for a little while." I know I am lying, but it's a soft lie to ease the pain of parting from the last link to my old life.

I take his hand, weaving my fingers through his one last time in an attempt to remember him, to remember what he was to me, and all he might have been.

"Amelia is a wonderful person," I say. "Better than me."

Owen's face lights with a brief, embarrassed smile. "You can't have thought I was going to spend my whole life pining after you?"

"I'm glad to know you won't. Now, on my signal."

I am already several yards away when the ball from Owen's musket rips through the corner of Grant's tent and the report wakes nearly everyone in the camp. Expecting a Cherokee attack, men scramble for their weapons, and the sentries pull back, as I thought they might. As planned, my shot from the rifle ignites a line of powder laid down on the opposite side of the camp from where Malcolm is being held. In the dark, the escort party can't tell they are firing at an imaginary enemy, and many of their shots go wild. Scrambling toward Malcolm, I look back once and see Owen enter the tent Amelia and I shared. That's as it should be, then, but I feel a pang of grief for the two of them, the dear friends I will never again see. I wish I could have said goodbye to Amelia, but leaving her innocent of my most recent wild scheme is the last kindness I can offer.

Malcolm is bound to the tree, helpless to free himself and certain prey for whatever comes, human or animal. I crawl toward him, dragging the rifle and my old kitchen basket, which is heavy with food from the supply wagon. I pull out the knife Grant gave me and saw through the cords that bind Malcolm to the tree. His muscles unwilling to hold him, Malcolm slumps against me. I hook my hands under his arms and lower him to the ground, where I cut quickly through the cords that bind his wrists.

"You can rest later," I whisper. "We've got to move. Stay down. Crawl."

"Catriona," he says. "What are you doing?"

"You saved my life once." I hand him the rifle because he can carry it more easily. "I'm—repaying a debt. Come on."

Malcolm looks confused for a fleeting moment, but he recovers quickly, gaining speed as his muscles return to life.

"Where are we going?" he asks.

"Grant said North Carolina would be best. I'm inclined to agree with him. We'll have to stay off the main roads. We're going northeast, away from the war."

50.

September 21, 1760

Night

I lie beside Malcolm on a bed of pine needles dropped from the trees that surround us. Overhead, between the tossing branches, the stars are coming out one by one in the dusk. I shiver as the evening chill passes over me. Here in the mountains, daylight is the difference between comfort and cold, no matter the season.

"Are you cold, sweet?" Malcolm asks, and I nod. He curves his body around mine, pressing close and tightening the blanket that covers us. His right arm drapes over mine, our hands still bound by the strip of green silk I salvaged from the ruin of my home and a strip of cloth cut from one of Malcolm's shirts. I reach up with my left hand and stroke the fabric, tightening the knots that threaten to come undone.

"My father disapproved of handfasting," I say. Once there would have been bitterness and rebellion in my voice. Now it is only a statement. "Donald Campbell was right about that: my father was a great one for rule of law. He was against secret marriages. He thought all marriages ought to be announced and performed in a church. Or by a minister at least."

Malcolm's mouth nuzzles the back of my neck, spreading comforting warmth through my body. "What did he say about spending all your nights for three months on end with your lover without being married to him?"

I laugh and turn back to Malcolm. "I'm not sure it ever occurred to him that I would be in that situation."

"You didn't have to be," Malcolm says. He kisses my forehead, just at the hairline, the place he kissed me all those months ago, the first night of the ice storm. "I would have married you the day I met you. You're the one who wanted to wait."

"You can't have wanted to marry me then," I say. "You had some choice words about mortally wounded women, remember?"

Malcolm smiles. "All right. I felt sorry for you at first. I didn't fall in love with you until I had to stitch the wounds from the catamount. You didn't scream, but I knew how badly I was hurting you. I would have done anything to be able to stop. That was when I realized I loved you."

I sigh, fresh sadness sweeping over me. I don't know what I wanted to wait for after Campbell's death and our escape from Malcolm's regiment. Something, some sign, for the war to be over, to feel safe. "Malcolm?" I say. "I'm glad Campbell died the way he did. I'm glad I killed him."

"Are you?"

"Yes. He did horrible things, but still, he can't do them any longer. I'm sorry about the other man I killed, the Cherokee. I wish I hadn't had to do it. But Amelia ..."

In answer, Malcolm tilts my chin up and kisses me gently.

"You did what you had to do, sweet. This isn't a world that asks us what we'd like. We tend to save the people we know."

I kiss Malcolm fiercely, in the way I've learned tells him I want to be made to forget for as long as possible, and I do forget for a time.

But as Malcolm sleeps, I lie awake under the bright stars for a long time, remembering. My family. My home. Owen. The rifle lies beside me, the grain on the wood like the lines in the face of an old friend. My beloved brother, my Mark.

And all the rest of those whose threads were cut too soon. The Cherokee war goes on, as does the greater battle for the continent with the French. Yesterday, when we ventured into a settlement to trade, we learned what happened after our escape. Grant and Montgomery never pushed through to the Middle Towns. They tried, but the Cherokee repulsed them in the mountains, and Montgomery decided not to risk losing his entire force. I try not to feel guilty. I held up my end of the bargain I made with Stuart and Demere. It is not my fault the 77th could not make it through.

Fort Loudoun surrendered to the Cherokee at the beginning of August. The inhabitants were to vacate and retreat to Fort Prince George, but on the first morning they were attacked by a Cherokee war party. All the officers except Captain Stuart were killed, and many others. It's thought this was in retaliation for Coytmore's massacre of the Cherokee hostages at Fort Prince George in February. Blood vengeance. The survivors were taken hostage themselves to await slavery or rescue, but Captain Stuart was bought by his best friend, a Cherokee leader named Attakullakulla, who sold all his goods to raise Captain Stuart's price. It's rumored the two of them and Attakullakulla's family escaped north, heading for Virginia. Captain Demere was not so lucky. He was dismembered and scalped before death came as a welcome escape. All I can find to be thankful for is that Amelia left Fort Loudoun with me in May, for had she stayed she might have been among the lost.

I feel tears on my face, and I bury my head against Malcolm's chest, gripping his hand in its tangle of fabric, waking him. "Is this a real marriage?" I ask. "Does it count?"

Malcolm's fingers explore my hair, which has reached my shoulders but still tumbles so easily out of its braid. "It counts for us, and that's what matters. You said yourself the backcountry has its own rules. And a record of marriage would be a dangerous thing."

I had thought of waiting for safety to marry Malcolm, but there is no real safety for us and never will be. We must live in relative hiding for many years, if we want to have many years to live. Winter will come soon, and now that we have found a place to build a shelter, we must begin to build a life. I finger the pearls at my throat, concealed in their ribbons, my mother's last gift to me. To the right buyer, they will bring a good price. But not yet. For now, we must live like the outlaws we are, hidden deep in the forest. The best we can hope for is to shelter in each other.

EPILOGUE

April 25, 1775

The Waxhaw Settlements,
North Carolina–South Carolina Border

I step outside and look to the west, pulling my shawl around my shoulders against the wind that billows across the valley, pushing a sudden spring thunderstorm ahead of it. The sky has gone pink too early for the sunset. I search the rolling hills, peering through the storm haze. My men should have been home by now, but they have stayed later and later on the days they go into town. I know they are probably only talking, but the prickle of worry at the base of my spine won't end until I see them. The sky worries me. I don't want them caught in the storm.

I venture into the yard that forms the border between the house and the fields, and at last I spot them, two black silhouettes on the rise of the hill. Malcolm, his shape melting into that of the horse he's leading, and Mark, carrying the rifle across his shoulders with an easy grace that makes my throat catch at memories. At thirteen, Mark is as tall as his father already, for he inherited the height and the dark blond hair of another Mark Blair. My son's name is Mark Blair, too, for Malcolm began calling himself by my name, another layer of disguise between him and the British authorities.

I return to the door and call into the house for Bess. She appears, clutching an old newspaper in one hand and a kitten in the other. I tell her to put those down and start setting the trenchers for supper. She is eleven, and prettier than she knows. Far too pretty for her own good. She has her father's pale skin and dark curls, and I have begun to understand my own mother's careful watch over me, though I try not to imitate it so.

Some sense of foreboding pushes me forward, toward Mark and Malcolm, though I'd be hard pressed to explain what it is. I still my feet, wanting to wait, wanting to cherish these last moments before they tell me whatever it is they know. But when Mark spots me, he hands the rifle off to his father and sprints down the hill, clutching a newspaper tight against the wind.

"Mother!" he calls. My heart sinks at the jubilation in his voice. I wish he had inherited my brother's caution along with his looks.

He fetches up against me, and I catch him in my arms and look up at him, seeing at once the baby whose life I fought my own body for, the child who toddled along tied by the wrist to my apron strings, the man biding his time in the corners of Mark's face. He is too excited to speak, and by the time he draws breath, Malcolm has caught up with him.

"Shots," says Mark. "Fired at Lexington and Concord, in Massachusetts."

My heart falls into my stomach. How I had hoped it would not come to this.

I lay my hand on his chest. "Wait," I say, taking the newspaper. "Put up the horse for your father, and then you can tell me about it."

When our son is out of earshot, I look up at Malcolm. "Well?"

Malcolm grimaces. "I'm afraid it's quite true, sweet. The British troops in Boston marched to steal the militia supplies in Concord, and the militia met them. Eight men of the Massachusetts militia killed at Lexington alone." He points to the newspaper. "See here. One Jonathon Harrington, fatally wounded, dragged himself home and died on his own doorstep."

I cover my face with my hands, but still all I can see is Malcolm or Mark doing the same thing, dying on the doorstep of this place I have made safe.

"Was it a slaughter?" I ask, grasping at my last hope. *You cannot fight Britain. You can't. They will destroy you. Look what they did to Boston for its little rebellions. Please don't try.*

"No," says Malcolm. "The redcoats were a bit surprised at the way farmers could fight." He shrugs. "It's not like we're dealing with the Prussian army, sweet. Then . . . but the British can be beaten."

"What is it? What's happened?"

I turn around. Bess is in the doorway, her slim face serious with worry. Mark has returned from stabling the horse, and he tells her before I can stop him.

"All right," I say, crushing the newspaper in my fist. "Enough. Massachu-setts has nothing to do with us. Let's eat our supper before it gets cold."

I usher my family into the house ahead of me and seal the door against the first fat raindrops, as though that will protect my children from the storm.

Author's Note

The Last Sister began as the answer to a challenge. I was told historical fiction for young adults had little chance of finding a publisher or an audience, so I approached this project by importing the elements that generally make for appealing young adult fiction: a violent, alien world; a love triangle; a protagonist challenged by events outside her control. I tried to avoid the things that tend to turn readers away from historical fiction: general didacticism, extensive use of unfamiliar dialects, and the privileging of famous people and events over the fictional characters' experiences. I began with a story about a young woman driven from her home into an unfamiliar and perilous landscape, and I started to think about when, why, and how that might have happened.

The Blair family is a bit of an anomaly. Settlers poured into backcountry South Carolina in the 1750s, most of them coming not from Atlantic ports but down the spine of the Appalachians from Virginia, Pennsylvania, and other points north in family groups or otherwise close communities. The vast majority of these settlers had little, if any, education and lived in extreme poverty. In exchange for relatively affordable land and freedom from the Church of England, they formed a human shield between the prosperous lowcountry and the risk of attack from a variety of unpredictable frontier forces, including representatives of both Native American and European nations. Reading and writing have formed the backbone of my life, so I wasn't sure I could write authentically from the perspective of someone who was illiterate, with relatively little knowledge of the world outside her own settlement. Further, I wanted readers to gain some perspective on how backcountry South Carolina and the Anglo-Cherokee War fit into Great Britain's global quest for empire. As I considered how an educated, middle-class woman might find herself in this place, I decided to make Catie Blair the daughter of a missionary whose idealism and curiosity overwhelm his common sense—not an uncommon failing among academics, and many eighteenth-century clergymen were also dedicated humanities scholars. In the mid-eighteenth century, several Presbyterian ministers attempted to establish schools and churches along the frontier, and Philip Blair is part of this movement. He is also someone whose general liberalism would have led him to educate his daughters as well as his sons. Catie's fascination with the story of the Fates derives from the emphasis many eighteenth-century academics placed on classics scholarship—the literature, language, and legacy of ancient Greece and Rome.

It's impossible to understand an era well enough to write historical fiction simply through focused research on the specific time period in question. I found I needed to delve several more centuries into the past to understand the various people groups who appear in this novel. The story of the war is much more complex than the word "Anglo-Cherokee" makes it sound, as if it were literally the English versus the Cherokee. In fact, there weren't many ethnically English people on the frontier at all: they tended to live nearer the coast. Many of the backcountry settlers were Scots-Irish, ethnic Scots whose ancestors had been displaced to Ireland in the seventeenth century and who had begun immigrating to America in waves in the first half of the eighteenth century. Mixed among them were a few highland Scots, members of a separate group that came directly from Scotland, some transported after the Jacobite Uprising of 1745 and others rack-rented out, or forced off the land by the intentional raising of rents to unsustainable levels. (Landlords did this in order to clear land for more profitable cattle and sheep farming.) Middle-class lowland Scots like Philip Blair, actively attempting to assimilate with the dominant English culture, did not find themselves on the frontier without good reason. Similarly, there were many subgroups among the Cherokee, and many cultural distinctions and prejudices were to be found among the Lower Towns, the Middle Towns, and the Overhills.

Catie is the daughter of two worlds, of a largely forgotten (in North America, anyway) ethnic split between the English and the lowland Scots, and she has grown to womanhood among a largely Scots-Irish population with some highland Scots influence. I imagined that such a background might lead her to interrogate her own identity in a shifting world.

The Blairs' ethnic and social identities would have made their position in the backcountry extremely precarious. Many backcountry settlers lived in close communities of family groups who had known each other for generations. To be outsiders in a place where connection to other people is literally the difference between life and death is to be completely without protection. As I learned more about people like the Blairs, it seemed increasingly feasible that their presence would be resented and that the community might turn on them.

I didn't need to invent a violent, alien world for Catie. While the Blair family and most of the other characters are fictional, the world they inhabit was very real. Outside of Catie's personal story, the historic events depicted and referenced happened as the characters describe. It is a cliché of history that governments start wars and individuals want peace, but in South Carolina in 1759, the opposite was true. Engaged in a conflict with France for control of North America and already expending military resources in a war on the European continent, Great Britain desperately needed an alliance with the Cherokee nation. In turn, the Cherokee had become increasingly dependent on British trade goods over several preceding decades and could ill afford to lose access to the firearms, powder, and shot that had helped make them a dominant regional power. So neither government wanted a war, but neither government had much control in backcountry South Carolina, and hostilities escalated through the latter half of the 1750s. If anything, the violence was worse than I have depicted. No one on the frontier, regardless of gender, age, status, or any other identity, could afford to be a noncombatant. I nearly stopped writing several times because I didn't see how anyone survived. But of course, some people did, and Catie Blair became one of them.

I knew Catie's journey to Fort Loudoun would be interrupted by a terrible accident, and the cougar allowed me to bring attention to the fact that not all the dangers of the backcountry came from other humans. Large predators were common, and though it was and still is rare to actually see a cougar, settlers recognized the possibility of their killing and dragging off farm animals and even children.

I also knew Catie would die of her injuries without help, but at first I wasn't sure what form that help would take. Should it come from the Cherokee? From a trader? From the French? The character of Malcolm Craig allowed me to widen the lens to take in more of what was happening in other parts of North America and in Europe during the Anglo-Cherokee War. Through Malcolm's experience, I was also able to introduce the highland regiments that would be important in the final quarter of the novel. The crushing of the Jacobite Uprising of 1745, the raising of the highland regiments to fight in North America, and the disaster at Fort Duquesne all happened as he describes. Malcolm, and Catie's initial reaction to him, also allowed me to explore the great prejudice against the highland Scots among other white ethnic groups, especially the English and the lowland Scots.

Many of the characters with whom Catie interacts at Fort Loudoun and Fort Prince George were real people. While their interactions with Catie are obviously fictional, the situations in and around the two forts are historically accurate. Attakullakulla, Connecorte, and Kanagatucko were all headmen among the Cherokee. Captain Demere and Captain Stuart led their respective companies at Fort Loudoun until the surrender of the fort and the subsequent attack in August 1760, and Stuart was married to a Cherokee woman named Susannah Emory. Lieutenant-Colonel James Grant led the doomed attack on Fort Duquesne, was taken prisoner and later released by the French, and served as second-in-command to Colonel Montgomery in South Carolina in 1760. In one of those little coincidences that mark the union of research and fiction writing, I didn't discover that Grant liked to set high-stakes traps for his enemies until I had already had him set one for the fictional Donald Campbell.

I have taken artistic license at two major points. First, I encountered some discrepancy about the date of death of Fort Loudoun's surgeon, so I situated it in early April for purposes of this narrative. Also, many stories circulated about atrocities committed by warring factions, and the one Grant repeats about French treatment of prisoners at Fort Duquesne probably is not true. However, he might have heard and believed it.

The story of the Anglo-Cherokee War, the highland regiments, the siege and fall of Fort Loudoun, and the days when backcountry South Carolina was the frontier is as fascinating as any I have found in many years of studying history, but it is not very well known. In *The Last Sister* I have tried to emphasize the difficulties of understanding a situation when we are in the middle of it, the complexities of human motivations, and the many ways people become tangled in forces that can be understood only in hindsight. I've heard it said that it's hard to study history and remain an optimist, but the many voices I've encountered from the past have convinced me of what Catie tells Grant in their final conversation—that most people really are doing the best they can with the cards they've been dealt. On the days when the problems of the world seem unsolvable and insurmountable, to do the best we can anyway still seems like an admirable goal.

Selected Sources

It would be impossible to discuss every aspect of the Anglo-Cherokee War in a novel and a brief author's note, so I hope readers will be interested in finding out more. I encountered many excellent sources during my research process and have listed a variety of accessible sources here for the use of students, educators, and general readers. While most of these sources are directed at an adult audience, I have designated those designed for the middle grades with an asterisk. Older readers may also find these useful for the valuable images they provide. Any mistakes found in the text are my own and are not the fault of these or the other sources I consulted.

Nonfiction Books

Akins, Bill. *The Unicoi Turnpike Trail: A Path through Time.* Etowah: Tennessee Overhill Heritage Association, 2008.

Edgar, Walter. *South Carolina: A History.* Columbia: University of South Carolina Press, 1998.

Glasse, Hannah. *Everlasting Syllabub and the Art of Carving.* From *The Art of Cookery Made Plain and Easy.* 1747. New York: Penguin, 2011. Great Food.

Grant, George. *The New Highland Military Discipline of 1757.* 1757. Alexandria Bay: Museum Restoration Service, 1995. Historical Arms Ser. 10.

*Hensley, Alexia Jones. *Unsung Heroines of the Carolina Frontier: A Curriculum Resource.* Columbia: South Carolina Department of Archives and History, 1997. Document Packet Number 9.

Kelley, Paul. *Historic Fort Loudoun.* Vonore: Fort Loudoun Association, 1958.

McCulloch, Ian M., and Timothy J. Todish, eds. *Through So Many Dangers: The Memoirs and Adventures of Robert Kirk, Late of the Royal Highland Regiment.* 1775. Fleischmanns: Purple Mountain, 2004.

*McCulloch, Ian Macpherson. *Highlander in the French and Indian War, 1756–67.* Oxford: Osprey, 2008. Warrior 126.

———. *Sons of the Mountains: The Highland Regiments in the French and Indian War, 1756–1767.* Vol. 1. Fleischmanns, N.Y.: Purple Mountain, 2006.

————. *Sons of the Mountains: The Highland Regiments in the French and Indian War.* Vol. 2. Fleischmanns, N.Y.: Purple Mountain, 2006.

Moore, Peter N. *World of Toil and Strife: Community Transformation in Backcountry South Carolina, 1750–1805.* Columbia: University of South Carolina Press, 2007.

Oliphant, John. *Peace and War on the Anglo-Cherokee Frontier, 1756–63.* Baton Rouge: Louisiana State University Press, 2001.

*Tunis, Edwin. *Colonial Living.* 1957. Baltimore: Johns Hopkins University Press, 1999.

Webb, Jim. *Born Fighting: How the Scots-Irish Shaped America.* New York: Broadway, 2004.

Weir, Robert M. *Colonial South Carolina: A History.* Columbia: University of South Carolina Press, 1997.

*Wilbur, C. Keith. *Revolutionary Medicine: 1700–1800.* 2nd ed. Guilford, Conn.: Globe Pequot, 1997. Illustrated Living History Ser.

Other Fictional Accounts

Craddock, Charles Egbert (Mary Noailles Murfree). *The Story of Old Fort Loudon.* New York: Macmillan, 1899. Online Reader file.

Guy, Joe D. *Indian Summer: The Siege and Fall of Fort Loudoun.* Johnson City, Tenn.: Overmountain, 2001.

Websites

"Dress the Part." *A Day in the Life.* Colonial Williamsburg Foundation, 2008. http://www.history.org/History/teaching/dayInTheLife/webactivities/dress/dress.cfm

Fort Loudoun. Fort Loudoun State Historic Area, 2012. http://fortloudoun.com/

Ninety Six National Historic Site. National Park Service, United States Department of the Interior, 2013. http://www.nps.gov/nisi/index.htm

About the author

A native of Greenville, South Carolina, COURTNEY MCKINNEY-WHITAKER holds a bachelor's degree in history from the University of South Carolina Honors College, a master's of library and information science from the University of South Carolina, and a master's in English from Illinois State University. She lives in Illinois with her family. Visit her website at www .adventuresinmypetticoat.com.

CPSIA information can be obtained at www.ICGtesting.com
Printed in the USA
LVOW11*2145031014

407242LV00002B/3/P